Date Due

Paige	Weber	6-2	
Shannon	Kaiers	6-0	
Katie			

EDWARD BLOOR
TANGERINE

SCHOLASTIC
Signature

AN IMPRINT OF
SCHOLASTIC INC.

NEW YORK TORONTO LONDON AUCKLAND SYDNEY
MEXICO CITY NEW DELHI HONG KONG

ISBN 0-439-28603-4

24 23 22 21 20 19 18 17   4 5 6/0

Printed in the U.S.A.   40

First Scholastic paperback reissue, June 2001

THE SOFT PARADE, words and music by Jim Morrison.
© 1969 Doors Music Co. All Rights Reserved. Used by Permission.
WARNER BROS. PUBLICATION U. S. INC., Miami, FL 33014

Text set in Palatino.
Designed by Camilla Filancia.

Dedicated to

JUDY BLOOR BONFIELD

Successful hills are here to stay.
Everything must be this way.

—THE DOORS,
"The Soft Parade"

The house looked strange. It was completely empty now, and the door was flung wide open, like something wild had just escaped from it. Like it was the empty, two-story tomb of some runaway zombie.

Mom called out to me, "Take the bag, Paul. I want to have one last look around."

I said, "I just did. I didn't see anything."

"Well, maybe you didn't look everywhere. I'll just be a minute."

"I looked everywhere."

"Wait for me out by the car, please. We can't have the new owners thinking we left a mess behind."

I picked up the garbage bag and hauled it out to the curb. We'd already packed up our sleeping bags, suitcases, and two folding chairs—all neatly wedged into the back of Mom's Volvo wagon. Now only this ten-gallon, self-tying, lemon-scented garbage bag remained, and we planned to toss it into the Dumpster behind the 7-Eleven. But first Mom had to make sure that I didn't overlook anything. She was worried that the people who bought our house, people who we've never met, would find a McDonald's swizzle stick and think less of us.

Once we dump this garbage bag, that will be it. That will be the last evidence that the Fisher family ever lived in Houston. Dad and my brother, Erik, are already gone. They've been living in Florida for a week now, with the sleeping bags, suitcases, and chairs that they stuffed into Dad's Range Rover. The rest of our furniture left yesterday, professionally packed by two guys who came to really hate Mom. By now it should be over halfway to our new address—a place called Lake Windsor Downs in Tangerine County, Florida.

I set the garbage bag down and leaned against the station wagon, staring east, directly into the rising sun. I'm not supposed to do that because my glasses are so thick. My brother, Erik, once told me that if I ever look directly into the sun with these glasses, my eyeballs will burst into flame, like dry leaves under a magnifying glass.

I don't believe that. But I turned back around anyway, and I looked west down our street at the receding line of black mailboxes. Something about them fascinated me. I leaned my chin against the top of the station wagon and continued to stare. An old familiar feeling came over me, like I had forgotten something. What was it? What did I need to remember?

Somewhere behind me a car engine started up, and a scene came back to me:

I remembered a black metal mailbox, on a black metal pole.

I was riding my bike home at dinnertime, heading east down this street, with the sun setting behind me. I heard a loud roar like an animal's, like a predator snarling. I swiveled my head around, still pedaling, and looked back. All I could see was the red sun, huge now, setting right over the middle of the street. I couldn't see anything else. But I could hear the roar, even louder now, and I recognized it: the roar of an engine revved up to full throttle.

I tilted up my sports goggles to unfog them. Then I turned back and saw it—a black car—just an outline at first, then clear and detailed. It came right out of the sun. I saw a man hanging out of the passenger window, hanging way out. He had something pulled over his face, some kind of ski mask, and he was holding a long metal baseball bat in both hands, like a murder weapon.

Then the gears ground, the tires squealed, and the car leaped forward at an impossible speed. I swiveled back, terrified, and pedaled as hard as I could. I heard the roar of the car closing in on me, louder and louder, like it had smelled its prey. I shot a glance into my bike mirror, and there it was—half a block behind, then ten yards, then one yard. The man in the ski mask leaned farther out the window. He pulled the bat back and up. Then he brought it forward in a mighty swing, right at my head. I dove to the right, landing on my face in the grass, just as the baseball bat smashed into the mailbox, exploding it right off its pole. Voices inside the car screamed—animal-fury screams—as the crushed black metal clattered across the street.

I scrambled back up. I left my bike there, its wheels spinning, and ran for home. I ran in absolute terror, listening for the sound of the car squealing back around to come after me again.

I burst through the front door, crying hysterically. My goggles were twisted back around my head. I spun around and around looking for Mom. Then Mom and Dad were both in front of me, holding on to my shoulders, trying to calm me down, trying to understand the word that I was saying over and over.

It was "Erik." I was saying "Erik."

Dad finally understood. He looked right into my eyes and asked. "What do you mean by 'Erik'? Erik what, Paul?"

I stammered out, "Erik. He tried to kill me."

Mom and Dad let go of my shoulders and stepped back. They looked at each other, puzzled. Then Dad raised his arm up and pointed to the right, into the dining room. There was Erik. He was sitting at the dining-room table. He was doing his homework.

Dad eyeballed me for a few seconds, then he went out front to look for my bike.

Erik called over, "There he goes. Blaming me again."

Mom took me into the kitchen and got me a glass of water. She ran her finger under the strap of my goggles and slipped them off. Then she said, "Honey, you know how it is with your eyesight. You know you can't see very well." And that was that.

But I *can* see. I can see everything. I can see things that Mom and Dad can't. Or won't.

Mom's voice broke into my remembrance. "Paul?"

My chin was still pressed against the car. She was standing next to me. "Paul? Are you with us?" I leaned back as she beeped the auto alarm and opened the tailgate. "You're remembering all the good times you had here. Aren't you?"

I shook my head to clear it. I reached to pick up the garbage bag. My arms felt weak. I muttered, "I was remembering. I was remembering something that happened."

She held up a white cigarette butt and said, "You don't know anything about this, do you?"

"No."

"I found it in the garage, behind the water heater."

I opened up the garbage bag enough for her to slip it inside. I said, "Good work, Mom." She walked quickly back up to the house, laid her keys inside the foyer, and pulled the door firmly closed.

And that was that. The keys were locked in. The zombie was locked out. And we were on our way.

part 1

part 1

Friday, August 18

For Mom the move from Texas to Florida was a military operation, like the many moves she had made as a child. We had our orders. We had our supplies. We had a time-table. If it had been necessary to do so, we would have driven the eight hundred miles from our old house to our new house straight through, without stopping at all. We would have refueled the Volvo while hurtling along at seventy-five miles per hour next to a moving convoy-refueling truck.

Fortunately this wasn't necessary. Mom had calculated that we could leave at 6:00 A.M. central daylight time, stop three times at twenty minutes per stop, and still arrive at our destination at 9:00 P.M. eastern daylight time.

I guess that's challenging if you're the driver. It's pretty boring if you're just sitting there, so I slept on and off until, in the early evening, we turned off Interstate 10 somewhere in western Florida.

This scenery was not what I had expected at all, and I stared out the window, fascinated by it. We passed mile after mile of green fields overflowing with tomatoes and onions and watermelons. I suddenly had this crazy feeling like I wanted to bolt from the car and run through the fields until I couldn't run anymore. I said to Mom, "This is Florida? This is what it looks like?"

Mom laughed. "Yeah. What did you think it looked like?"

"I don't know. A beach with a fifty-story condo on it."

"Well, it looks like that, too. Florida's a huge place. We'll be living in an area that's more like this one. There are still a lot of farms around."

"What do they grow? I bet they grow tangerines."

"No. Not too many. Not anymore. This is too far north for citrus trees. Every few years they get a deep freeze that wipes them all out. Most of the citrus growers here have sold off their land to developers."

"Yeah? And what do the developers do with it?"

"Well . . . they develop it. They plan communities with nice houses, and schools, and industrial parks. They create jobs—construction jobs, teaching jobs, civil engineering jobs—like your father's."

But once we got farther south and crossed into Tangerine County, we *did* start to see groves of citrus trees, and they were an amazing sight. They were perfect. Thousands upon thousands of trees in the red glow of sundown, perfectly shaped and perfectly aligned, vertically and horizontally, like squares in a million-square grid.

Mom pointed. "Look. Here comes the first industrial park."

I looked up ahead and saw the highway curve off, left and right, into spiral exit ramps, like rams' horns. Low white buildings with black windows stretched out in both directions. They were all identical.

Mom said, "There's our exit. Right up there."

I looked ahead another quarter mile and saw another pair of spiral ramps, but I couldn't see much else. A fine brown dust was now blowing across the highway, drifting like snow against the shoulders and swirling up into the air.

We turned off Route 27, spiraled around the rams' horns, and headed east. Suddenly the fine brown dirt became mixed with thick black smoke.

Mom said, "Good heavens! Look at that."

I looked to where she was pointing, up to the left, out in a field, and my heart sank. The black smoke was pouring from a huge bonfire of trees. Citrus trees.

I said, "Why are they doing that? Why are they just burning them up?"

8

"To clear the land."

"Well, why don't they build houses out of them? Or homeless shelters? Or something?"

Mom shook her head. "I don't think they can build with them. I don't think those trees have any use other than for fruit." She smiled. "You never hear people bragging that their dining-room set is solid grapefruit, do you?"

I didn't smile back.

Mom pointed to the right and said, "There's another one."

Sure enough. Same size; same flames licking up the sides; same smoke billowing out. It was like a Texas football bonfire, but nobody was dancing around it, and nobody was celebrating anything.

Then, in an instant, in the blink of an eye, we crossed over from this wasteland into a place carpeted with green grass, with trees along both sides of the road and flower beds running down the middle of a median strip. We could see the roofs of big, expensive houses peeking up over the landscaping.

Mom said, "This is where the developments begin. This one is called the Manors of Coventry. Aren't they beautiful? Ours is a little farther in."

We went past the Villas at Versailles, which, if anything, looked even more expensive. Then we saw a high gray wall and a series of wrought-iron letters that spelled out LAKE WINDSOR DOWNS. We passed iron gates and a pond of some kind. Then we made a couple of turns and pulled into a wide driveway.

Mom announced, "This is it. This is our house."

It was big—two stories high—and very white, with aqua trim, like a Miami Dolphins football helmet. A new wooden fence ran around both sides to the back, where it met up with that high gray wall. The wall, apparently, surrounded the entire development.

9

The garage door opened up with a smooth mechanical hum. Dad was standing in there with his arms open. He called out, "Perfect timing, you two. The pizzas got here five minutes ago."

Mom and I climbed out of the car, stiff and hungry. Dad came outside, clicking the garage door closed. He put an arm around each of us and guided us toward the front, saying, "Let's do this the right way. Huh? Let's go in the visitors' door."

Dad led us through the front door into a tiled foyer two stories high. We turned to the left and passed through an enormous great room with furniture and boxes piled all around it. We ended up in an area off the kitchen that had a small, round table and four chairs. Erik was sitting in one of the chairs. He waved casually to Mom. He ignored me.

Mom waved back at him, but she was looking at the boxes stacked in the kitchen. She said to Dad, "These boxes are marked DINING ROOM."

Dad said, "Uh-huh."

"Uh-huh. Well, I marked DINING ROOM on them so the movers would put them in the dining room."

"OK. Erik'll put them over there." He looked at me and added, "Erik and Paul."

Mom asked, "Did the movers break anything?"

"No. They didn't break a thing. They were real pros. Nice guys, too."

Mom and I each grabbed a chair. Erik opened a pizza box, pulled out a slice, and started stuffing it into his mouth.

Mom said, "How about waiting for the rest of us, Erik?"

He gave her a tomatoey grin. Dad passed out paper plates, napkins, and cans of soda. Once Dad sat down, the rest of us started to eat.

Everybody's mouth was full for a minute; then Mom said to Dad, "So? What have you been doing?"

Dad wiped his mouth. "Work. Trying to get organized

up there. Trying to get in to see Old Charley Burns." He looked at me. "He's a real character. You'll have to meet him. Spends half his life at the stock-car races. He's crazy about stock-car racing."

Mom said, "You mean he's really not there? You can't get in to see him because he's not there?"

"Right. He's really not there. He's up at Darlington, or at Talladega, or at Daytona."

Mom was concerned. "And that's OK?"

"I don't know that it's OK, but that's the way it is. He's the boss. He makes his own hours. He told me I can make my own hours, too." He looked over at Erik. "That'll be good for us. I'll be able to go to football practice every day."

I thought to myself, *OK, here we are. How long did it take Dad to get to his favorite topic, the Erik Fisher Football Dream?* I'd heard it all before. Too many times. And I was about to hear it again. I tried to head him off by asking him something, anything, but he was too fast for me. "It's a great opportunity for you boys, too. Erik will get the exposure he needs in the press. The *Tangerine Times* is crazy about high school football. And we're just down the road from the University of Florida—you know, the Gators? In fact, Old Charley is a big Gators fan. And Florida State and the University of Miami aren't far away. These big-time Florida schools like to draft Florida boys for their teams."

That was that. Dad was now off into the Erik Fisher Football Dream. As soon as I got an opening I said, "May I be excused? I'd like to go find my bedroom."

Dad said, "Sure thing. You're at the top of the stairs, to the right. Erik's down at the other end. And you have two guest rooms in between. You guys should never hear each other."

I retraced my steps through the great room, went up the stairs, and turned right. I had to squeeze into my bedroom past a stack of boxes. I switched on the light and saw one

11

that had PAUL'S SHEETS written on it, so I opened it and made up my bed. Then I found my computer carton and set it up on the desk. When I got around to putting my clothes away in the dresser, I came across a box that said ERIK'S TROPHIES. I felt a surge of anger, Mom's anger, at the moving guys for doing that. I picked it up and carried it out to the top of the stairs.

Erik was standing down in the foyer. He had the front door cracked open. He was talking to a group of kids—at least two girls and one guy—telling them that he would see them later.

I put the box down quietly and hurried back into my room. I turned on the computer, got into my private journal, and wrote until about eleven o'clock. Then I lay down on the bed and fell asleep—but I woke up almost immediately. Someone was running down the hall. It was Erik. I heard him run down the stairs, go out the front door, and pull away in a loud car.

I couldn't get back to sleep. My mind started racing like an engine. I started thinking about our old house. Then I started thinking about a zombie, a pissed-off zombie. Dragging one foot behind him. Keeping to the right. Taking his time. Slowly, surely, stalking his way down Interstate 10.

Saturday, August 19

I woke up in the dark to the sound of an explosion. I groped around for my regular glasses—unable to find them in this new bedroom, upstairs in this new house. Then my glasses suddenly appeared on the nightstand, illuminated by a flash of lightning.

I'd no sooner pulled them on when another explosion made the windows rattle and the walls shake. The lightning once again filled the room, painful and surprising, like the flash of a camera in my face. I waited for more explosions to follow, but none did, and I fell back asleep.

I woke up again at seven, still wearing my glasses. I walked down the stairs, unbolted the front door, and stepped out into the morning air. It wasn't what I expected. The air had a gray tint to it, and a damp, foul smell like an ashtray.

Smoke, I thought. *Something around here is on fire.*

I walked back inside and turned left, toward the sound of a television. Mom was sitting on a stool at the high counter that separates the kitchen from the rest of the great room.

"Mom, I think something's on fire around here."

"What? Where?"

"Step out front and take a look. And smell the air."

Mom slid off the stool and hurried out the front door. She made it exactly as far as I had when the smoke stopped her in her tracks.

"Where's it coming from?" she cried, shuffling backward in her bedroom slippers. She stared at the top of the house, looking for flames.

"I don't know. I'll check around back." I pulled my T-shirt up to cover my mouth and nose and ran off into the blowing gray smoke. I circled completely around our new house, but I couldn't see the source of the fire.

Mom was on her way back inside. "I'm calling the Fire Department."

"What about Dad and Erik? Should I wake them up?"

"They're up already. They're up and out. They went to Gainesville to look at the football stadium."

"Gainesville?"

"That's where the University of Florida is, honey."

"Oh. I guess we don't need to save them, then," I said as I started to feel the walls for heat. "You know, it could

13

be the electric wiring inside the walls. It could smolder for a while in there and then burst into flame."

"It could?" Mom replied in horror. She snatched up the portable phone and dialed 911, talking as she followed my hand's progress along the wall of the great room.

"The builder of this development certainly should have known how to wire a—Hello! Yes, I want the Fire Department." Mom felt the wall with her free hand. "Yes! There's a fire at...Oh, Paul! What's our address? Lake Windsor Downs! What is it? Run outside and find the house number!"

I sprinted out, read the black numbers over the garage, sprinted back in, and shouted, "1225!"

But Mom had already dug out a contract and was reading into the phone, "1225 Kensington Gardens Drive, Lake Windsor Downs. What? Where is it? It's in Tangerine! It's just outside of Tangerine!" Mom listened for another ten seconds, turning red. Then, at the end of her patience, she yelled into the phone, "What more do you need to know? It's the place with the smoke pouring out of it. Get somebody out here!" She listened again, said, "Yes, please hurry," and hung up.

We resumed our search of the house and waited for the approaching wail of the fire engines. Twenty minutes later Mom picked up the phone to call the Fire Department again as I peered out the front window.

"Wait, Mom!" I shouted. "I see them. They're on the other side of the development."

Mom and I ran outside and watched an old red fire engine cruising slowly up and down the streets.

The fire engine turned in our direction. We waved and hollered and managed to attract the driver's attention. When the engine rolled up in front of our house and the driver got out, we saw that he was alone. He didn't look to be much older than Erik. He had on knee-high black-and-yellow boots, a pair of cutoff shorts, and a white shirt that had TANGERINE VOLUNTEER FIRE DEPARTMENT—WAYNE written over the breast pocket.

He waved to us and smiled brightly. "Y'all the ones who called about the fire?"

Mom turned and pointed at our house. "Yes! Yes, right here."

The young man didn't move. "Where's the fire at, ma'am?"

Mom directed her voice at him like a laser beam. "You get in there and answer that question for yourself, young man. I called you twenty minutes ago. Is our house about to burst into flames while we're standing out here?"

"Any of your walls or doors feel hot, ma'am?"

"No."

"Then I'd say you don't need to worry. You don't got a fire. Just a bunch of smoke."

"Smoke? Smoke from where?"

Without a moment's hesitation, the young man's left arm shot up and pointed to the open field just beyond the wall at the end of our street. "Right out there. It's the muck fire."

"It's the what?"

"Muck fire, ma'am. That field probably got hit by lightning last night. Stirred up the muck fire."

"Last night? So . . . how long is this fire going to burn?"

The young man laughed out loud and threw up his hands. "It's been burning for as long as I can remember."

Mom's mouth dropped. She stared at him in disbelief as he continued cheerfully, "Muck fires don't go out. They're burning all the time. Burning right there under the ground, all the time. Sometimes the rain'll damp them down, but they're still smoldering. Y'all ever hear of lignite?"

Mom and I shook our heads dumbly. Wayne continued, "Well, that field's full of lignite. Lignite is, like, one step before coal. There's hundreds of miles of it under here."

Mom turned to me with a look of pure puzzlement. "Well, I'm sure your father was never told about any of this. I'm sure the Homeowners' Association will want to know about this."

"Oh, they know about it, ma'am. Lots of people call us when they first move in here. We wind up having to explain it to them."

I watched Mom struggling to understand this. "You explain it to them?"

"Yes, ma'am."

"And then what do they do?"

The young man laughed again. "They learn to live with it, I guess. When the wind's up like this, they gotta stay inside, keep the windows closed."

"You're saying that there's no way of stopping this fire?"

He shook his head. "Late summer like this, if you want to stop the muck fire you got to stop the lightning from striking. They ain't figured out how to do that yet."

Watching this, I suddenly had to admire this Wayne fellow. He was relentlessly cheerful, even in the face of Mom's rising anger. I knew she wanted to grab him by the ear and march him down to that field to put out that muck fire once and for all. But she couldn't. She couldn't do anything except turn to me once again and vow to bring this "muck fire situation" to the attention of the Homeowners' Association.

"Y'all have a nice day!" Wayne called. Mom and I turned together to look at him. With a happy wave he climbed back into the fire engine and pulled noisily away.

Saturday, August 19, *later*

Dad and Erik were gone all day. Our house never did burst into flames, but the thermometer on the patio, hanging there in the direct sun, did climb to over a hundred degrees.

16

A vicious thunderstorm hit in the late afternoon and knocked out our power for about ten seconds. That was just long enough to make Mom and me have to go around the entire house resetting all of the alarm clocks, VCRs, computers, and stereos.

After supper I opened the garage door and walked my bike out toward the street. The air was hot and damp, but there was no smell of smoke. The wind was blowing west now, toward the Gulf of Mexico.

You can actually see the wind here. It whips around full of white construction sand, the sand that covers the streets and the unsold lots. The same white-sugar sand that whipped through our development in Houston and the one before that, in Huntsville.

I turned left and pedaled against the sand toward the front of the development. Our street is about half filled with houses now. The development has grown from the west side to the east side, and we're on the last street before the east wall. Every empty lot on our street has a Sold sign on it, though, so Lake Windsor Downs will soon be complete.

I stopped at the model homes area—four houses surrounded by the same white picket fence—and pulled off my glasses to clean them. Lake Windsor Downs offers four choices to home buyers, each named after a British royal family: the Lancaster, the York, the Stuart, and the Tudor. Mom absolutely loves that. I'm sure that's why we live here instead of in the Estates at East Hampton, or the Manors of Coventry, or the Villas at Versailles. Mom will soon be describing people like this: "They're the two-story Lancaster with the teal trim," or "They're the white Tudor with the red tile roof."

I replaced my glasses and started off again, riding parallel to that high gray wall. I stopped for a few minutes to watch two guys unloading thick squares of muddy sod from a flatbed truck. They plopped the squares down over the white-sugar sand, like pieces of a jigsaw puzzle. When they pulled away a new white Stuart had a new green lawn around it.

I pedaled up to the iron gates. They open onto a two-lane entranceway with a cement island in the middle. There's a fancy little guardhouse on the island, like something the kings and queens in history would have built to keep out the serfs, or the Vandals, or whoever. It isn't keeping anybody out now. It's empty inside, but I could see a dirty ashtray and a wastebasket full of soda cans.

Just inside the entranceway is a big pond: Lake Windsor, I suppose. I started around it on my bike. It's a perfectly round blue lake with a border of grass between the water and the road. I thought I heard a splash in the water, but I couldn't see anything moving. I rode completely around the lake in one minute and then headed toward home.

As soon as I turned onto our street, I saw a black Jeep Cherokee parked in our driveway. A heavyset man in shorts was talking to Mom. She was pointing at the top of our house and smiling. When I pulled up next to them, she was saying, "So naturally I thought I'd see flames shooting out of the roof!"

The heavyset man turned toward me, nodding his head in sympathy. "Yeah. When that muck fire kicks up, it can be a real stinkaroo. Hello, young man."

"Hello, sir."

"Paul," Mom said, "this is Mr. Costello. He's the president of the Homeowners' Association. This is my son Paul."

I said, "Pleased to meet you."

Mom added, "He lives in the brown-and-beige Tudor on the west side."

I shook Mr. Costello's outstretched hand and said, "I was just up at the lake. Just now."

"Is that right?" He smiled. "Did you see any of the koi?"

"The what?"

"The fish! Koi. Japanese carp. They look like giant goldfish."

"No. No, I thought I heard something, but I didn't see any fish."

"You get up there early in the morning and check out those koi. They're really something to see. We had them flown in from Atlanta. Stocked the lake full of them."

Mom asked, "The lake? Is that Lake Windsor?"

Mr. Costello laughed. "I guess it is now. It's not an official lake. It's man-made. Any new development like this has to have a retention pond for storm runoff. We decided to make the lake a centerpiece, a showpiece, for our community. We stocked it with the koi and added plenty of green space around it for strolling or even picnicking." He reached over and squeezed my elbow. "No fishing, though, OK? Those koi are high-priced fish."

Just then Dad and Erik turned the corner and pulled into the driveway. As usual when Erik appears, the attention switched from me to him. Dad and Mom started to tell Mr. Costello about what a great football player Erik is, but Mr. Costello was ready for them. He has a football-playing son of his own, and he hopped into his Jeep Cherokee to go get him.

They all wound up in the great room, near the fireplace. I sat on a stool near the kitchen. Mr. Costello's son is named Mike. Mike and his father talked about the football program at Lake Windsor High with a great deal of pride. Mr. Costello pointed out, "We've only had the program for ten years, and we've already surpassed the program at Tangerine High. No big-school football players are coming out of Tangerine High anymore. The Lake Windsor Seagulls are now the dominant team in three counties. They're rewriting all the county record books."

Dad said, "What position do you play, Mike?"

Mike Costello spoke very well, like one of those football

guys who make United Way commercials. "Coach Warner and Dad and I made a decision last year. Coach had enough linemen, but he had no backup at quarterback. He's been working with me, and now I'm number-two quarterback on the depth chart."

Mike's father turned to Mom and explained, "That means he's the backup to Antoine Thomas."

But no one in my family needs to be told what "number two on the depth chart" means. If Mom had chosen to, she could have explained to Mr. Costello what it *really* means. As backup quarterback, his son Mike would be handling the snaps and holding the ball for the placekicker—in this case, Erik Fisher, a placekicker who can hit with deadly accuracy from fifty yards. If Mom had chosen to, she could have explained to him that Mike Costello's backside would be featured in the local paper often as he held the ball for this new placekicking sensation. But she didn't.

Mike was very friendly. He told Erik that he "had heard about him already from the coach" and that he "was looking forward to working with him."

Erik smiled and said, "So Coach Warner told you that you'll be my holder?"

Mike answered, "Coach wants me in there as the holder so we can have the option—either we can kick the ball, or we can fake the kick and have me roll out and run or pass."

Erik was still smiling, but he said, "Coach Warner knows what I can do. He can send anybody out there to pretend to kick a field goal. When I go out there, it'll be for real."

Mike shrugged and said, "That'll be the coach's call. Won't it?"

Erik locked eyes with him for a second, then backed off. "Yes, of course it will."

I thought to myself, *Way to go, Mike*. But I had to admit Erik was right. I've heard Coach Warner talk to Dad enough to know he's counting on Erik to be an impact player, a star.

I guess part of that stardom will come at Mike's expense. I can see Mike Costello's future. I can see the *Tangerine Times* photos of the sensational senior placekicker Erik Fisher and his anonymous holder. (Dad has the clippings from Houston of the sensational junior placekicker Erik Fisher and his anonymous holder, a kid whose name totally escapes me now.) There will be no football glory in Mike Costello's future. But does Mike, or his father, really care? They certainly don't care the way Dad and Erik do.

Dad told them that he graduated from Ohio State. But he added that he always regretted not being big enough to play football there. Mike's dad told us that he graduated from FSU, and from FSU's School of Law. He didn't add that he regretted anything.

Both Costellos seemed to be impressed by Erik. They both asked about his high school exploits back in Houston. They both admired the gold varsity ring on his hand. Dad boasted that Erik was the only sophomore in his high school ever to receive one.

Erik was as phony as he needed to be. He asked some questions about Lake Windsor High's student government, and about its National Honor Society. He asked about early-acceptance programs at different universities in Florida.

Mike told us that he had already been accepted into FSU's School of Engineering, so I don't think he's too worried about his future in football, or in anything else. Actually, he seems a pretty decent guy, for a football player. But who knows? He's bound to change, in one way or another, once he gets caught up inside the Erik Fisher Football Dream.

Monday, August 21

It took me a long time to fall asleep last night. I was thinking about this: Erik's arrival is going to change the football season at Lake Windsor High School. Dad's arrival is going to change how things are done in the Civil Engineering Department in Tangerine County. Mom's arrival will change the Homeowners' Association in Lake Windsor Downs. So what about me? Will I make the difference between winning and losing for the middle school's soccer team?

I have this sense that great things are expected of us here. Dad calls this a "booming area," but it's no Houston. It's not even a Huntsville. It's like we're major leaguers who've been sent down to a minor-league city for a while. We're expected to do great things here and then move back up to the big leagues.

I got down to breakfast just as Dad was leaving. He was halfway out the door, and he did not look happy. He was lecturing Mom: "You ought to file a complaint against that fireman. You ought to call the county and complain about the slow response time. Then you ought to complain about them sending some jerk kid out here who doesn't know what he's doing or what he's talking about."

I don't know why, but I immediately rose to Wayne's defense. "He sure seemed to know what he was talking about, Dad. He sure knew all about the muck fire."

Dad snapped back, "No professional shows up twenty minutes late wearing cutoffs. If he worked for me, he'd be fired."

Then he was out the door, leaving me with my unanswered questions: *Fired for what, Dad? For telling us the truth?*

For telling us something that you didn't know? That you should have known?

After breakfast I joined Mom in one of the guest bedrooms. We'd taken on the job of unpacking the boxes. We had already worked our way through the great room, the living room, and the dining room.

"Shade and storage space," Mom said, "are the two things that you do not get in Florida. People pack up their northern homes with their attics and basements and tiny upstairs rooms that nobody ever uses, and they move into these Florida homes that are as wide open as cathedrals. All the house space down here is devoted to air and light, nothing to storage."

Mom had, of course, anticipated this problem. Before the movers came we had set aside everything that we would not use "on a regular basis" in Florida. All of these items are now stacked in a climate-controlled storage space just west of here, out on Route 22. We probably have as much stuff out there as we do here in the house, including most of Mom's antiques, which "just aren't Florida."

It occurred to me, as we unpacked the things that *are* Florida, that Mom might actually hate moving here. But of course she will never tell me about it. Just like she would never have told Grandmom and Grandpop about hating any of those moves of her childhood. Mom would never waste her time complaining. Just like she would never waste her time worrying about the past.

Later in the afternoon we drove up Route 89, past new developments with new walls and guardhouses, past a long row of high-tension wires, to the adjoining campuses of Lake Windsor High School and Lake Windsor Middle School. All the way there we seemed to be riding side-by-side with black storm clouds.

"I hope we get in before this rain starts," Mom muttered as we turned at Seagull Way into the enormous blacktopped

23

parking lot of the campus. We drove past the long, window-less two-story high school and around the football stadium to the middle school. The middle school office is located in a one-story building that looks like the younger brother of the high school building.

We made it inside just as the first bolts of lightning cracked around us. While Mom gave my name to the secretary, I looked through a glass door at a field full of small wooden shacks. They take up most of the space be-tween this main building and the steel bleachers of the high school football stadium. "I wonder who gets put into those shacks," I said, turning toward Mom. She was now standing with a tall, thin woman with jet black hair.

The woman eyed me coldly and said, "All seventh and eighth graders are in portable classrooms. The main building is for sixth graders only."

Mom did not look pleased. The woman continued, "I'm Mrs. Gates. I'm the principal here at Lake Windsor Middle School."

Mom extended her hand. "I'm Caroline Fisher. This is my son Paul."

"Hello, Paul," she said. "What can I tell you folks about Lake Windsor Middle?"

"We were hoping to see exactly where Paul will be going next week. He has problems with his eyesight—he's legally blind—so we were hoping to make a dry run today."

Mrs. Gates looked hard at my glasses. She seemed to be trying to think of a way out of this, but she finally said, "I see. I see. All right, let's take a quick tour."

Mrs. Gates and Mom took off at a fast walk. I followed slowly, angry at Mom for calling attention to my eyesight. She wanted a tour of the place because she's nosy and wants to see everything for herself. It wasn't because I can't see, because I can. I can see just fine.

"We call this the Building," Mrs. Gates explained. "It

contains the main office, the cafeteria, the library, and the sixth-grade classrooms."

"Don't you have an auditorium?" Mom asked.

"The cafeteria doubles as the auditorium."

"What about a gym?"

"When we need to, we use the high school's gymnasium."

"But where do you have your PE classes?"

"Oh, we always have physical education outdoors, on one of our fields."

"And when it rains?"

"Then we have it indoors, in the classrooms."

"Surely they don't do jumping jacks in those wooden portables."

"No. On a rainy day the PE teachers will most likely concentrate on other parts of their curriculum, such as health care or good nutrition."

We were outside now, facing the portables. There must be forty of them, all connected by a system of wooden walkways—the kind of boardwalks you see at the beach—only these stretch over some sick-looking grass and a lot of brown dirt.

Mrs. Gates was speaking rapidly. "Each portable is, of course, air-conditioned. As you can see, all of the buildings on our campus are grounded with lightning rods for our afternoon storms."

Mom eyed the field with alarm. "How would you ever know if there were some emergency out here?"

Mrs. Gates turned to her and asked, "Like what?"

I froze. Even I could hear the annoyance in that voice.

Mom locked eyes with her. "Does it really matter like what? Do I really have to provide you with an example of what constitutes an emergency?"

Mrs. Gates retreated. "No, of course not. Each portable is connected to the main office by a telephone and a public-address system, and each has its own pull alarm in case of fire."

We all stared at the crisscross of wooden walkways until Mrs. Gates asked, "What brings your family to Tangerine?"

"My husband's job. He's the new Deputy Director of Civil Engineering for the county."

"I see."

Large drops of rain started to fall around us, so we headed back inside. Mom prompted me, "Paul? Do you have any questions?"

"Yes. Do you have a soccer team?"

"We do. We have an excellent soccer program—a boys' team and a girls' team. We play against all the schools in this area. Are you a soccer fan?"

"I'm a soccer *player*." I corrected her. "I play goalie."

We were now back at the main office; Mrs. Gates led us through into her private office. "Mrs. Fisher, I'd like to get you to fill out an IEP for Paul—an Individualized Education Plan. Being vision impaired, Paul is entitled to take part in our IEP program. Basically we identify Paul's situation, set specific goals for him to achieve, and note any special needs he might have."

Mom started to read the form. I stepped outside to show that I wanted no part of that conversation. I spotted a glass trophy case and went to check it out. The biggest trophy was for last year's boys' soccer team. It said, FIRST PLACE, TANGERINE COUNTY SPORTS COMMISSION.

Mom came out of the office briskly. We ran through the cold rain to the car. Once we were inside and belted up, she said, "So, what do you think of Lake Windsor Middle School?"

"I don't know," I mumbled, staring out the window.

We drove back past the field of portables, but Mom suddenly hit the brakes.

"Look at that!" she cried.

The field was now completely flooded, like a rice paddy. The brown water had risen to within inches of the wooden walkways. We both shook our heads in disbelief.

Then I decided to answer her question about the school. "I guess if they have a decent soccer team, I'll let them slide about not having indoor classrooms and not having a gym."

"Yeah!" Mom sputtered. "Not having a gym, or an auditorium. Two more facts apparently overlooked by your father. And what am I supposed to do? Send you to school every day in rain gear? With an umbrella?"

Mom would never say it, but I bet we were thinking the same thing. *What else has Dad "overlooked" about Tangerine?* We drove on in silence, except for the pounding of the rain, from the flooded campus of Lake Windsor Middle School to the flooded streets of Lake Windsor Downs.

Wednesday, August 23

All four of us were back at the high school–middle school campus today. The head coach, Coach Warner, was holding a three-day tryout camp for the football team before the start of the school year.

Erik, of course, didn't need to try out, but he was there anyway. Dad had brought Erik to meet Coach Warner earlier in the summer. Dad had knelt down and held the ball for Erik to drill fifty-yard field goals, one after another, while, according to Dad, the coach's jaw had dropped lower and lower.

Now Dad and I were standing next to the coach—not that either one of them was aware of me. I was watching a huge bird of prey circling overhead, like a hawk. But it wasn't a hawk. I knew that. It was an osprey. (I know the difference because of a science project I did last year. Could a vision-impaired person tell the difference?)

The players were doing calisthenics under a troubled-looking sky. As black clouds gathered in the west, Coach Warner explained to Dad, "I've never had a good place-kicker before, but I sure could have used one last season. We lost four games by a grand total of seven points."

"Those days are over," Dad assured him.

"Antoine Thomas was the whole show last year. He was the go-to guy on every play. He ran for over a hundred yards eight times."

"That's pretty impressive."

"I even had him running back kicks. But I'm not going to do that this year. He's just gotten too valuable. If Erik can give us five or six points a game, then I can save Antoine for quarterbacking."

"Oh, Erik can give you that. He averaged nine points a game last year, and he was only a junior. He scored fourteen points in one game. That was the game when he kicked the forty-seven-yard field goal."

I remembered that game back in Houston. Erik was on the front page of the sports section the next day. I think it was the proudest day of Dad's life.

Dad told Coach Warner the thing about Ohio State—how he regretted that he hadn't been big enough to play football there. Coach Warner nodded sympathetically, like he agreed this was some kind of tragedy in Dad's life. I don't understand that.

Then again, I don't understand why Dad loves football. I've played football, real football, in the junior league. It's boring. You just stand around most of the time waiting for somebody to tell you what to do. And in the end, some guy like Erik who hasn't even worked up a sweat can come in and grab all the glory. It doesn't work that way in soccer.

Erik used to play soccer. He was really good, too. This was back in Huntsville, back when he was nine and ten years old. He took all the penalty kicks for his team. That's

28

how he learned to kick so hard, drilling those penalty kicks into the back of the goal net. When we moved to Houston, when Erik was eleven, he realized that football was the star attraction. He took to kicking a football, soccer style, into a small net that he set up in our backyard. Day after day, in rain and cold and heat, Erik worked on perfecting a two-step kick.

Up until then, Dad wasn't much into sports. Once Erik started getting good, though, Dad became transformed. He started talking about his high school football career and, of course, his regrets about college. He became obsessed with football, especially with placekicking. He learned how to hold the ball for Erik, spinning the laces away. For a while, he tried to get me to hike the ball to them. But I never really cooperated, and they soon dropped me from the routine.

We watched the Lake Windsor players break into groups for timed sprints. Mom came up and stood with us for a minute. I knew that she was really there to tell me to get in the car because a thunderstorm was coming. She said, "A storm's coming," to Coach Warner, but he just smiled and agreed with her, "Sure is!"

Mom pointed out some people to me. There was Mike Costello, and there were his father and his brother standing on the other sideline. There was Arthur Bauer, the guy Erik had over to the house yesterday. There was Antoine Thomas, the quarterback.

Mom quickly grew impatient to get me to the car. On the way to the parking lot, she said, "Those boys shouldn't be out there in a thunderstorm."

"They have to play in all kinds of weather, Mom. Sometimes you get caught in a blizzard. Sometimes you get caught in the rain. It's part of football. It's part of soccer, too."

"Why can't they practice in the morning, when it doesn't rain? This is ridiculous. When you know that it's definitely going to rain at exactly the same time every day, you can't really call it getting caught in the rain, can you?"

I had to agree. "I guess you're right. It's like the afternoon tree-watering time around here. But there aren't any trees anymore."

We climbed inside the car just as the first big drops of rain rapped against the roof.

"Look at your father! What is he doing out there?"

"I don't know."

"He's just going to stand there and get soaked?"

"Looks like it."

"This isn't Texas. They have their own weather in Florida, and we all need to change our attitudes about it. People shouldn't stand outside in this kind of rain. Just listen to that!"

The rain was beating down so loud now that it was hard to hear Mom's voice.

I sat thinking for a minute and then hollered, "I'll bet the people who used to live here, the people who grew the tangerines, were really happy with this weather. That's why they were here, right? To grow tangerines?"

"Do you mean, it's nice weather here if you're a duck?"

"Yeah. Or a tangerine. But now it's all upside-down, you know? It's all messed up. The rain clouds show up every day, just like they're supposed to, but there aren't any tangerine trees. Just people. And the people have no use for the rain clouds. So the clouds go around looking for all the tangerine trees. They can't find them, they get mad, and they start thundering and lightning and dumping the rain on us."

I had the feeling Mom knew what I was talking about, but all she would say is, "Clouds don't get mad, Paul."

We sat in the beating rain noise for a few minutes, then it abruptly stopped, like some annoying little kid had stopped banging on a pan. The sun came out, and the steaming heat rose up all around us. "Great," Mom muttered. "Now it's sauna time."

"You need to lighten up, Mom."

"Oh, is that right? You're the one getting attacked by disappointed rain clouds. Why don't you lighten up?" Mom looked in the rearview mirror and added, "Look! Soccer players!"

I turned around and, sure enough, behind the field of portables was a small group heading toward the middle-school soccer field.

"That's Mike Costello's brother in front. His name's Joey. Go ahead, Paul, catch up to them. Teach them a few things."

"Yeah, maybe I will."

I hopped out and followed the group. There were four guys ahead of me kicking a ball around. I walked up and stood right in the goal.

Joey Costello said something like, "Hey, how's it going?" and kicked one at me. Then the other three kids fanned out in a semicircle in front of the goal. I caught Joey's kick and rolled the ball out to the next guy so he could take a shot. I caught his kick, rolled it to the next guy, and so on. They weren't very good. Not one of them seemed to know how to kick. They didn't drive the ball with their insteps, they just stubbed it with their toes. I had no trouble stopping everything they kicked at me.

I never did hear the names of the other guys. But when they got tired of playing, we walked back together toward the football field parking lot. Joey said, "Are you coming out for the Lake Windsor team?"

"Oh yeah. I'll be there."

"You gonna play goalie?"

"Yeah. How about you?"

"Fullback, I guess. I played some goalie last year, but I never got into a game."

"When are tryouts?"

"I don't know." Joey turned to the other guys. "When are tryouts? Anybody heard?"

Everybody shook their heads or said, "No." Joey said, "Listen to the morning announcements. They'll tell you when."

"All right," I said. "I'll catch you guys later." The four of them continued toward the other side of the field, still stubbing the ball along the ground ahead of them. I saw that Mom and Dad were waiting at the car, so I hustled over there.

I said, "Where's Erik?"

"He's getting a ride home with Arthur Bauer," Dad answered.

"How did your soccer playing go?" Mom asked.

"No sweat," I said. As we rode back, I thought about how easy it was, and how easy it was going to be. If Joey was the best they could do for a goaltender, then I already had the job. I wondered if he had changed his mind about playing goal again after watching me today. I wouldn't doubt it. I wondered if he saw that a major leaguer was here to play a season or two in the minors.

Monday, August 28

Today was the first day of school. I left the house at seven-thirty to walk to the front of the development and catch the bus. The smoke was thick and strong smelling. I walked past dark green Dumpsters filled with plasterboard and scrap metal, past blue portable toilets parked along the construction lots. It occurred to me that I've never lived in a development that was finished. I have always lived with overflowing construction Dumpsters and portable toilets sitting on boards.

I turned right at the end of Kensington Gardens Drive and walked parallel to the high gray wall. Something started to bother me almost immediately. The gray of the wall drifted along in the left side of my vision—distracting me, troubling me. What was it? Something about the wall? Something about a bus stop? Something that I needed to remember? My steps slowed down, and I came to a dead stop, frozen there like a windup toy that had run out of torque.

Then a scene came back to me. Just like the other morning in Houston. Entirely on its own, a scene came back to me:

I remembered another bus stop. And a shiny yellow school bus.

I was standing at the back of a line of kids, waiting to board the bus for one of my first days at kindergarten.

Mom had driven me to school on the actual first day. This was the first day when I would be accompanied by no one except Erik, my fifth-grade brother. But Erik did not accompany me for long. He was standing at the front of the school-bus line with his fifth-grade friends when one of them turned, made a gesture, and called to me, "Hey, Eclipse Boy, how many fingers am I holding up?"

I didn't realize at first that the boy was talking to me, and I had no idea what he meant. Erik and his friends laughed about the joke, then the bus doors opened and we all filed in. I can't put all of the details in order now, but it became clear to me later that, for some reason, the big kids on the school bus were calling me Eclipse Boy.

The fact is we did have an eclipse that summer, around three weeks before school started. Based on that, Erik was telling his friends this story: The reason for the Coke-bottle glasses on my eyes was that I had stared at the sun, unprotected, during that eclipse.

The story puzzled me then, and it puzzles me now. I do

not remember doing any such thing. And yet when I search through our family photos, I can see that I never wore glasses of any kind before that summer. But right after the eclipse, I was wearing these thick lenses that I now call my regular glasses.

Puzzled or not, I went right along with the story. I even told it myself. It gave me a special kindergarten identity. It made me somebody. I was the boy who had not listened and who was now paying the price. *Look at me if you dare!* Teachers and other adults seemed to value me as an example. I was the living proof that you shouldn't look at an eclipse or you'll go blind; that you shouldn't play in an abandoned refrigerator or you'll suffocate; that you shouldn't go swimming right after you eat or you'll get stomach cramps and drown.

So there I sat on that yellow school bus—Erik Fisher's younger brother, Eclipse Boy, visually impaired and totally incapable of following in his brother's footsteps.

The scene faded. I stood still for another minute, trying to remember more, but nothing would come. Then I made myself turn away from the wall, and I made my legs move again, one step in front of the other, to the end of the street.

As I turned the corner, I was surprised to see other kids standing next to the guardhouse. In my two weeks here, I had never seen any other kid in Lake Windsor Downs, even though I had ridden my bike up and down all of the streets at all times of the day. Now here they were, spread out in a lazy line, about ten kids of various sizes.

I quietly took my place at the end of the line, next to a guy who was slouching so badly that I thought he might actually fall over. He wasn't alone, either. Everyone seemed to be depressed, to be sorry to be there. I wondered if that was just an act, or if they really didn't feel any excitement about the first day of school.

"What's up, goalie?"

I turned, startled to find that someone was standing right behind me. I hadn't seen him coming. It was Joey Costello. I held out my hand and said, "It's Paul. Paul Fisher. You're Joey, right?"

"Right," he answered, shaking my hand.

"I met your brother over at my house. I met your father, too."

"Yeah, they said something about that. They said your brother can kick fifty-yard field goals."

"Right. Yeah, he can."

"Mike says Coach Warner has him holding the ball for him. His name's Erik, right?"

"Yeah. I had a feeling Mike might be holding the ball for Erik when he told us he was the backup quarterback."

Joey thought for a moment, then said, "Mike's getting a bad break, you know. Mike's a good player, but he's a lineman, not a quarterback. And now he's playing behind Antoine Thomas, the best quarterback in the state. He'll never get to play unless something bad happens to Antoine. And then everybody'll be mad because Mike ain't no Antoine."

"Yeah. He can't win."

The bus turned into the entranceway and stopped in front of us. When we climbed on, Joey sat with one of the soccer players from the other day. I found an empty seat near the back and pulled out my class schedule. The school had sent us a computerized schedule that showed my six periods, teachers' names, and classroom numbers.

With the schedule had come a map of the high school–middle school campus, which I appreciated, and a hand-written note to Mom from Mrs. Gates, which I did not. It said, "Vision-impaired students should report to the office for assistance." That made me mad. What did she plan to do? Assign me a dog and a cane?

The bus turned into the campus and drove around to a circular driveway that said BUSES ONLY. I looked again at my schedule, feeling jittery. It said, "Homeroom 8:15–8:25, Portable 9." I moved along with a big crowd of kids, circling the main building and funneling into the wooden walkways that led to the portables.

I found the one that said P-9 with no problem whatsoever. There was a green sign on the door that said, MS. ALVAREZ. I climbed the three wooden stairs and opened the door. Ms. Alvarez gave me a cheery "Good morning" and told me to find an empty desk.

The class seems to be made up of the same type of droopy kids that had stood with me in the bus line. In contrast, Ms. Alvarez has a lot of enthusiasm. She told us she was "truly excited to be here on the first day of a new year." She went on to tell us that we're her first homeroom ever, and that she's looking forward to starting each day with us. We sat there and stared at her without much reaction, but she smiled bravely through it, and we passed the first ten minutes of the school year together. She asked us to all take out our schedules and check them. Mine said, "Science 8:30–9:25, Portable 12."

Ms. Alvarez read some announcements from a computer printout, but there was nothing about the soccer team. The speaker in the room crackled to life with the sound of a gong being struck. This was our signal to funnel out again onto the wooden walkways. We had four minutes to get to our next class, but it took me less than one.

I climbed up a set of stairs marked P-12, where the green sign said, MRS. HOFFMAN. Mrs. Hoffman was standing right inside the door, scowling and holding a seating chart. She's clearly at the other end of the teacher food chain from Ms. Alvarez. As she would soon tell us, she has been teaching science for twenty years. She asked my name and then directed me to the last seat in the first row. The kids in this room seem a little more lively.

Just five minutes into Mrs. Hoffman's class there was a knock on the door. A girl came in holding a block of wood with the word PASS painted on it. She whispered to Mrs. Hoffman, who checked her chart, looked toward me, and said, "Paul Fisher, go with this young lady, please."

What could I do? I got up. I followed the girl out the door and onto the walkway. I said, "Where are we going?"

"Mr. Murrow's office."

"Who's Mr. Murrow?"

"He's the head of guidance."

We went to a small office inside the main office. A man with a brown suit and thick glasses like mine was sitting at a desk. He had a pile of those IEP forms spread out in front of him. He said, "And what is your name?"

"Paul Fisher, sir."

He found my IEP form. "All right, Paul, this is Kerri Gardner, one of our school volunteers. Kerri will act as your eyes, so to speak, until you've learned your way around our campus."

"I can see fine."

He seemed genuinely surprised. "You can?"

"Yes, sir. I've been to two classes already."

Mr. Murrow looked back at my IEP form and then at me. He said, "Well, perhaps since you're new to our school, Kerri could just take you around for the first day. What harm could that do?"

I didn't know what else to say. I didn't know how to describe the harm that that would do to me. Nothing more came out of my mouth, so he said, "Why don't you two go on back to Mrs. Hoffman's class."

I followed Kerri Gardner back to P-12—actually, to the wooden steps outside of it. That was where I finally found my voice. I stopped still and said as calmly as I could, "Look. I'm sorry. I don't mean to mess up your job, but there's no reason for anybody to show me around. OK?"

She looked at me, puzzled, so I explained, "There's nothing wrong with me. This is a mistake. I can see just fine."

Kerri answered matter-of-factly, "So then what's with the glasses?"

I reached up and fingered the thick plastic frames. I finally answered, "I had an accident. I had some kind of damage to my eyes when I was five years old."

Kerri clearly did not mind being released from her duties. She thought for a moment, lowered her voice, and said, "Look. I'll hold on to the pass until the end of the day and then turn it in. Nobody'll know."

"OK, thanks."

Kerri started off but turned back to ask, "What was the accident? What damaged your eyes?"

"I don't know. I mean, I'm not sure," I replied.

She took off again, leaving me thinking. *Why didn't I answer that question? I used to have an answer ready to that question. I used to tell people that I once stared too long at a solar eclipse.*

But if that's the truth, if that really happened, why can't I remember it?

Wednesday, August 30

I'm in my room now, at the computer, listening to the sound of Erik kicking a football into a net in the backyard. It's a short, violent sound, like some big guys holding up some little guy and punching him over and over in the stomach. *Poomph. Poomph. Poomph.*

The Erik Fisher Football Dream seems to be materializing. Arthur Bauer is holding the ball for him today, crouching low and spinning the laces away, just like Dad, just like Mike Costello. Arthur is a senior, like Erik. Unlike Erik, he seems to have no special talent for football. And yet here he is, a third-string benchwarmer kind of guy, holding the ball for the great Erik Fisher.

Arthur has a sister named Paige, who is a sophomore and a cheerleader. Paige is down there, too. She is clearly going to be Erik's girlfriend. Arthur's girlfriend is named Tina Turreton. She's sitting next to Paige. Tina is a junior and, of course, a cheerleader.

The four of them are hanging out in the smoke of a late-afternoon muck fire ignited by an early-afternoon lightning strike. *Poomph. Poomph. Poomph.*

Mom has already done her research on Erik's friends. She pumps him for information over dinner every night, and he tells her whatever she wants to know: Arthur and Paige Bauer are the yellow Stuart with the brick front. Their father is a building contractor and a major in the Army National Guard. They moved in three years ago. Tina Turreton is the white York, like ours, but with avocado trim. She's only lived here a year.

They're a strange foursome, sitting back there in the smoke. Basically they pay no attention to each other. The girls are on the cement patio, sitting at the redwood picnic table, doing homework. The boys are on the grass, kicking the ball into the net. *Poomph. Poomph. Poomph.*

I guess Paige and Tina want to date football players, so these two will do. Erik and Arthur want to date cheerleaders, so these two will do.

I watched them all pull up to the house in Arthur Bauer's truck, then I hurried upstairs. Arthur has a white Toyota Land Cruiser that he's jacked up and put big tires on for "mud runnin'." That's what they do around here. They take their jacked-up trucks out into the swamps and "mud run." When they can't do that, they run up and down the dirt road behind our wall, the perimeter road. Arthur's truck has a big spotlight mounted on top, at the center of the windshield, so he can go mud running at night.

Now he can take Erik mud running. And he can take Erik to practice. And he can take Erik wherever else Erik says to take him.

You see, Erik doesn't drive. Can you believe that? One of the greatest things about high school is that you can drive. All by yourself. You're *free*. But Erik doesn't drive. He has never even expressed an interest in driving. Tell me that isn't strange.

From my bedroom window I can see them all clearly, especially Arthur Bauer. And I can predict his future. Arthur is about to get his big break, his chance to be somebody at Lake Windsor High. Let's face it, Arthur Bauer is no Mike Costello. He is not the backup quarterback to Antoine Thomas. He has not already been accepted into FSU's School of Engineering. He has never really accomplished anything, until now. This is his shot at the big time. He will somehow, with Erik's help, beat out Mike Costello for the job of holder on placekicks. It will be Arthur's backside featured in the newspapers, holding the ball for Erik Fisher's fifty-yard field-goal attempts.

According to Joey Costello, Arthur has never even gotten into a game. Now he'll be out there when the crowd is roaring, and the cameras are flashing, and the game is on the line. What will Arthur do for an opportunity like that, for that kind of fame and glory? What will Arthur do for Erik, his sponsor, his benefactor, his ticket to the big time? Let's face it. He will do anything. He will do anything that Erik asks. He has found himself a place in the Erik Fisher Football Dream, and he will do anything to stay there.

I've always been afraid of Erik. Now I get to be afraid of Erik and Arthur.

Thursday, August 31

In addition to my regular glasses, I have special goggles, prescription goggles, for playing sports. They're made out of some kind of astronaut plastic that could crash-land on Venus and not break. Nothing can break them. If the dinosaurs had worn these goggles, and the Earth had been bombarded by mile-wide asteroid boulders, the dinosaurs would still have died, but their goggles would be intact. Nothing can break these goggles.

The reason I bring this up is that Ms. Alvarez read the announcement this morning that tryouts for the soccer teams, boys' and girls', will start tomorrow. I have my goal-tending gear—the prescription goggles, knee pads, and elbow pads—in a drawer in my room. I just checked the drawer to make sure everything was ready. I didn't want to find out tomorrow that my gear was all packed away in our climate-controlled storage place on Route 22.

Mom and I took some stuff to the storage place today. Mom is not adjusting well to the smoke from the muck fire. She took down her mother's drapes from the dining room and packed them up with her grandmother's quilts from the bedrooms. "I won't have them ruined by this smoke," she told me as I lugged the boxes out to the car. "We'll put them back out when your grandparents visit in December."

My grandparents are Mom's parents. Dad's parents died when he was young—his father when he was ten, and his mother when he was a freshman in college. Dad never talks about them. It's like they never existed.

Mom doesn't talk much about hers, either. I know that my grandfather retired from the army as a master sergeant. He still works as a security guard in an office building. My grandmother always ran a day-care business out of her home, wherever that happened to be, right up until last year. Mom says that's where she inherited her own organizational skills.

Mom is now donating those skills to the Homeowners' Association of Lake Windsor Downs. Mr. Costello asked her to be on the Architectural Committee. It's a powerful position. If you have any plan to improve your house, even if it's just planting a new tree, you have to have it approved beforehand by the Architectural Committee.

Because of this, Mom has taken to spotting irregularities whenever we drive into or out of the development. She's taken to saying stuff like, "Look at the trim color on that Lancaster. That's not a regulation trim color. It looks like pea soup."

Today she said, "Look at the mailbox on that Tudor. That's not a Tudor-style mailbox."

I said, "Lighten up, Mom."

"Don't tell me to lighten up. These people all read and signed the regulations before they bought houses here. Those regulations are serious, Paul. This development has a certain look to it. If you like that look, then you buy a house here. If you don't like that look, then you buy a house someplace else."

"What harm could it do to have a non-Tudor mailbox?"

Mom thought about that one. "Not much, I suppose. I won't send them a letter about the mailbox, because the one they have doesn't look bad. But if twenty more houses decided to put up twenty different styles of mailboxes, it'd start to look like a shantytown around here."

Mom suddenly got very serious. "Paul, I'm talking as somebody who never, ever, lived in a nice house growing up. Or even lived anywhere near a nice house. This is not a joke to me. Your house is your family's biggest investment. And you have to protect that investment."

At the storage place, Mom showed her ID to an elderly guard, who waved us on. I unlocked our bin, pulled up the sliding metal door, and stacked the boxes inside. On the way home I turned the conversation to the soccer tryouts.

Mom actually had a good suggestion. She said, "You should call that Joey Costello boy. You two could run some laps tonight. Maybe we can get a soccer-team car pool going with them, too."

I called Joey as soon as we got back, and asked him if he wanted to start running. He said he runs every night at six-thirty, and I could meet him at the guardhouse if I wanted. I said OK and hung up.

That was odd. If he ran every night, why had I never seen him?

Anyway, Joey turned out to be pretty funny. Up until now he'd been a little stiff. We started to run with the sand at our backs and just a trace of smoke in the air. On our second lap he pointed to a house, a white Stuart on a corner lot. He said, "You see that house? Mr. Donnelly and his son live there. They've been hit by lightning three times."

"No way."

"Absolutely. Three times. Are they losers or what?"

I had to laugh when I noticed the sign on their front lawn. "Hey, look! It's for sale!"

"Yeah. Like they've got a prayer."

"I don't know. When you're looking at a house, does anybody tell you bad stuff like that?"

Joey said, "No way. They'd never mention it."

"What if you found out?"

"They'd tell you that it was a good thing. They'd tell you that, statistically, it's the safest house in the whole development. Maybe in the whole world. There's almost no chance that this house will ever get hit by lightning again."

I looked back over my shoulder at the receding Stuart. "It'll get hit again. And again. And I'll tell you why."

"Why?"

"The lightning. It knows that spot."

"What are you talking about?"

I pointed at an empty lot full of sugar sand. "Think about this place. After they plowed under all the tangerine groves, what did they do?"

"Who? What did who do?"

"The developers. The construction guys. What did they do?"

"I don't know."

"They leveled everything out with bulldozers. Right? They brought in tons and tons of that white sand and dumped it here. Then they landscaped over everything."

"Yeah. So what?"

"So let's say that that corner house used to be the highest ground around here for miles. Maybe it was at the top of a rise with big trees on it. So that's where the lightning always used to strike."

"Then it must've had big *dead* trees on it."

"Whatever. This was the highest spot, and it worked like a lightning rod. Now, you could bring back those developers, and the construction guys, and the engineers, and ask them to point out where the highest spot around here used to be. Not one of them would know. But the lightning knows. It hits right where it's always hit. It's just that some fool has stuck a house there." I pointed back toward the front of the development, toward the four English royal-family models. "Who knows? Maybe someday, after all this crumbles away, the trees will be back, and these storms will make sense again."

We completed our second lap. Joey was looking at me a little strangely. He said, "See you tomorrow."

"Right. Tryouts are at four. You need a ride home?"

"Nah, I'll catch a ride with Mike."

"OK."

44

I started off, but Joey was struggling with something. He finally said, "Hey, uh, Fisher . . . I don't think lightning is that complicated. I don't think it knows anything about anything."

I thought about that. "Yeah. Maybe I'm exaggerating."

But maybe I'm not.

Friday, September 1

My last class of the day is language arts, with Mrs. Bridges. If you think we're slugs in the morning with Ms. Alvarez, you should see us by sixth period. Some kids actually fall asleep, but I don't think they're completely to blame. By the time we get to sixth period, the portables' air conditioners have been struggling along for seven hours, with the doors constantly opening and closing. We're sweating buckets by then. We're wilting. Even Mrs. Bridges's perm is wilting by then.

But today, when the speaker crackled on and the gong bell sounded, I was filled with new energy. I hefted up my gym bag and set off for the soccer tryouts.

Just to the south of the portables is a baseball diamond with a scoreboard that says, LAKE WINDSOR MIDDLE SCHOOL—HOME OF THE SEAGULLS. The soccer field is to the left of that, next to a stretch of undeveloped land.

As I left the wooden walkways Joey fell into step with me, and we jogged together to the fields.

"You're a pretty good goalie, right?" he asked me.

"Right," I said.

"Then I'm going out for fullback."

"Hey, we need at least two goalies. What if I get killed?"

"You're not gonna get killed. I'll play fullback. I like fullback. You get to knock people down."

"Suit yourself."

45

Joey pointed to a circle of kids near the sideline. "Check out Tommy over there, the kid with the ball. He's from the Philippines. Awesome display, man. Awesome."

I looked over and recognized a kid from my homeroom, Tommy Acoso. He had a group of guys standing around watching him, like he was a juggler. We stopped to watch him, too. He kept hitting the ball straight up in the air with his head, feet, and knees, never letting it touch the ground, just keeping it going and going and going. Sometimes he would make it stop dead, right on his forehead. It *was* an awesome display. Not all of these guys were the toe stubbers who I had played with last week.

"That's Gino over there," Joey whispered. "Gino Deluca. He'll be the captain this year. No doubt. He was a co-captain last year. Scored twenty-two goals."

I saw a big guy—big for a soccer player—with long, curly black hair. He was driving penalty kicks into the net from twelve yards out. I asked Joey, "Where's he from?"

"I don't know. New Jersey, I think."

Gino kept hammering penalty shots into the upper left corner of the goal while a tall kid in a gray sweatshirt retrieved the ball and rolled it back. Gino is obviously a major leaguer. He's the kind of guy you have to have on a soccer team in order to win. The guy who wants to take the penalty kicks. The guy who's hungry to score the goals.

The head coach is Mr. Walski, an eighth-grade teacher. He blew a whistle, and we all moved toward him. He looks more like a baseball-basketball guy to me, but he coached the soccer team last season, and he knows most of the seventh and eighth graders. He's tall and nearly bald. When he spoke, it was in a raspy voice. "I want to congratulate you guys on making the team."

There was a scattering of laughter.

"For those of you who may not know it, our policy in the Lake Windsor Middle School soccer program is this:

Everybody makes the team, everybody practices, and everybody gets a uniform. However,"—and he paused here for emphasis—"that does not mean that everybody is, as we say, 'on the bus.' Everybody cannot, and I must emphasize *cannot*, go to every away game. We have a small team bus, and we have restrictions due to insurance. We can only take fifteen kids to the away games. That's our policy. You're a part of this team from day one, but your part may be to play in practice games only and to dress for the home games only. Does everybody understand?"

There were nods around the group. The coach continued, "OK, let's get started. Gino, you're the captain. Take them twice around the field. Then we're going to break into sixth-, seventh-, and eighth-grade groups and start calisthenics. Let's move out."

I ran with Joey and about thirty other guys, twice around the field. "That means half of us are dog meat," Joey muttered.

"What are you complaining about? You're on the team."

"Fifteen kids are on the real team, and fifteen kids are dog meat. I was dog meat last year, and it was a drag. I don't want to do that again."

"Hey, it makes sense to me. Why drive all these extra guys to a game when there's no chance they're going to play?"

"Yeah? That's easy for you to say."

After calisthenics, we broke into groups to kick the ball around. I had no reason to do that, so I found my gym bag and got out my goggles, knee pads, and elbow pads. Gino and some other eighth graders were back at the goal kicking shots at the kid in the gray sweatshirt. I walked up next to the goal and stood there until they couldn't help but notice me.

The kid in gray checked out my goggles and said, "Yow! It came from Mars!"

The eighth graders laughed, but when I didn't go away Gino said to me, "You here to play, or you here to model sportswear?"

"To play."

Gino motioned and the kid in the gray sweatshirt stood off to the side. I moved into the goal, dead in the center, and placed my heels on the chalk line. A kid with red hair was next in line to kick. He took a shot that rolled wide of the goal. I never even moved.

I was waiting for Gino, and he knew it. He called for the ball and then placed it with care on the penalty line. He stepped back three paces and looked right at me. I got down into my goalie crouch, a coiled spring ready to release. Gino shouted like a samurai, took two quick steps, and started his powerful kick. I sprang up and to my right, exactly where I had watched him kick every other penalty shot. I heard the sound of his foot walloping the ball, and then I felt it smack against my right wrist. The ball flew away from the goal as fast as it had flown in. It sailed toward the far sideline. I hit the ground and popped up immediately, ready for more.

Gino looked at the ball bouncing away in the distance and then looked back at me. He seemed genuinely surprised. "Whoa!" he said quietly, and gave me a thumbs-up sign with both hands.

The kid in the gray sweatshirt hung around by the goal for another minute. Then he casually walked out and joined the others in the line, waiting for a turn to kick one at me.

The coach didn't see any of this, but I knew I had just landed the job. I was now the Lake Windsor Middle School goaltender. First-string goaltender. On-the-bus goaltender.

Tuesday, September 5

Mom and I had just returned home from the supermarket. We were unloading her station wagon, carrying bags of groceries from the garage into the kitchen, when Erik and Arthur pulled up in the Land Cruiser. There was mud splattered all over the sides, all over the tinted windows, and even up on that center spotlight. Erik got out of the passenger side and walked up to Mom, slowly and solemnly. Arthur got out and followed him. Erik stopped just inside the garage and said, "Mike Costello is dead, Mom. He got killed at practice today."

Mom and I stopped still, the supermarket bags weighing down our arms. Neither of us moved, or knew what to do next. We stared at him, speechless, until he continued in the same voice. "He was just standing there in the end zone. He had one hand on the goalpost, leaning on it, and *kaboom*! There was a crack, and a flash, and he went flying through the air. He landed right on his back, right there on the goal line."

By now Mom was staring hard at him, trying to understand the point of this speech. "Erik? The boy...the boy who was here?—Mike? Is dead?"

"Dead before he hit the ground. Arthur and I went over and looked at him, right?"

Arthur spoke up. "Right."

"The whole left side of his hair was burned off. Singed right off, you know?"

Mom still did not seem to comprehend. She struggled for words. "What...what...Erik, tell me exactly what you did."

"Me? Nothing. There was nothing I could do. Coach

Warner, all the other coaches, they surrounded him. They started banging on his chest."

Arthur added, "Bangin' on him."

"Doing CPR. Everybody was going nuts. Dad started running up to his car phone, dialing 911."

Mom said, "Your father? Your father called 911?"

"Yeah. Ambulances came. Cop cars came. They had this power-pack thing, you know?"

Arthur said, "Jump-startin' him."

"They were trying to jump-start his heart. They were sticking needles in him. Everything! But nothing worked, because he was already dead. He was dead before he hit the ground."

"What about Jack? Jack Costello? Was he there watching all of this?"

"No, I didn't see him. I think his brother was there." Erik looked over at Arthur. "Was that his brother?"

Arthur said, "Yeah," and seemed to fight back a smile.

Erik continued, "His little brother freaked out. He went crazy. He kept trying to take off Mike's shoes. I thought the coach was gonna have to smack him. He wouldn't get out of the way. Just kept trying to get his shoes off. Did you see that?" Erik looked at Arthur again, who covered up his face with his hand.

Mom picked up the phone. She tried to reach Dad—first at his mobile number, then through his office beeper—but she couldn't.

I asked her, "Should I call Joey?"

"No. No, we can't call the Costellos now. We can't intrude on them now." Mom banged out another number on the phone. "I'm going to try the school."

There was no answer at the school, either. Mom stood there staring at the bags of groceries. She looked like she was going to pass out. The ring of the telephone made her jump. It was Dad, calling from the hospital. He told her basically the same story that Erik had, right down to Joey Costello and the problem with Mike's shoes. Joey and his parents were at the hospital, and Mike had been officially pronounced dead. Dad said that everyone there was in a state of shock.

I know I was. I carried my bags of groceries on into the kitchen and set them down. Then I heard a strange sound. It was the sound of voices in the backyard. Happy voices.

I looked through the patio doors and saw Erik and Arthur. They were laughing. I stepped closer to the doors, and I could hear Erik saying, "Did you see his hair? Did you see the side of his head? He got Mohawked, man!"

Arthur said, "Mohawked."

I watched them in disbelief. How could they be happy? Who were these two people? Then I realized it: They were the two people who will benefit from Mike Costello's death. And they were celebrating it. Erik grabbed at Arthur's shoes and screamed in a high-pitched voice, "The shoes! Gimme the shoes!"

I turned to look for Mom. She was still in the garage, on the phone with Dad. She saw none of this. She heard none of this.

I turned back to watch the cruel comedy routine on the other side of the glass. There they were, Erik and a nasty friend. Just like I remembered them in Houston. Nothing had changed except the name of the friend.

I felt sick and confused. I asked myself, *How could this happen? How could this happen to Mike Costello? He was a nice guy. He was number two on the depth chart. He was already accepted into the School of Engineering at FSU.*

And I answered myself, *Here's how: because Mike Costello didn't fit into the Erik Fisher Football Dream . . . Mike would never, could never, have been sitting out there with Erik and laughing at such a thing.*

Now Mike is dead.
But the Dream lives on.

Wednesday, September 6

Mom seemed to think they would be canceling classes at the high school today and sending everyone home early because of the tragedy with Mike Costello. Mom was way off on that one. They didn't cancel classes. They didn't even cancel football practice.

I watched the football practice from a distance. I stood in a goal on the soccer field, looking through the back side of the football stadium bleachers. Different pockets of players were doing different drills. It all looked very violent today. Over here they were shouting and hitting a tackling dummy. Over there they were hurling their bodies at a blocking sled, trying to drive it backward. In the middle of all this knocking down and getting knocked down and getting back up again, I could see Erik standing at the fifty-yard line, untouched by it all. Calmly, deliberately, he drilled his field goals between the upright posts in the end zone. But Mike Costello was not there to spin the laces away from the kicker and set the ball down. Mike Costello was on a slab at the undertaker's. No, there was another backside in the distance today—Arthur Bauer's.

Naturally, Joey Costello was not at soccer practice, or at school. I expected to hear something about Mike over the loudspeaker, but the only announcement they read was about reduced tickets to a carnival that's coming to Tangerine. No "Pray for Mike Costello" or "Pray for Joey Costello." Ms. Alvarez, though, wrote his address on the chalkboard and urged everybody who knows Joey to send a card to the family.

A couple of guys at soccer practice were talking about the accident. They said that the principal of the high school, Mr. Bridges (husband of my language arts teacher), read an announcement. Mr. Bridges said the Student Council planned to do something special to honor Mike's memory. He didn't say what that something was. It obviously wasn't canceling football practice.

Mom and Dad are at each other's throats arguing about all of this—the football practice, the lightning, the kind of place we live in now. Mom is determined to call the parents of each and every football player, get them together, and have them refuse to send their sons to any more afternoon practices.

Dad, apparently, is arguing the other side. Coach Warner now refers to Dad as one of his "football fathers." Dad likes that, and I think he is afraid of doing anything that might mess up his status. Mom's reply was something like, "Dead boys don't kick footballs."

Soccer practice was a colossal drag. We spent most of the time playing a pointless (and goal-less) scrimmage game— the sixth and seventh graders versus the eighth graders. I hate games like that. The ball never gets near the goal. Two teams full of clueless toe stubbers keep kicking it back and forth at each other, never going twenty yards past either side of midfield. The kid in the gray sweatshirt played goal for the eighth graders. He had a shutout going, too.

It's obvious to me that there are only a handful of real players on this team. Our side had Tommy and me. Their side had Gino and a couple of big guys playing fullback. Everybody else who got the ball just kicked it away in a panic. We have absolutely nobody at midfield. That's why the pointless, toe-stubbing battle continued to rage. There is no in-between on this team. We have two great strikers in Tommy and Gino, one great goaltender in me, and a freezer full of dog meat. Maybe when Tommy and Gino get together on the front line they can feed off each other. I sure hope so.

While I was standing there in the goal waiting for something to happen, my mind started to wander. I started thinking about Joey and what he must be going through. I wondered what I would be like in Joey's place. What if my brother had landed on the goal line with the left side of his hair singed off? What if Erik was the body at the undertaker's now? How would I feel about that?

I would feel relieved. I would feel safer. But I would feel sorry, too. Erik is a part of that eclipse story. I know he is. Erik is a part of whatever it is that I need to remember. I don't want Erik to die and take his part of the story with him.

Thursday, September 7

Mom began her telephone campaign at 9:00 A.M. She had a list of all the numbers in Lake Windsor Downs. She called everyone she knew of who had a son on the football team.

After a few hours of this, she was interrupted by a call from Dad. The principal of Lake Windsor High School, Mr. Bridges, had called him. Mr. Bridges told Dad that he was getting complaints from parents about the afternoon football practices. Dad and Mr. Bridges arranged to have a meeting at our house tonight with Coach Warner and anyone else who wanted to come. Mom acted surprised, hung up, then returned to her list and called back everyone who had expressed interest. She asked them all to meet at our house at 7:45.

After dinner I helped Mom arrange couches and extra chairs in the great room. Erik went out with Arthur. For a while I could hear them racing up and down the perimeter road in the mud, then they were gone.

By 7:55 twelve parents had arrived. They sat in the great room with Dad and made small talk about the Japanese fish in our lake, stuff like, *Are the koi disappearing from the lake? Are they dying? Is someone fishing in the lake at night? Could there be an alligator eating the koi?*

Mom answered the door at 8:05 to Mr. Bridges, a short round man in a blue suit, and Coach Warner, who was wearing a Lake Windsor High pullover. Mom showed them to a pair of chairs next to the fireplace, facing the crowd. She thanked them for coming, then took a seat next to Dad on the couch. Coach Warner sat down, but Mr. Bridges remained standing to speak.

"You probably know me. I'm Bud Bridges. I've been principal of Lake Windsor High since the doors opened here ten years ago. And I have to share with you that this tragic accident is the worst thing that's happened to me as a principal. Mike Costello was a fine young man, a young man I'm proud to say I knew. His loss is a personal loss for me."

"Let's make sure he's the last one we lose!"

Everyone in the room looked at Mom, who had startled them with this interruption.

Mr. Bridges recovered quickly. "Amen to that. I met with the Student Council officers today. They have decided to dedicate this year's Senior Awards Night to Mike Costello and to plant a tree in his memory in our entranceway."

Mom leaned forward. "Mr. Bridges, can we count on you to stop these afternoon practices during thunderstorms?"

Mr. Bridges looked over at Coach Warner. "I've discussed this with the coach, and I'll let him address that."

Mr. Bridges sat down, but Coach Warner did not get up. He spoke quietly from his chair, directly to Mom. "Ma'am, I also took Mike Costello's death personally. I knew Mike well. I knew him as a football player and as a leader. I know that Mike was dedicated to this team and would not want to see it destroyed because of this tragic accident." The coach cleared his throat. "And that's really what you're talking about, ma'am, the destruction of this team. There really is no other time to practice, so we would be a team that did not practice. There are some boys who play for me, boys like Antoine Thomas, who are counting on football, and on this football season in particular, to get them into college. College is not going to happen for them without football. That's just a hard fact. I know some of you have the means to send your kids to college anyway. I'm just saying that not everybody is in that situation."

Mom remained hunched forward. "We're not saying, Don't practice. We're saying, Don't practice when lightning might strike and kill a player."

"Ma'am, there has never been another boy injured by lightning in our program. And we've been practicing in the same place at the same time for ten years now. It was an accident, a tragic accident...Somebody gets killed in their car out on the highway, it's tragic and we mourn the loss of that person, but we don't stop all traffic from ever using that highway again. We don't close it down. We recognize it as an accident."

Mom sat upright. She pulled a small black notebook out of her pocket. "Coach Warner, you may be interested in this information. This is from the *Tangerine Times*, August first: 'Tangerine County is the lightning-strike capital of the United States. More people are killed by lightning in Tangerine County per year than in any other county in America.' That's not 'any other county in Florida,' Coach. That's 'any other county in America.' And there have indeed been other football players killed—one at Tangerine High and one at St. Anthony's High. A cross-country runner was killed here two years ago by lightning. A sophomore from Lake Windsor High was killed stepping off of her school bus last year. Being struck by lightning is one of the top causes of accidental death in this area."

Coach Warner looked down, like he was thinking. When he looked back up at Mom, he seemed to have made up his mind. "Ma'am, if you choose to remove your son from the football program based on that information, I will understand. He can turn in his playbook and uniform to me or to one of my assistant coaches."

I looked at Dad, sitting back on the couch next to Mom. His whole body was stiff, rigid, like he was dead. What would he do? Would he publicly take Coach Warner's side against Mom? Or would he defend her and anger Erik's coach?

I would not find out the answers to these questions, because it was Mom who spoke up. She was not ready to give up, either. Mom was not ready to pull the plug on the Erik Fisher Football Dream that drove our lives. "Why can't you hold your practices in the morning, for the safety of all? I understand that these boys, and you coaches, and we parents, are all dedicated. We can dedicate ourselves to getting the boys to the football field at six-thirty. That way they can practice for an hour, take showers, and be ready for class at eight."

Coach Warner replied slowly, "Ma'am, I can't ask these players and their parents to give up their sleep, to disrupt their lives, to come out to practice football at six-thirty." He paused to collect his thoughts. "We have kids who can only get to school by bus. Those kids could no longer make practice. Again, this is about doing the right thing for everybody involved. Not all of my players have parents at home, with cars, who don't need to be at work themselves by six-thirty in the morning."

Mom was angry now. She pointed her black notebook at him. "You seem to want to make this a rich-versus-poor or a have-versus-have-not issue, right? But a bolt of lightning is not aware of a kid's parents' income when it hits him. That's what we're talking about here, if you'd care to listen. We're talking about kids placed in harm's way every day because of when *you* schedule your practice."

Coach Warner looked down again. He wasn't going to budge. Mr. Bridges was looking more and more nervous.

Arthur Bauer's father said, to no one in particular, "It's the same thing with soldiers. They gotta train in all kinds of weather so they'll be ready for anything."

A long and tense silence followed. It was broken when a large man, larger than Coach Warner, stood up. He had a reddish gray crew cut and a big head and neck, like a football player's. When he spoke, though, it was with a surprisingly high voice. "I'm Bill Donnelly. My son, Terry, and I live at 6200 Kew Gardens Drive. Some of you may know my house, or know about it. It's the one that's been struck by lightning three times. Each time it was at about four o'clock in the afternoon. My son plays football at Lake Windsor High, and I'm very proud of that. But I have to agree with Mrs. Fisher. We live in an area where this lightning-strike stuff is a reality." He stopped and addressed the coach directly. "I'm willing to drive my son to practice at four o'clock in the morning if I have to. And I'll take part in any kind of car pool we set up, to make sure that every kid can get there." He turned then and looked right at Mom. "I can't sell my house because of this lightning thing. I can't get an insurance agent to write me a homeowners' policy. But I don't really care about any of that. I care about my son and what might happen to him. I can't even imagine what Jack Costello and his wife are going through tonight."

Mr. Donnelly sat down, and the rest of the room finally came to life. Other parents leaned over to Mom to tell her that they'd take part in a car pool, too.

Mr. Bridges stood up to speak. He had to wait until the

talking died down. "Well, all right, I think that's a good suggestion. What we can do now is present this suggestion to all the parents. We can contact the parent or guardian of each player and ask them to respond to the question, Should we move football practice to the early morning? Coach, does that work for you?"

Coach Warner was quick to agree. "Of course. We can try that. Me and my staff are certainly willing. We'll ask all the parents, and if the majority want to do that, then that's what we'll do." He paused to look at Mom. "Personally, I'd prefer another solution."

Mom replied immediately, "Which is?"

"Which is that we continue to practice in the afternoon, but we call a halt to it whenever there is lightning in the area."

"That's every day, Coach. Every day at four o'clock."

"No. It is not every day. At this time of the season we might have rain every day. We might have rain during some of our games, too. But that does not mean that there is lightning striking in the area every day."

The coach stopped, and no one else spoke. Mr. Bridges took the opportunity to sum up the meeting. "Then we're all agreed on this course of action. We need to present this suggestion to the parents of all the players. If the majority want to move practice to the morning, we'll work together to solve the transportation problems that some boys might have."

People around the room started mumbling, and the meeting broke up. Mom thanked Mr. Bridges and Coach Warner for coming. They exited quickly. Other parents lingered for a short time at the door, thanking Mom. Mom made a point of thanking Mr. Donnelly, right in front of Dad, "for speaking up in support of our children." Dad pretended to be saying good night to someone else, but I'm sure he heard. By 8:30, the house was empty of guests. Mom, Dad, and I worked silently to restore the furniture and straighten up the great room.

Mom headed upstairs first. She said good night to me, but she pointedly ignored Dad. When I went upstairs, he was standing alone by the fireplace, staring at the spot where Coach Warner had been sitting.

Friday, September 8

I'm not going to dwell on this. I'm just going to say it and get on with my life.

I was standing in the goal at soccer practice taking shots from some of the starting players, mostly eighth graders. They've all picked up on what the kid in the gray sweatshirt said about my goggles. They all call me Mars. That's OK with me. I've been called worse. What's important is that I'm a player, and they all recognize that. I'm their starting goalie, right?

So I was standing in the goal, wearing the red pullover goalie shirt, handling some pretty easy shots. Gino was over on the sideline talking to Coach Walski. I saw them kind of looking at me, and then Gino came running over and yelled, "Hey, Mars! Is your name Paul Fisher?"

"Yeah."

"Coach wants to see you."

"All right." I figured this was it. This was going to make it all official. The coach was going to tell me how impressed he has been by my play in goal, and so on. I hustled over to the sideline. "Coach Walski? You wanted to see me?"

"Are you Paul Fisher?"

"Yes, sir."

He looked at his clipboard and flipped through some

pages until he found a memo. "Uh, Paul, you have an IEP. Is that correct?"

"Yes, sir."

Coach Walski looked pained. "I'm sorry to tell you this, Paul, but you're not eligible for the program."

"Sir?"

"You can't play. You can't play soccer for Lake Windsor Middle School."

"What are talking about—'can't play'? I can play! I'm one of the best players here!"

"No. No, I mean you're not eligible to play. I have a memo from Mr. Murrow saying that you're in a special program for the visually handicapped. Is that right?"

"So what? I can see fine!"

"That's not the point."

"I don't understand what you're talking about."

"We have to carry insurance on every boy and girl in the program or we can't play. Period. If we lose our insurance, we lose our program. I'm sorry, but there's no way we can justify putting a visually handicapped student in the goal, of all places, where he could get his head kicked in." He looked at me like I was crazy to think otherwise. Then he added, "Come on now."

I screamed, "No, you come on now! You see if you can kick my head in! You see if you or anybody else here can get one ball past me—one ball!"

Coach Walski pulled back. He changed his tone. "Paul, I'm sorry. I know you're upset. I know you're disappointed. But try to understand this. It'd be the same situation if you had a heart murmur, or a hernia, or whatever. I have to play it straight with the insurance company. If any kid has any physical problem, I have to report it. And I know that this condition of yours will not be acceptable to the insurance company. Again, I'm sorry."

He got even sorrier a few seconds later. I still can't

believe what I did. I knelt down on that sideline, took off my sports goggles, and started to cry. I didn't say another word. I just put my head down and cried and sobbed.

Coach Walski was as much at a loss as I was. Neither of us knew what to do next. He just stood there and watched me. I heard him call an assistant over and tell him to organize a scrimmage. Coach Walski stood a little off to the side and waited. I finally stopped. I wiped my face with my goalie shirt, put my goggles back on, and walked from the field to the parking lot.

I stood in the bus shelter until five, when Mom pulled up in the station wagon. Dad was right behind her in the Range Rover. Mom rolled down the passenger-side window. "What are you doing here? Are you all right?"

"I got kicked off the team."

"What? What happened?"

"Coach Walski said I'm in a program for the handicapped so I'm off the team."

"That's . . . that's outrageous! He can't do that."

"Well, he just did it. He said they can't get insurance for me because I'm in a handicapped program. You know all about that. Right, Mom?"

"Me? What do you mean?"

"You told them I'm handicapped! You told them I'm visually impaired!"

"Darling, you are. I just told them the truth."

"That's not the truth. I can see! Don't you know that? Why did you fill out that stupid form when you know I can see? You saw me play in Houston. You saw me make thirty saves in one game! Did I look visually impaired then?"

"Paul, darling, I did not know that the IEP form had anything to do with playing on the soccer team. I would never have filled it out if I did. I know how important this is to you. Listen, now. Your father will straighten this out with Coach Walski." She turned off her engine, got out, and went back to speak to Dad.

I didn't listen, but I guess she explained the situation, because Dad got out and walked to the soccer field. I remained standing in the bus shelter, watching the black outline of an osprey slowly crossing the sky to its nest. It was clutching something that flashed brightly, reflecting the sun. I said to myself, *There goes another one of your koi, Mr. Costello.*

Mom was watching me, but she didn't say anything. Did she really believe that Dad was going to straighten this out?

We both watched Dad talk to Coach Walski, and we both watched him walk back to the station wagon. He stood at the passenger window, between Mom and me, and said, "All right. Here's the deal. They have a problem with the insurance. They can't put Paul in the goal because of his vision. *However!* Coach Walski does want you to manage the team. He hasn't appointed a manager yet for this season, and he wants you to take the job. He said to tell you that you'd be 'on the bus.' You'd be in charge of the team and the equipment for every game, home and away."

I looked at Mom's face. At least she understood. At least she had a clue.

I didn't argue. There was nothing left to say. I looked back at Dad and told him calmly, "I'm not a water boy, Dad. I'm not a team manager. I'm a player." Then I climbed into the back of the station wagon, and we all started for home.

After a few miles, Mom whispered, "Darling, do you want me to go speak to Mr. Murrow?"

I said, "What for?"

"To tell him that your vision has improved."

"Why? Do you believe that?"

We drove in silence for a while. Then she answered, "Yes, I do. I do believe it. And I do remember those games in Houston. You were the best goaltender in that league.

I was terrified to let you play, but you turned out to be the best goaltender in that league." I looked up at the rearview mirror and saw tears in her eyes. "Paul, all I can do is apologize, and promise that I'll never mention your eyesight to anyone ever again."

I was too hurt and angry to tell her that I appreciated those words. That those words helped. But they did.

Friday, September 8, *later*

The obituary in the *Tangerine Times* said that Mike Costello would have a public viewing tonight and a private burial ceremony tomorrow. I was actually looking forward to going. For one thing, I had never been to what Mom was calling a Catholic wake. But also I was feeling very, very low about myself and about the soccer team, and I realized that Joey was the only person I knew who was feeling worse. He was someone who even I could feel sorry for.

I squeezed into my blue suit, and Mom, Dad, and I drove in the Volvo to O'Sullivan's Funeral Home on Route 89. As we drove, I pointed out the steady series of osprey nests, each at least ten feet in diameter, built along the tops of the high-tension wires. Dad said, "They ought to get rid of those things."

"Why, Dad?"

"Why? They could short out the power for the whole town. That's a crazy place to build a nest."

I thought to myself, *Maybe so, but at least the osprey don't have to smell the muck fire. And their streets don't get flooded every time it rains.* I wondered if their nests ever got hit by lightning.

We pulled into the parking lot of the funeral home. There were lots of 4 × 4s and sports cars. All of the football players and a lot of the seniors who knew Mike Costello had come.

Erik was in the parking lot, too, with a big group of kids around him that included Paige, Arthur, and Tina.

As we walked inside I began to get a scared feeling in the pit of my stomach. I had never seen a dead body. I had never been in a funeral home. There was a powerful scent of flowers—too powerful—as we paused in the lobby. Two separate viewings were happening. The viewing for "Michael J. Costello" was taking place in the room to the right.

As soon as the wooden doors opened, I could see him— Mike Costello. He was laid out in a casket. He had bright lights over him; his right side was facing the public. The casket was steel gray, with a white satin interior. I was really amazed. Here I was, looking at an actual dead person, a person who I had seen alive just days before. Mike Costello looked terrific. He looked like he was lit from within, like a wax statue in a football hall of fame.

I didn't know how to behave. I had never been through anything like this before, so I copied Mom and Dad. They walked up to the casket and knelt on the padded kneelers. They said a short prayer and got up. I waited for them to finish, then I knelt down alone at the casket. Closer up, Mike Costello didn't look so terrific. There was no hair on the left side of his head. There was no hair on his left hand, either.

I got back up and looked for Mom and Dad. They were waiting behind another couple for a chance to speak to Mr. and Mrs. Costello. I walked up and stood with them. I was surprised to hear how light their conversation was. They weren't even talking about Mike. They were talking about the lake at our development and about what might be happening to the koi. I looked around for Joey, but I didn't see him. I saw football players and cheerleaders and Student Council types spread out all over the room. Mr. Bridges was there. So were Coach Warner and the other football coaches.

When it was our turn to talk to the Costellos, Mom

expressed how sorry we all were about the terrible accident. I just muttered, "I'm sorry," and shook hands with them. Mrs. Costello said, "Joey will be glad to see you here. I know he wants to talk to you. He wants to ask you something."

The room was just about filled, mostly with high schoolers and adults. But then I did see a group of middle school kids coming in, and Joey was with them. A girl from my math class named Cara, Cara Clifton, gave him a big hug right in front of everybody. In fact, she kind of hung on him. Then she and the rest of the middle school kids went over and found seats. Everybody in the room seemed to be sitting down.

Joey was alone for a minute, so I went over and said, "How's it goin'?"

"Hey, Fisher. It's goin'. It's goin'. What's happening at soccer practice?"

"I don't know. I got kicked off the team."

"Yeah. Right."

"No, no kidding. I really did. I got kicked off."

"No way!"

"Yeah way."

"Uh, look. The priest just came in. I gotta go sit down. But I want to hear about this. I gotta ask you something, too."

I went over and sat with Mom and Dad. A young priest came in and started saying the rosary with everybody. We didn't know what that was all about, but we sat there with our heads bowed and said some of the prayers. Then the priest spoke about Mike. He talked about what a good guy he was. What else could you say about Mike? I don't know anybody, except Erik and Arthur, who wouldn't say that about him. A lot of people in the room were crying. A whole lot of people.

After the priest left some of the kids left, too, and some

of the adults got up and started to talk again. We stayed in our seats for a while. Mr. Donnelly went back to the casket and knelt there, with his eyes tightly closed, for a long time. Mom pointed out people from Lake Windsor Downs—a gray-and-white Tudor, a York with a circular driveway. Paige was talking to a man I recognized from the football practice meeting. He was her father, Arthur Bauer, Sr. Mom pointed out Tina Turreton's mother, too; she looked like she could be Tina's older sister—very young-looking. I recognized a few of the other parents who had come to the meeting in our great room, but I don't know their names.

After a few minutes we walked out into the lobby. That's where I saw Joey again. He had one arm around Cara Clifton, who was crying uncontrollably; he was shaking hands with Coach Warner with his other arm. A couple of guys from the soccer team were there, too, a couple of the toe stubbers. They obviously hadn't heard that I was off the team. One of them said, "What's up, Mars?" which I didn't mind at all. That nickname is all I'm ever going to get from the Lake Windsor soccer program.

Kerri Gardner came up and put her hand on Cara's shoulder. She looked over at me and said, "Hi." She explained to Cara that their ride was waiting and they had to go. Then she turned back to me and said, "I hear you're a great soccer player." I just stood there, unable to think of anything to reply. Cara let go of Joey, asked Kerri for a tissue, and the two of them left.

Joey joined his mother and father near the door, where a line had formed to say good-bye. It must have been a tough thing to stand there and say something to every one of those people, but that's exactly what they did. When Mom and Dad got up there, the Costellos started asking them about the meeting in our great room—how it had gone and who had said what.

Joey picked up our conversation where it had left off. "So how did you get kicked off the soccer team? I thought you were on the bus."

"I *was* on the bus. At least I think I was."

"Walski kicked you off?"

"Yeah. I don't know. Sort of. Murrow sent him this memo saying that I'm in a handicapped program, a program for the visually impaired. He freaked. He said he'd lose his insurance policy or something."

Joey was shaking his head. "Oh, man. Man, that's cold. Maybe my dad can file a lawsuit for you or something."

"Is that right?"

"Yeah. He's a lawyer. He can file a lawsuit. It's gotta be against your civil rights. Your parents are paying taxes so you can go to this school, right? Why shouldn't you be allowed to play on the school team?"

"You're right."

"It's not your fault if you're a geek."

"Thanks. Thanks a lot."

"Hey, you know what I'm saying."

"Yeah. Yeah."

"Look, do you want to go the carnival with us to-morrow?"

I was shocked to hear Joey say that. I answered, "Uh, isn't tomorrow the funeral?"

"Well, the funeral is first thing tomorrow morning. My mom thinks it's a good idea that I go out and do something with my friends tomorrow afternoon. 'Life goes on,' she said. We've been doing nothing but all this funeral stuff, you know, since it happened. So she says I need to get out and do something to take my mind off it." He looked over toward his parents. "They're more worried about *me* now than they are about Mike. You know what I'm saying?"

I looked at Joey's parents, then at mine. He asked me again, "So are you up for it? For the carnival?"

"Yeah, sure. I guess. I don't know anything about it. I heard the announcements about it at school."

"It's pretty cool, for Tangerine. It's low-rent, but it's cool, in a low-rent kind of a way. I'll call you tomorrow afternoon."

"Yeah. All right."

Mom and Dad and the Costellos finished their conversation. I wish I knew what they talked about. It must have been serious, because Mom and Dad didn't exchange another word all the way home.

That was all right with me. I needed time to think. I looked out the window at the starry night, at the high-tension wires and the osprey nests, and I thought over and over again about what I could have said back to Kerri Gardner.

Saturday, September 9

Life goes on, all right.

When I came downstairs for breakfast, Mom and Dad were arguing. Mom was sitting on a stool at the kitchen counter. Dad and Erik were standing in the doorway, ready to exit. Erik was letting Dad do all the talking.

"Look, there's nothing wrong with me taking Erik to practice this morning."

Mom clearly did not agree. "You don't schedule a football practice on the morning of your team captain's funeral."

"It's a private funeral. We were not invited to attend that funeral."

"That's not the point. You should show respect for the family by canceling practice on the morning of the funeral."

Dad had heard enough. "Well, Coach Warner did not think that was appropriate, so he didn't do it. The season begins in one week, and we need to get out there."

"*You* need to get out there?"

"That's right. Every team in this county is practicing this morning, and so are we. And while we're at it, Coach Warner did not *schedule this practice on the morning of the funeral*. These weekend practices have been scheduled all along. It's not fair for you to say that the coach doesn't care about his players, or that he doesn't care about Mike Costello, just because he continues to do his job."

Mom didn't reply, so Dad and Erik completed their exit.

Mom's final word on the subject was to me. "Coach Warner cares so much about his players that he pushes them out into the lightning every day."

Joey called at 2:30. Mom answered the phone. She offered to drive us, so Joey showed up at our door at 2:45. Mom asked him how the services went. He said, "Fine," and that was that. We didn't talk about it again. Life went on. We got into Mom's car and drove to the carnival.

I was curious to finally see the town of Tangerine. In the time we've lived here, we've driven in every direction but this one. We've gone west to the supermarket, south to the mall, north to the schools, but never east to the town. As we headed up Route 89, Joey said, "My dad told me that this all used to be tangerine groves, as far as the eye could see. It was the tangerine capital of the world."

Mom turned off the highway at Route 22 and drove east through the citrus groves. The air was filled with a remarkable scent.

Joey said, "What is that smell? That's gross."

I said, "You're crazy. I love that smell. That's the citrus. Something is in bloom now. Huh, Mom?"

Mom said, "I don't know, honey."

We drove for another mile. We passed a cluster of lime green houses made out of cement block. I said, "Check out that color, Mom. You'd better notify the Architectural Committee."

Mom was not amused. "This isn't a development, Paul."

"Then how come the houses are all the same color?"

Mom thought about that and replied, "Maybe you're right. Maybe this is some kind of early development. Maybe the owners of the packing plant built those houses for their workers."

"The migrant workers?"

"No. I don't think so. The migrant workers would come and pick fruit for a few weeks and then move on. But there must have been permanent workers, citrus packers, who lived here year-round. Like Joey was saying, this used to be the tangerine capital of the world . . . Now the tangerine industry is dead. Look. Over there. That's the old packing plant."

It was strange to see an old packing plant, to see an old anything. But it was also comforting to hear that something around here has a history. That something actually belongs here.

It makes sense. I can see how it worked: The citrus packers walked from those lime green cement-block houses into that packing plant—that huge and magnificent structure. It must have been built, red brick by red brick, to be the most magnificent building the workers had ever seen, like a European cathedral.

So why did it stop working? When did it all go wrong? Whose fault was it? Maybe the people from the lime green houses just got tired of walking into this building every morning. Maybe they stopped seeing how magnificent it was. And now it's gone. It's all over. Someplace else is now the tangerine capital of the world.

We didn't see much else of the town, because suddenly, right in front of us, were the rides and tents of the carnival. "Low-rent" was a compliment for this thing. It was set up in a big field of dirt, next to a sign that read TANGERINE FLEA MARKET EVERY SUNDAY. Mom dropped us off in the parking lot, which was another field of dirt across the road. She said, "Are you boys sure you want to get out here?"

"Yeah!" Joey laughed. Maybe he thought Mom was kidding.

Mom sighed. "OK. When do you want to be picked up?"

"I don't know. Joey, what do you say? Seven o'clock?"

Joey thought about it. "Yeah. That's cool."

Mom called, "All right. I'll see you two right here, on this spot, at seven o'clock. Be careful."

"We will, Mom. Bye."

As we waited to cross the busy road, Joey handed me a discount ticket and said, "They're from Coach Walski."

Just outside the entranceway I saw a group of guys with a soccer ball. They were good. Three of them were doing the juggling bit with a ball, like Tommy Acoso does, but they were passing it back and forth, too. I stopped to watch for a minute, and a kid called over to me, "Hey! Give me one of those tickets!"

"I only got one," I said.

"Yeah? So I only need one. Hand it over."

Joey grabbed my elbow and hustled me away. "C'mon, man. Don't mess around with those guys. They're from Tangerine Middle."

"So?"

"Don't talk to them, and don't look at them." We handed over our tickets and passed through a turnstile. "They have gangs in Tangerine Middle School. They have kids with guns, man. Real gangstas. Some of them have AK-47s."

"No way."

"Hey, don't believe me. Just don't mess with them, 'cause I ain't bailing you out."

We walked quickly past the Octopus and another ride that looked like a swinging-ax pendulum. Joey called out, "There they are! There's Cara and Kerri and the guys!"

I was thrilled. I had been secretly hoping this would happen. Cara came up and put her arm around Joey right away. Unfortunately nobody, Kerri included, paid much attention to me. The three guys, who I sort of knew from classes and lunch, were all talking about going to a freak show in the back of the carnival. Cara and Kerri were saying things like "Oh, gross" and "No way."

Everybody was disappointed when we actually got inside the freak show, called Wonders of the World. Everybody except me. I was really fascinated as I prowled through the dark, partitioned rooms of the exhibits. They were mostly photos, but there were some wax statues, too. The exhibits had names like the Woman with a Third Eye, the Buffalo Man, and the Frozen Fräulein.

I lost the rest of the group when I stopped to read about the Boy Who Never Grew. According to the sign, this boy stopped growing at the age of five, but he went on to live to the age of eighty-nine. And although he was studied by the top doctors in Europe, he remains a mystery to this day. No one ever discovered what happened to him to cause this strange affliction. I peered into the eyes in the photo for a long, long time.

When I came out of Wonders of the World, blinking in the sun, my classmates were all gone. The guys who I had seen at the entrance with the soccer ball were there, waiting to go in. They were too busy karate-kicking at each other to notice me.

I turned left and headed toward the big double Ferris wheel. I watched it being loaded, seat by seat. The wheel rotated up, and I saw Cara and Joey close together on a seat. It rotated again, and I saw Kerri. She was sitting with one of the guys from the group. A guy named Adam. A guy who doesn't wear glasses and who knows how to talk. I spun around and walked the other way, eventually stopping at a snow-cone place. After about half an hour by myself, I caught up with the group again. No one had noticed that I was gone. Kerri wound up going on the Caterpillar with Adam, too. I didn't go on any rides.

Seven o'clock finally came. I went and stood at the entrance. I could see that Mom was already parked in the lot. Joey kept me waiting for ten minutes, then ran up and said, "You ready?"

"Yeah. I've been ready."

We crossed the road and climbed into the air-conditioned car. Mom cried out, "Look at that!"

We looked, and we saw the gang of soccer kids from Tangerine Middle all climbing into the back of a light green, classic Ford pickup truck.

"Yeah. Cool truck," Joey and I said, almost at the same time.

"No! No!" Mom continued. "Look at the truck and tell me what's wrong with this picture."

We looked again, and I noticed the words TOMAS CRUZ GROVES, TANGERINE, FLORIDA written on the door. "Do you mean that they spelled Thomas wrong?"

"Honestly, Paul!" she snapped. "Can't you be serious when I ask you a question?"

"But I am being serious."

Mom pointed at the pile of kids, who were now riding toward the exit. "Seatbelts! They're not wearing any seatbelts. Not one of them. And how could they? They're all bouncing around in the back of that truck like a bunch of golden retrievers."

"Well, that's up to them, right?"

"No, that is not up to them! That is against the law. One good bump and they'll all break their necks! Why do we bother passing safety laws? People will still throw six kids into the back of a truck and then drive them out onto the highway."

Mom drove in silence all the way home—angry about the driver of the pickup truck. It doesn't take much these days to make her angry. I was feeling pretty miserable myself—about Kerri Gardner, about soccer, about my whole life here. I remembered the face of the Boy Who Never Grew, the face of that eighty-nine-year-old little boy. I remembered the fear in his eyes. I know that fear. It's my fear. They may as well stick me in there next to him.

A picture came to me, nasty yet satisfying. I could stop trying to be what everyone else is and accept being a freak. They could open a new exhibit, starring me. A modern exhibit called the Children Who Wouldn't Listen. Stomach Cramps Boy, who went swimming right after lunch. Refrigerator Door Boy, sealed forever to stay fresh. And Eclipse Boy, studied by the greatest doctors in Europe but still a mystery to this day.

Monday, September 11

I was up for a long time last night, listening to the rain. It was still raining when Mom dropped me off at the guardhouse. I stood next to Joey, but neither one of us had much to say.

Lake Windsor Middle School is a very uncomfortable place to be when it's raining. Hundreds of kids crowd into the walkways between classes. The kids with umbrellas smack them into each other. The kids without umbrellas panic because they're trapped in the cold, pounding rain, unable to move behind the kids with umbrellas.

I was one of the kids with umbrellas, even though the coolest guys don't carry them. Of course, the coolest guys don't have to take off their glasses and dry them before they can see again, either.

It was still pouring during third period when a kid came into my math class in P-19. He was soaking wet and holding one of those wooden office passes. The teacher, Mr. Ward, called me up to the front and said, "You're wanted in Mr. Murrow's office right away."

I let the kid with the pass share my umbrella as we crossed over the ocean of mud and ducked into the building. When we got to Mr. Murrow's office, I noticed Mrs. Gates and Coach Walski standing with him next to his desk. Lined up on a long couch against the opposite wall were Joey, Adam, and the other two guys from our group at the carnival. I went over and sat with them.

Mr. Murrow started speaking. He was angry. "I want you boys to tell me exactly what happened at the carnival on Saturday." He paused and then added, "You were all at the carnival on Saturday, were you not?"

Nobody answered until Joey spoke up and said, "Yes, sir. We were there."

Joey didn't say anything else, so Coach Walski intervened. "We know that you were there, boys, because I gave you all tickets. That's how we've all come to be in Mr. Murrow's office today. Now, maybe you don't know what this is all about, so I'll tell you. Mrs. Gates got a phone call on Saturday from the Sheriff's Department."

Mr. Murrow picked up the story from here. His tone was more reasonable now, more like Coach Walski's. "The Tangerine County Sheriff's Department received a complaint from the owners of the carnival that one of their exhibits was vandalized by boys from a soccer team. They called Mrs. Gates and asked her to help find out exactly what happened to the exhibit." He checked the name on a piece of paper. "The Wonders of the World exhibit."

Joey was quick to respond. "Hey, we didn't do anything wrong. We were in the exhibit, yeah. But we didn't do anything to it."

Everybody on the couch agreed, except me. I knew immediately what had happened, and who had done it. I really didn't want to rat out those soccer guys, but I was the only one who had seen them going in. It had to be me. I raised my hand up limply and said, "I think I know who did it."

All three adults turned to me. Mr. Murrow said, "OK. Who did it?"

"When I came out of the exhibit, I saw a bunch of guys from Tangerine Middle going in. I think they were soccer players."

"Why do you think that?"

"Well, sir, they were carrying a soccer ball."

The three adults looked at each other, and then they smiled. The rest of us started to relax. Joey said, "Yeah, I saw those guys, too, on the way in and on the way out. They were bad news, no question about it."

Coach Walski said to Joey, "Did you recognize any of them from our game last year?"

Joey was certain. "Oh yeah. They were definitely from that team. I think they were all starters. I never saw them going into the freak show, so I didn't know who you were talking about at first. But yeah, definitely, they're the guys you're looking for."

Mrs. Gates seemed relieved and happy. She said, "Thank you very much, boys. I guess we've solved this mystery. I wish they were all so easy to solve."

Mr. Murrow added, "I'm glad it was just a case of mistaken identity. I didn't think you guys would do anything like this. All right, why don't you go ahead and get back to class. And thank you, too, Coach."

Coach Walski told him, "I know the coach at Tangerine Middle. Her name's Betty Bright. Call Betty and tell her what happened. She'll round those kids up."

Mr. Murrow picked up the phone as we all piled out into the hall.

Nobody said anything. When we got to the outside door, I asked Joey if he wanted to walk under my umbrella. Adam and the other two kids were too cool to have umbrellas, so they took off and ran through the rain toward their portables.

I stopped still when we got outside the building, right at the entrance to the boardwalk. This whole thing was really bothering me, so I said to Joey, "Hey, we ratted those guys out."

Joey seemed puzzled. "Yeah. So what? They're never gonna know who we are."

"Oh no? Who knows what Murrow's gonna say to this Betty Bright. He might tell her our names."

"No way. It's not like we're testifying in court or filling out affidavits. Our names aren't on anything."

"Listen to yourself. You sound like a lawyer."

"Oh, give me a break, Fisher! Do you want to take the rap for something that you didn't do?"

"No."

Joey paused for a moment and asked, "So how come you took off at the carnival?"

"I don't know." I paused, too. I finally said, "That Adam kid, is he going out with Kerri Gardner? Is that the deal?"

"Adam? Adam's a geek."

"So what does that mean? Is he going out with her or isn't he?"

"Not that I know of. Why? Do you want to go out with her?"

"No. Why should I?"

"Well, hey, she obviously likes geeks. Why shouldn't you?"

I stood there, trying to think of a comeback, when suddenly, I heard a *whoosh*ing sound, like the sound you get when you open a vacuum-sealed can of peanuts. Then the brown water that had puddled up all over the field began to move. It began to run toward the back portables, like someone had pulled the plug out of a giant bathtub. Next came a *crack-crack-crack*ing sound. The boards began to come apart, and the loose mud under the walkways began to slide toward that giant bathtub drain.

One after another the doors of the portables opened and the teachers looked out, staring into the dense rain, trying to spot the cause of all this commotion. Mr. Ward opened the door of Portable 19. He stepped out onto the porch and looked around back. Across the field, the kids from Ms. Alvarez's portable came walking out with their belongings, in single file, like they were supposed to do in a fire drill. Other teachers saw that and started their kids out, too. But suddenly there was a larger sound. A louder *whoosh* turned every head and opened every eye in that rainy field. Then the walkways started to heave up and down, making terrible splintering noises.

Immediately kids started screaming and vaulting over the handrails, landing in the ankle-deep mud. Another *whoosh* and more violent cracking sounds followed. Then every seventh and eighth grader started to pour out of those portables, some still calm, some panicking.

There was instant and total chaos in the back row, the one nearest to the football field, because the portables themselves were starting to break apart and move. The kids came diving out, jamming in the doorways, pushing into the backs of other kids, knocking each other flat on the disintegrating boardwalk. They knocked each other into the moving mudslide that was now swirling in a circle around them.

"What is it?" I yelled to Joey. "An earthquake?"

"No! Sinkhole, man! It's a sinkhole! It's opening up under the field. Look at 19!"

I looked and saw the entire portable being swallowed up by the mud, its roof now where its porch steps should be. I yelled, "That's my math class!"

Joey shouted back over the din, "They must all be trapped in there!"

I didn't even think about it. I yelled back, "Come on!"

We ditched my umbrella and jumped out of the way as the first panicked wave reached the building. We pushed around the bottleneck of screaming kids forming at the door. Stepping carefully, we sloshed and fought our way through the mud to Portable 19.

We joined some eighth graders in a kind of bucket brigade extending from the field down into the sinkhole. They were grabbing the hands of the kids who were trapped in the portable and pulling them up, step-by-step, to the edge of the hole. Some of those guys must have been ten feet below ground level at this point, and the sinkhole was still deepening and spreading. The mud continued to swirl around us in a rapid clockwise motion.

Empty of kids, Portable 16 fell right over, roof first, into the far end of the hole. Portables 20 and 21 were balanced on the rim of the crater, about to go.

Joey and I dug our heels into the mud about halfway down toward the bottom of the hole. We pulled and grabbed at kids as they made their way up the slippery incline to the top. Some of them were so frightened that they didn't want to let go of us, but we pushed them along anyway, up to the next guys. I lost my balance twice and fell into the mud, but I managed to right myself quickly. My glasses were so caked with mud that I could no longer see anything clearly. I must have pulled twenty kids up before I heard Mr. Ward's voice yell, "That's it! That's everybody! Let's get out of here!"

Those of us in the middle of the line helped the guys from the bottom to climb out. Then they pulled us up. I heard Mr. Ward yell again, "There go 17 and 18!" and I heard the sounds of portables 17 and 18 splitting apart. The *whoosh*ing was getting louder, and I felt afraid for the first time, afraid that we might all get sucked down and drown in the mud. We moved out in a tight group, holding on to each other through the field of moving slop and splintered boards.

Finally we pushed our way inside the main building, out of the rain. I tried to clean my glasses on my sopping, filthy shirt. No way. Someone snatched the glasses away from me, right out of my hands. It was a big guy, with a towel, and he proceeded to wipe them clean. He said, "Mars, my man! Good work out there."

I knew that voice. I said, "Thanks, Gino."

He placed them carefully on my head and said, "It sucks what they did to you, Mars. I told Coach Walski that, too. You're the best seventh-grade, four-eyed Martian goalie in the entire county."

"Thanks, Gino. I appreciate that."

He started to move on with his towel, but he turned to add, "They should have bent the rules for you, Mars. They bend the rules for *other* guys, lots of them, so they should have bent them for you." I watched Gino head off into the sea of muddy and miserable kids.

Sirens started to wail outside. Then the loudspeakers crackled to life. "This is Mrs. Gates. We are experiencing an extreme emergency. Please listen carefully and do exactly as I say. First, any injured student should come immediately to the office. No student who is *not* injured should attempt to come to the office at this time. All other students should move calmly and quietly to their afternoon bus stops or pickup points. School buses have already been dispatched to drive you home. If you cannot go home at this time, you should proceed out the front entrance and walk to the high school gymnasium."

Mrs. Gates repeated this speech twice more as I worked my way out the front door and turned left to my bus stop. I hooked up with Joey again there. He said he'd heard that there were kids with broken arms and legs all over the office.

A convoy of ambulances, police cars, and fire engines turned into the entranceway, their sirens wailing and their lights flashing. The rain continued to hammer down, pounding on the long line of kids trudging north, around the football stadium, toward the high school gymnasium.

Our bus pulled into the circular drive and we climbed on board patiently and politely, slopping mud all over the aisle floor and the seats. The bus driver said she had instructions to take all of us right to our doors.

I was shivering and my teeth were chattering by the time I got home. I let myself in through the side door to the garage and went into the laundry room. I peeled off my shirt, socks, shoes, and pants and dumped them all into the washing machine. Then, wearing only my undershorts, and streaked head to foot with mud like one of those lost guys from the Amazon rainforest, I went in to break the news to Mom.

Monday, September 11, *later*

At four o'clock Grandmom and Grandpop called from Ohio to tell us we were on the national news—on CNN—so Mom turned it on. They already had live footage shot by a news helicopter. It showed the whole campus, then it zeroed in on the field of portables and the focal point of the sinkhole.

I was surprised, and even a little disappointed, at how small the crater was—only about fifty yards across. I was also surprised to hear that only a dozen kids were treated at the Tangerine County Medical Center, and all for minor injuries. Nobody was dead. Nobody was even kept overnight for observation.

The local news at six o'clock opened with the same helicopter shot. But they also had interviews with Mrs. Gates,

Mr. Ward, the sheriff, and a group of eighth graders who had been in the Portable 19 rescue brigade.

They were followed by a geologist from the University of Florida, Dr. Judith Something. She explained that the above-normal amounts of storm runoff (rain) had caused an underground cavern to form and then collapse. When it collapsed, everything on the surface above it collapsed, too—in this case, the area of the field that contained Portables 16 through 21.

The reason this sinkhole had done such massive damage to the school was that all the portables were connected by wooden walkways. Yeah. Tell me about it—all that cracking and splintering! None of the news coverage could recapture that.

Dad came home angry and agitated. Reporters had been calling Dad's office, the Department of Civil Engineering, asking how a school could be built over a huge sinkhole. Old Charley Burns was out of the office at a stock-car race, so Dad had to take the heat. Dad tried to find the geological surveys for the Lake Windsor campus, but he couldn't. He had to tell the reporters that he didn't know where they were. One reporter had had the nerve to ask him, "How can you not know what's going on in your own office?" He was especially angry about that.

The eleven o'clock news featured the same exact reports. That's when I got a call from Joey. He said, "I heard that a whole home ec class got buried alive in Portable 18. They're just not telling us."

"No way. Who told you that?"

"Cara."

"She's hysterical."

"Yeah. You're right. She is. I gotta go." And he hung up.

I gotta go, too. I'm wiped out. But I feel good about today.

I faced down danger today, maybe even death. When

disaster struck, we all had to do something. In a way, we all had to become someone. I'm not saying I was a hero. All I did was slide around in the mud and try to pull people up. But I didn't panic and run, either.

I'm still afraid of Erik. I'm afraid of Arthur now, too. But today I wasn't a coward, and that counts for something.

Tuesday, September 12

The *Tangerine Times* printed a special pullout section on the Lake Windsor Middle School sinkhole. The photos were spectacular. They had one huge shot of the splintered walkways sticking up in all directions, like Godzilla had just trampled through there.

The newspaper ran a letter from Mrs. Gates to the parents of all seventh and eighth graders. We're all supposed to attend a special disaster meeting on Friday night at seven-thirty in the high school gymnasium. The letter said that "state and county officials are planning to attend," and that "they are currently working out an emergency relocation plan that will be presented at this meeting."

I'll bet they are. Think about it: There are 25 portables that are completely trashed, completely out of commission. Let's say there are 25 kids assigned to each of those portables. And each kid has 7 class periods a day. That's 625 kids and 175 class periods to relocate. Awesome.

I was shocked to read that the sixth graders are supposed to return to school on Thursday. Thursday! The main building of the middle school and all the buildings of the high school have been certified as "structurally safe" by a team of engineers hastily assembled by Old Charley Burns. It turns out that Old Charley was in Daytona, but now he's back. And he is "taking personal charge of the case." (I'm sure that's fine with Dad, who wants nothing to do with the case, or with Old Charley.)

The field of portables, of course, has been certified as a disaster area. The engineers condemned everything "within a hundred-yard radius of the focal point of the sinkhole," which was right under Portable 19. The condemned area includes all of the portables, of course. But to the south it also includes a corner of the soccer field and all of the baseball diamond. To the north it includes nearly all of the high school football bleachers that back up onto the middle school.

There's extra land to the south, so the soccer field can be moved. But what about those steel-frame, thirty-row-high, hundred-yard-long high school bleachers? They're not moving anywhere. They're condemned. Period. The football stadium has just lost half of its seating capacity. And Erik Fisher, the soon-to-be-famous placekicker, has just lost half of his audience.

Thursday, September 14

Dad is the new Director of Civil Engineering for Tangerine County.

It happened quickly. Channel 2 ran an *Eyewitness News* special report about Old Charley Burns last night at 6:00 P.M. Dad had Old Charley's job by noon today.

The *Eyewitness News* team really kicked butt. It turns out that in the ten-year, multi-million-dollar building boom on the west side of Tangerine County, Old Charley's department never denied *one* request for a permit. They never sent out one inspector, either. They let the developers hire their own inspectors and even fill out their own inspection reports. They let the developers conduct their own geological surveys, too—including the missing one for the Lake

Windsor campus. And they maintained "the most relaxed building code in all of Florida for construction methods and materials."

So what has Old Charley been doing instead of inspecting new development plans? According to the *Eyewitness News* team, he's been "living the high life—either at a Florida Gators game or at a stock-car race." The University of Florida Alumni Association lists Old Charley as a "Bull Gator" contributor. He even has his own skybox. He has a skybox at Daytona, too. And he is an honored guest at Talladega, at the Charlotte Motor Speedway, and at various other race sites around the southeast.

According to the *Eyewitness* team narrator, "Charley Burns lived the high life. Yet his salary remained that of a civil servant. So where did it all come from—the skyboxes, the expensive trips, the big contributions? It came from the developers—on the side, off the books, under the table. They wanted Charley Burns out of the way, so they sent him to Charlotte, or to Darlington, or to Talladega. While he was gone, the Estates at East Hampton, and the Villas at Versailles, and Lake Windsor Downs, and the middle school–high school complex all went up—unsurveyed, unsupervised, and unsafe."

By the time the report was finished, Old Charley was roadkill. There wasn't enough left of Old Charley to hose off the driveway. At first Dad said he was worried that he'd be "tarred with the same brush." But a county commissioner called him right after the broadcast and talked to him for over an hour. Then, like I said, he got the job today.

I heard Dad promise the commissioner that "every new construction site will be thoroughly inspected and regulated from now on." So I guess it's the end of the multi-million-dollar building boom west of Tangerine. The end of an era. The Old Charley Burns era.

Dad never mentioned Old Charley in his conversation

with the commissioner. He never mentioned him when he told Mom, Erik, and me about the job offer, either.

It's the end of an era, all right. And it's like Old Charley Burns—the former Director, the racing fan, the real character—no longer exists.

But that's Dad. You're either at the center of his world, or you're nowhere. There is no in-between.

It's the Dad era now.

Friday, September 15

Mom and Dad and I drove up to the high school tonight to hear about the emergency relocation plan. I expected to hear that we were going to be out of school for a month or two, or maybe even six.

I guess we all thought that, because Mom had been calling every private school within driving distance. She was trying to sell me on a local Catholic school called St. Anthony's. The boys there have to wear blue pants, white shirts, and blue ties.

Mom was selling, but I wasn't buying. "Mom, we're not Catholic," I pointed out.

"That doesn't matter. I talked to the principal, Sister Mary Margaret. You don't have to be Catholic to go there. It just happens to be a Catholic school."

"What are you saying? It's just a coincidence that only Catholics go there?"

"Maybe you don't know everything about it, Paul. Would you please listen? Ten percent of their students are not Catholic. And the sister told me that she's been flooded by calls from Lake Windsor Middle, so you'd be with kids you know."

"There are about three kids that I can stand at Lake Windsor Middle."

"Well, I'll bet you Joey Costello's parents have called there."

"Sure. I'll bet Joey Costello's parents know what a rosary is, too."

Dad snapped at both of us. "I think this discussion is a bit premature, don't you? The school officials say they have a plan worked out. So let's all hear what it is. Until then let's have some peace and quiet."

Dad is stressed to the max about this sinkhole business. His department is getting dozens of phone calls from magazines, and wire services, and TV producers. He's talked to people from as far away as Australia and Japan. In so many words, he gives them all the same message: "Old Charley Burns did it. Now Old Charley's gone."

That's why the county commissioners want Dad onstage with them at the meeting tonight. They want everybody watching to get the message: "Old Charley Burns did it. Now Old Charley's gone."

When we got to the high school there were about a thousand parents and kids entering the gymnasium. We saw the Costellos getting out of their Jeep.

While our parents talked, Joey muttered to me, "Check it out. Some of these geeks still have mud on them."

I said, "Did you see the news?"

"Yeah. Can you believe it? If we hadn't gone home on that bus, we'd have been on TV with Mr. Ward and the rest of the 'rescue brigade,' right? They'd be making a movie about us."

"Yeah. Right."

"We'd have been heroes." Joey looked away. He clenched his jaw and added, "Mike would have been proud of what we did, I'll tell you that."

"Yeah. I'm sure he would have."

"OK, here we go. I'll catch you tomorrow."

"OK."

We split off from the Costellos and moved into the gymnasium. There were no seats at all. The pullout bleachers had not been pulled out, so everybody had to stand. We worked our way in as far as we could, stopping about twenty yards from a small stage.

Dad spotted the county commissioner who backed him for Charley Burns's job. The commissioner was a big guy with a big gut and a big bald head. Dad waved to him and then pushed his way steadily forward up onto the stage until he was standing next to him. Mom and I stayed down on the floor.

After a few minutes Mrs. Gates walked to the microphone and tapped it. "I want to begin by apologizing for the standing-room-only conditions, but it was the only way to get all of us in here tonight. I want to thank Mr. Bridges, the principal of Lake Windsor High School, and all of his staff. They, along with our own remarkable middle school staff, have been working nearly round the clock since Tuesday morning."

The people in the crowd applauded in appreciation.

"I don't need to tell anyone what happened here on Monday. But I do want to assure you that none of our students were seriously injured. And that's because every student behaved in a very mature way. The fact is, many students showed a great deal of courage out there. They helped to keep a natural disaster from becoming a human disaster, and they, too, deserve our applause."

There was louder applause this time. I strained to see Joey, but I couldn't.

"I want to introduce the people up here on the stage." Mrs. Gates then went on to introduce about twenty people: the Commissioner of This, the Coordinator of That, the Superintendent of Something. When she got to the Director of Civil Engineering and read out Dad's name, the crowd buzzed ominously.

Finally she got to the part that everyone had come to hear. "All these people, in conjunction with the State Department of Education in Tallahassee, have helped to devise this emergency relocation plan." Mrs. Gates stopped and held up some papers. She looked over the crowd. "I cannot stress too strongly that this is all temporary. This is a plan to hold us over until we've fixed our problem—fixed it quickly, fixed it completely. The Department of Civil Engineering"—she stopped and looked down at her notes—"under the new direction of Mr. Fisher, has a small army of contractors at work out there. They will make sure that the sinkhole is completely stabilized and that there is *zero* chance of this ever happening again." Mrs. Gates paused, but no one applauded.

"Now. The estimated timetable for repairs to our school, and that means restoring everything to just the way it was, is three months. Our target date for returning to normal life at Lake Windsor Middle is January eighth, the start of the new term. For the remainder of this term, we will all go by this emergency relocation plan, which goes into effect on Monday."

Wait a minute! Whoa! I couldn't believe what I was hearing. *Monday?* I had figured on a month's down time at the very least. Now, basically, we had the weekend off, and then we were due back in school.

Mrs. Gates turned to page two of the plan and began to read the details. They added up to this: All the eighth graders would have to squeeze into the high school; all the seventh graders would have to squeeze into the middle school.

Parents around me whispered to each other and acted like they understood.

Mrs. Gates should have quit while she was ahead, but she continued. "Unfortunately this means that the middle school will have to run on a split shift for the rest of this term, with class periods reduced to forty minutes. Sixth graders will begin at seven-thirty A.M. and end at one P.M. Seventh graders will begin at one-thirty P.M. and end at seven P.M."

An unfriendly-sounding rumble began in the crowd.

Mrs. Gates spoke again quickly. "We understand what a strain this will put on everyone, but I ask you to remember that this is only until the end of the term. We also understand that this plan simply will not work for some families. That is why seventh-grade parents will have another option."

Mrs. Gates turned and pointed to a black woman in a blue suit. "Dr. Grace Johnson, the principal of Tangerine Middle School, has agreed to take in any of our seventh graders for the remainder of this term. Lake Windsor students who choose to go there will be absorbed into the existing class schedule at Tangerine Middle School, which is the same as our normal class schedule. Those of you who choose this option, however, will have to provide your own transportation."

The crowd noise started to increase.

Mrs. Gates said, "Seventh graders, please do not leave without a split-shift schedule." She then closed the meeting by saying, "That's all for now. Remember: We're all in this together, and we'll come out of this an even stronger Lake Windsor Middle School family. Good night."

As the people around me started toward the exits, I stood rock still, looking up, like I was looking toward the heavens. It was a miracle. I could not believe what had just happened.

Dad found us in the crowd and said, "Come on. We can talk about all this in the car."

"No. No!" I shouted above the noise. "We have to talk about it here. The miracle happened here!"

Mom looked at me curiously, but she sided with Dad. "Come on, Paul. The car is quieter, and we need quiet. This is a big decision to make."

I was elated, and I wasn't budging. "What's to decide?" I faced down Mom and Dad in the middle of that gymnasium. "Mom, you ruined my life at Lake Windsor Middle when you turned in that IEP. This is your chance to un-ruin it! Dad, I don't mind if you never pay any attention to me for the rest of my life, just give me this chance! I won't complain about Erik, ever. Just give me this chance. Both of you. I want to go to Tangerine Middle School, and I want to go with no IEP."

I looked at Mom, and I knew I had her. She couldn't resist me, not after what had happened with Coach Walski. I looked at Dad, and he seemed puzzled. Not angry, just puzzled. He said, "What's this about me never paying attention to you? Maybe during football season I'm more wrapped up with what Erik's doing. That's true. But the rest of the time I pay equal attention to you boys."

"Football season and soccer season happen at the same time, Dad. It's OK with me if you can't pay attention to both. Just let me go to Tangerine Middle. Do you understand? I wouldn't be the water boy there. I'd be the goalie."

Dad started nodding—slowly at first, but then he picked up speed. Mom looked at me with her nervous smile, but she nodded right along with him.

The heavens had opened up for me.

part 2

part 2

The first day of school. Take two.

Mom drove me into Tangerine this morning at seven-thirty. We drove past the lime green houses and the citrus packing plant. We passed through a small downtown area and then pulled up to a concrete building that looked like a block-long post office. We parked across the street, and I reminded her, "I'll be at soccer practice until five. I hope."

"I hope so, too," Mom replied. "Look, I really should go in with you this morning. There must be transfer forms for me to sign."

"No, there aren't any forms for you to sign. All I need is my computerized class schedule from Lake Windsor Middle. No forms. No mothers."

Mom was staring across the street and not liking what she saw. There were two small groups of guys karate-kicking at each other outside the building. There were larger groups, too. Menacing-looking gangs, just standing around, watching the karate kickers go at it. Mom said, "Look at that! Why isn't this area being supervised?"

"Hey, that's no big deal. That's just what some guys do, Mom."

"At the entrance to the school? What kind of first impression is that?"

"They do that wherever they are. Lighten up. I'll see you at five."

"Yeah. If you live."

I walked around the karate kickers and the gangstas and pushed open a heavy wooden door. I saw that I could go straight, toward the first-floor classrooms, or I could climb the stairs on the left, toward what seemed to be the office. I went left and started up the worn marble stairs, thinking how unusual it was to find stairs like these in Florida. For that matter, the whole building was unusual. I hadn't been on the third floor of anything since we moved here.

The school's office was located at the top of the first flight. The principal herself was standing just inside the glass doors. She walked right up to me and said, "I'm Dr. Johnson. Who are you?"

"Paul Fisher, ma'am."

"And you're from Lake Windsor Middle School, I presume?"

"Yes, ma'am."

She took my schedule from me and read it carefully. Then she turned around and called into one of the side offices, "Theresa! Come out here and take this one."

A small, skinny girl with brown hair tied back in a ponytail came out of the side room. Dr. Johnson said, "This is Paul Fisher. Paul, this is Theresa Cruz. She'll be your escort for your first day at Tangerine Middle School. She'll be your escort for your second day, too, if you want. After that you'll be responsible for getting around on your own. But Theresa will continue to be a resource person for you, for any questions that you might have."

I said, "All right. Thank you, ma'am." I paused. I don't know why, but I just felt I had to say it. I said, "It's nice to be here."

Dr. Johnson gave me a huge smile. "Well, it's nice to have you here."

It was pretty much downhill after that.

Theresa Cruz had very little, or nothing, to say. I followed her silently from class to class. She would introduce me quietly to each teacher, and we would sit down together.

I tell you, it was eerie. Like a science fiction story. Like I had entered some kind of mirror universe. The subjects and the class times are exactly the same as in Lake Windsor

Middle, but the rooms and the people are completely different.

Tangerine Middle is a tougher school, no doubt about it. I got real nervous whenever we went out into the hall. If anything's going to happen to you in a school like this, it's going to happen in the hall. One big guy took his forearm and swatted me out of the way, like I was some kind of gnat. But I didn't take it personally. I just kept my head down, followed Theresa, and went where I was supposed to go.

My classes are all on the second floor. Basically the third floor is entirely the sixth grade, the second floor is the seventh grade, and the first floor is the eighth grade, with a few exceptions. The first floor also has the cafetorium which, obviously, doubles as the cafeteria and the auditorium. It's pretty gross. The cafetorium has a kitchen at the near end and a stage at the far end. In between are rows of wooden tables with wooden folding chairs. It's loud in there, like in some old prison movie.

Theresa stayed with me when we passed through the lunch line in the cafetorium. She even sat down with me to eat. To eat, but not to talk. I tried to get the lowdown on some of my new teachers, the inside stuff, but Theresa wasn't cooperating. I'd say something like, "So, how's this Mrs. Potter for science?"

And she'd say, "Pretty good."

"How's Mr. Scott?"

"Pretty good."

And so on. I finally gave up and ate my lunch. But afterwards I tried with the question that meant the most to me. "Do you know anything about the soccer team?"

Theresa pulled back a little and actually looked at me, surprised. She nodded and said, "Oh yeah. Yeah. My brother Tino plays on the team."

"Yeah? He's an eighth grader?"

"No. He's my twin brother. He's in seventh grade, too."

"Oh? Well, I was thinking about going out to practice today, to see if I could get on the team."

Theresa thought about this. "Yeah. You could do that. Tino won't be there today, though. He's still suspended. Victor, Hernando—none of those guys'll be there today. But I guess they'll still have practice."

I knew the answer to the next question, but I asked it anyway. "Why won't any of them be there?"

"Oh, they got into some trouble over at the carnival. Ms. Bright grabbed the whole bunch of them while they were sitting here eating lunch. She brought them up to Dr. Johnson, and they all got suspended for three days."

"So they'll all be back tomorrow?"

"Yeah. Tino, Victor, Hernando—all those guys."

"And they're all starters?"

"They're who?"

"They're starting players? On the soccer team?"

Theresa answered with pride. "Oh yeah. Victor, he's kinda like the star. Victor and Maya, they're like the two stars, you know? They score most of the goals. Tino scored two goals last year. I think Victor scored sixteen, and Maya scored fifteen. They both made the All-County Team."

"And who's the goaltender?"

"The goalie's Shandra Thomas."

"Shandra? That's a girl, right?"

"Yeah. Shandra's a girl. Maya's a girl, too."

"What? Don't you have a boys' team and a girls' team?"

"No. There's only one team. Boys, girls—they both can play on it. They're mostly boys. But some of the girls are good. They've played in the Y league all their lives and stuff. Maya learned to play over in England. That's why she's so good."

I was trying hard to process this information. I said again, "So Shandra's a girl?"

Theresa seemed to be enjoying this. "Oh yeah. There's four girls: Shandra, Maya, Maya's cousin Nita, and Dolly. They're all on the team. Then there's Tino, Victor, Hernando, and about ten other guys. They're good! They were second in the county last year."

After lunch we went back to our routine, with Theresa only speaking when she introduced me to a teacher. But at least we had broken the ice. I was starting to get a picture of this new place, and I was glad I had come here.

I'd say the most obvious difference between my new school and my old one is this: At Tangerine Middle, the minorities are the majority. I have no problem with that. I've always felt like a minority because of my eyes. The next-most obvious difference is the building itself. It's old. I have no problem with that, either, except that it has a disinfectant smell that kind of gags you. The textbooks are old, too. Really old. And they have stuff written in them. The teachers seem to have adjusted to this by not using them much. A couple of teachers have talked about class projects and group projects that are due. I guess I'll find out about those things soon enough.

I also figured out why Theresa was assigned to be my guide. We have exactly the same schedule, mostly advanced classes. My day went smoothly enough until seventh period, when I had an unpleasant surprise. My language arts teacher is Mrs. Murrow. Get this: Mrs. Murrow is married to Mr. Murrow, the head of guidance at Lake Windsor Middle. I'm going to work hard at not being noticed in that class. I don't want to risk his hearing my name and announcing, "That kid's handicapped! He needs an IEP!"

After the bell rang, Theresa and I walked downstairs and out the back door. To the left, behind a baseball backstop, was a green scoreboard. Across the top was written TANGERINE MIDDLE SCHOOL—HOME OF THE WAR EAGLES. We crossed over the bus lanes and headed down to a soccer field that was circled by an asphalt running track.

I could see a mixed group, girls and boys, taking turns shooting the ball at a big, tall girl in the goal. I said, "That's Shandra, right?"

"Yeah. In the goal. That's Shandra."

"Who are those other girls?"

"Who? You mean the ones standing together?"

"Yeah."

"That's Maya and Nita. Maya's the tall one. They're cousins. They're always hanging out together."

"And who's the other big girl?"

"That's Dolly. Dolly Elias. Her brother Ignazio was the captain last year." Theresa pointed at her and called, "What's up, Dolly?" It was the first time I had heard her raise her voice. Dolly waved back.

"Is she your friend?"

"Yeah. She rides home with Luis and Tino and me."

"Is Luis on the team, too?"

"No. No, Luis is grown-up. He's our big brother. He comes and picks us all up after practice. He picks up Hernando and Victor, too."

We crossed the field in front of Dolly just as she drove a perfect corner kick, five feet off the ground. Theresa walked me up to a tall, powerful-looking woman in a maroon warm-up suit. She said, "Ms. Bright, this is Paul Fisher from Lake Windsor Middle School. He wants to play on your soccer team."

Ms. Bright had to look down to meet my eyes. She said, "How long are you going to be with us, Paul?"

"Three months, ma'am. At least through the soccer season."

"Uh-huh. Have you played soccer before?"

"Oh yes, ma'am. All my life. I was starting goalie for my last school, back in Houston."

"Uh-huh. Well, let me explain something to you right from jumpstreet. You can be on my team. But you're not going to take the place of one of my starting players and then go back to your Lake Windsor Middle School. That's not going to happen. If you want to play backup to one of my starting players, then I'll be glad to have you."

"Yes, ma'am. That's what I want to do."

"Good. I need a backup in goal. Grab that red shirt and go down to the far end. We're about to start the scrimmage."

"Yes, ma'am." I ran down to the far goal, set my bag down, and pulled on my protective gear. With half the starters missing, the scrimmage was kind of a joke. I only touched the ball once. Needless to say, no one scored on me. Shandra had the same kind of game down at her end.

I can't describe how great it feels to have another chance. Nothing, nothing at all, is going to bother me. I'll play backup to Shandra Thomas and be happy about it. Goalies get hurt. A lot. They need backups more than anybody else. I've been hurt—had my hand stepped on, had the wind knocked out of me—and someone had to fill in for me. It happens all the time. I'll get into some games, no question about that.

Near the end of practice, I noticed a familiar truck pull up. It was the same pickup that I had seen at the carnival, the vintage green one with TOMAS CRUZ GROVES, TANGERINE, FLORIDA written on the side. A guy in jeans with a plaid work shirt got out and walked over to Theresa. He walked with a bad limp. This had to be her brother Luis. He had the same dark brown hair and eyes as Theresa. His head and hands seemed very large, even from where I was standing. After practice Theresa and Dolly climbed into the front of the truck with him and drove away.

I gathered up my gear and walked back into the building

alone. Just as I was about to push through the wooden front door, I heard, "There you are, honey!"

I turned and saw Mom coming down the stairs from the second-floor office. I watched her until she put her arm around my shoulder and started to lead me out. I had a panicked feeling, like my heart had stopped beating. But I managed to ask quietly, "Mom, what were you doing up there?"

We crossed the road and reached our car before she replied. "Dr. Johnson's secretary called me today, Mr. Know-It-All. It turns out you *do* need your paperwork from Lake Windsor Middle School in order to transfer here."

My heart began to ache. "My paperwork?"

"That's right. I had to drive up to Lake Windsor and get it. You can't imagine the chaos in that office!"

"Mom, who did you talk to?"

"Mr. Murrow, of course. He gave me your file, and I delivered it here. Now you're official." Mom unlocked the doors and we both climbed in.

I looked at her angrily. "I'm officially what?"

"A student at Tangerine Middle School."

"A visually impaired student? An IEP student?"

"No. Nothing of the kind."

I closed my eyes in despair. "So what happens when the head of guidance here opens my file and sees my IEP?"

"Nothing happens, Paul. There is no IEP in your file." Mom started the car and put it in gear. As we U-turned in front of the school, she added, very carefully, "Your IEP form disappeared somewhere between Lake Windsor and here. It's the kind of thing we should probably never mention again."

We rode in silence back through the downtown area to the highway. I finally said, "Maybe it was an osprey."

"What?"

"Maybe an osprey got hold of it."

"What are you talking about?"

"You know, my IEP. Maybe it's feathering some osprey nest right now."

Mom finally got the joke and smiled. "That would be a nice decorating touch."

"Yeah."

"Inconsistent with the scheme of the other nests, but a nice touch."

"Yeah. Something like that." As we headed west on Route 22, I began to feel a real sense of hope about Tangerine Middle School. After all, it was great luck getting Theresa as a guide. Getting Mom to ditch my paperwork was beyond luck; it was another miracle.

Things actually seem to be going my way. Finally. It's the Paul Fisher Soccer Dream. I wonder if Erik feels that way about his life here. But I wonder, too, if Mike Costello felt that way about his when he was leaning against that goalpost.

Tuesday, September 19

I followed Theresa around all morning again. Another big kid, a different one, banged me into a locker. Theresa didn't pay any attention to it, so I tried not to, either. I followed her into the lunchroom again, and we sat down at the same table as yesterday. Everything seemed to be cool. But then everything got uncool real fast.

A bunch of guys came over. I recognized a few of them from the carnival. Their leader, a stocky guy with curly hair and real oily skin, said to Theresa, "What's he doing here?"

She said, "This is the one I told you about. The one who wants to play on your soccer team."

The leader eyeballed me and snorted. "You? You think you can play on my team? What do you think this is, Lake

Windsor Middle School? You think we gotta take every chump who shows up? You think 'cause your mommy buys you a jockstrap you're automatically on my team?"

I looked at him calmly. I really didn't know if he was putting me on or if he meant what he was saying. He looked like he was about to dump his lunch tray on my head.

Theresa spoke up. "Chill out, Victor. I'm trying to eat."

Victor took the seat directly across from me, in my face. He continued, "Lake Windsor—that team's a joke, man. We're gonna bust you up this year. You got that big Italian kid, right? Thinks he's bad? He's a joke, man. He's nothin'. And the rest of you guys? . . . That makes you less than nothin'. Less than zero. That's you, Lake Windsor Man. Less than zero. You're a negative integer." He turned to one of the other guys and slapped hands with him.

Victor then turned his attention to his hamburger and took a big bite. I figured he wasn't really serious, he was just messing with me. I decided to take a chance. I said, "Hey, what do you expect? We play in a sinkhole."

Victor shot an angry look at me, but then he started laughing, nearly choking on his burger. The other guys took their cue from him and started laughing, too. "That's right, man. You crawled out of some kind of sinkhole. That's right." He took a drink of soda. "Hey, what's that big kid's name?"

"Gino."

"Right. Gino. Hey, Tino! They got a Gino, and we got a Tino." Victor reached across, high-fived with Theresa's twin brother, and went on. "I heard about your Gino. You ever hear about me? You ever hear of Victor Guzman?"

"Yeah. I heard about you. I heard you scored sixteen goals last year. I heard you were All-County."

Victor took another bite and said, "You heard right."

Everybody was quiet after that, so I said, "I worked out with the team yesterday."

"Fool, you didn't work out with the team! The team wasn't there yesterday."

I looked at Theresa. I decided to play dumb. "Right. Right. Where were you guys?"

Victor snorted. "Tell him where we were, Tino."

Tino answered to nobody in particular, "We were in jail. They put us in the vandalism jail."

My stomach suddenly knotted up. I said, "What? They put you guys in a jail cell?"

Tino looked at me like I had just said the stupidest thing he had ever heard and I was the biggest loser he had ever met.

Another kid at the table said, "Yeah, I heard you guys got busted. What was up with that?"

Tino answered, "Self-defense, man."

Victor laughed through a mouthful of hamburger. He swallowed and said, "Right. Right. Self-defense. Me and Hernando saw the whole thing."

Hernando added, "Self-defense, man. All the way."

Victor continued, "Did you go to the freak show? At the carnival? Did you see that dude with the big scar down his cheek and the big ax in his hand? Ax Man was his name. Me and Hernando are reading all about this guy on the sign. He chopped people up, right?"

Hernando filled in, "He chopped a whole bunch of people up, long time ago."

"Right. So we're reading about him, and Tino comes around the corner real fast and gets scared."

"Scared? No way!" Tino protested.

"So he screams, and jumps up in the air, and karate-kicks this Ax Man dude right in the stomach, right? And Ax Man snaps in half!"

"Right in half, man," said Hernando. "He's laying all over the floor."

"So we start yelling, 'You killed Ax Man! You killed Ax

Man! Let's get outta here!' And we all run outta that place!''

Victor, Tino, and Hernando started rollicking with laughter, reliving the moment. My stomach started to knot again. I said, "So how did you get busted?"

Victor stopped laughing. "How did we get busted?" He glared at Tino. "Stupid Tino here."

Tino snapped at him, "Shut up, fool."

"You shut up. He's carrying his soccer ball around all day, showin' off, you know? Like he's got something to show off."

"I told you to shut up."

"Yeah. You told me that. So they call up Betty Bright and they tell her that it was soccer players that trashed the Ax Man. She knows right away who it was, so she nails us."

The conversation soon turned to things that I didn't know about. I concentrated on my lunch, thinking, *Maybe you actually got away with ratting out these guys.* I certainly hoped so.

As soon as I got to practice in the afternoon, I could tell that things were different.

Victor Guzman is the leader out there. Everybody accepts that. He spurs on the offense all the time. He talks trash to the defense all the time. He wants the ball all the time.

Lake Windsor Middle had about thirty kids on its team; Tangerine Middle has fifteen. I make it sixteen. They don't even have enough players for two scrimmage teams. The starting front line plays against the starting defense. The other four kids play behind the front line, feeding them the ball.

I was in the far goal again. I may as well have been in Houston. I never touched the ball until right before the end of practice, when the coach called Shandra over to talk to her. The coach yelled down to my end of the field. "New guy! Paul Fisher! Get up here. Get in goal."

I sprinted up and took my place on the goal line. So far the front line had scored four times. But Shandra had made about fifteen saves, some of them really impressive. Now it was my turn to face the starters. Victor, Maya, and Tino are the main strikers. They play in the middle of the front line. Nita and a kid they call Henry D. play out on the wings.

Victor started in on me right away. "Paul Fisher? Hey, Fisher Man, you think this is trout season here or something? You think you're in some kinda tuna-catchin' tournament here?" Some of the others started laughing. "You're gonna be wearing those glasses on the other side of your head if you think that. This ain't no Lake Windsor Middle School, sucka. You're facing the War Eagles now!"

Nita set the ball up in the corner. She lofted a corner kick into the center to Maya, who controlled it and passed it along the ground to Victor. Victor caught it at full stride and drove a shot high and hard toward the goal. I saw it coming all the way. I sprang off my heels, forward and to the left. The ball stuck in my outstretched hands like they were Velcro. I landed flat on the ground, fully extended, holding on to the ball. A great save.

I looked over to check Betty Bright's reaction. She had her head down, talking earnestly to Shandra. She had missed the whole thing.

Suddenly, *wham!* A foot came slicing in front of my face, driving the ball out of my hands and into the goal. Victor pumped his fist into the air. He leaned over me and yelled, "You taking a nap, Fisher Man? Is this naptime at Lake Windsor Middle School? Too bad. You missed my goal!"

Tino came up behind him, shaking his head, "That's no goal, man. That's bogus."

Victor turned on him. "What are you talking about? That goal counts."

"No chance. That ball was dead."

"Yeah? You gonna be dead you don't shut your mouth."

"You shut your mouth, chump!"

"Hey, come here and shut it for me!"

Tino lunged at Victor. They bounced off each other and squared off in a snarling, karate-kicking scene, right above my head. Hernando tried to get between them and break it up, and Maya and Nita drifted out of the way.

The coach looked up and blew her whistle. She screamed at them, "You two didn't learn a thing, did you? Do you need another three days off? Do you need to miss the opening game of the season?" The combatants stopped fighting and glared at each other. "I see one more punch over there, you two are back on suspension. You hear me?" Victor and Tino continued to glare at each other, but the worst of it seemed to be over. The coach blew her whistle again. "That's enough for today. Everybody get here early tomorrow. I'm giving out the uniforms."

I picked myself up off the ground and followed everybody off the field. When we got to the bus lanes, the old green truck pulled up. Theresa and Dolly got into the front while Tino, Hernando, and Victor piled into the back. All seemed to be forgiven with them. They were already laughing about something. Probably about me.

When I walked out to the front of the building, I saw Maya and Nita waiting for their ride. I nodded as I walked past them. Maya said to me, in a musical voice, "That was an excellent save."

"Oh? Thank you."

"The goal would not have counted. You had the ball in your grasp."

"Uh-huh."

"The whistle would have blown."

"Thank you. I know better than that, though. I shouldn't have been lying there posing for pictures like that. I should have protected the ball."

A blue Mercedes pulled up and the two girls got in. Mom

pulled up right behind. She said, "So, are you on the team?"

"Yeah. I think I am."

She jerked her head toward the blue Mercedes. "Are those two girls on it?"

"Yep."

"Really? Girls? Are they the only ones?"

"Nope. There are two more."

Mom seemed genuinely impressed. "How nice. To have girls on your team. That's nice."

As we drove home, I relived everything that happened at lunchtime and at practice. Every word. Every action. I thought to myself, *It's not my team, Mom. Not yet anyway. Not by a long shot. And it's definitely not nice. But it's where I want to be.*

Wednesday, September 20

I got my uniform today. Joey brought his over after supper.

We went out back, through the patio doors. That was a mistake. It was a bad time to be outside. The muck fire was particularly strong. I could actually see it, and feel it, and smell it swirling over and into our yard. And mixed in with it, I could hear a sound, a predator's sound. It was the sound of Arthur Bauer's Land Cruiser on the other side of the back wall. It was the sound of Arthur and Erik accelerating, braking, and sliding through the mud on the perimeter road. I should have told Joey to come back inside, but I didn't. We laid our uniforms out on the picnic table, side-by-side, so we could compare them.

Joey's uniform is brand-new. It has light blue socks, white shorts, and a light blue jersey. The jersey has a white number 10 on the back and the word SEAGULLS written in cursive across the front. Pretty cool.

My uniform has obviously known some previous owners. It has maroon socks and shorts and a gold jersey with a thin maroon stripe on each side. The jersey has a black number 5 on the back and a round black patch over the heart, hand sewn, that shows a ferocious-looking eagle with arrows in its talons.

The smoke was starting to get to us, so we gathered up our stuff to go inside. I hadn't noticed that the predator's roar had stopped. Arthur and Erik had quit their mud running and driven around from the perimeter road to our driveway. I usually notice stuff like that, especially where Erik is concerned, but today I didn't.

Just as Joey and I turned around from the table, Erik and Arthur entered the backyard through the gate. Arthur ignored us and headed toward the patio door.

Erik, carrying all of his football gear, swiped at Arthur with his helmet and said, "Hey, check it out. It's Mohawk Man's brother."

Arthur stopped and stared at Joey. He answered on their cruel wavelength. "I didn't know Mohawk Man had a brother."

"Yeah you did, butthead. The shoes! He was trying to take Mohawk Man's shoes!"

The two of them started to laugh. Erik said, "It's the hair that fooled you. No family resemblance."

Arthur picked up the banter. "No. No resemblance. None at all."

"I wonder if he got his money back for those shoes."

"Yeah. Hey, there was nothin' wrong with those shoes. The kid had some money comin'."

Joey was clearly stunned by this exchange. He had no idea what they were talking about. But I did, and I felt sick with anger.

Erik and Arthur continued on through the patio doors, passing through them into Mom's world, changing their ghoulish routine about Mike Costello into one about the National Honor Society, or the student government, or some other bull for Mom's ears.

Joey turned to me with a pleading look. He said, "What are they talking about? Who's Mohawk Man?"

"Forget about it. They're idiots."

"No. Tell me. You obviously know."

Joey was right. I took a deep breath of the smoky air and explained, "Joey, they're making fun of your brother. They're making fun of Mike when his hair got burned off by the lightning. And they're making fun of you for trying to take his shoes off at the field."

Joey thought for a minute. Then he whispered, "That's what I thought they were doing." He sat down on the picnic-table bench. "I should've punched them out for that. I should've tried, anyway." He looked at me. "That's what Mike would have done. Mike had guts. He stood up to people when he had to." Joey's voice dropped even lower. "He wasn't a coward like me."

"Hey! You're not a coward. We saved people's lives at that sinkhole, right?"

"This is different. This is personal. It's about me. They *knew* they could do that to me. They knew I wouldn't do anything back."

"They're idiots, Joey. And they're just not worth it. You don't see me standing up to them, do you? I just let them be idiots."

Joey stared at the wall. "I know a lot of those football guys are laughing at me because of what I did. Because of the shoes. But I never, in a million years, thought they were laughing at Mike."

"Hey. Nobody who's worth thinking about is laughing at Mike. Or at you. Who are we talking about here? Erik? Erik's laughing at everybody. It's all a big joke to him. Arthur Bauer? He's a big zero. But now he's getting his chance, right? He's gonna hold the ball for Erik. But he's no Mike Costello. Nowhere near. He doesn't have the talent. He doesn't have the character. So what's he going to do? He's going to mock him. He's going to put him down. He'd never do it to Mike's face, so he's doing it this way. He's the coward, not you."

Joey may or may not have been listening. I don't know. Tears were pouring down his face. He tried to talk through them. "I wanted to explain to Coach Warner about the shoes. He—I guess he thought I had cracked up or something." Joey let the sorrow pump out of him now, like blood from an artery. "But—but I saw Mike lying there. Maybe I even knew he was dead. I don't know. I had to do something for him, somehow. Mike always felt better when he got his shoes off. That's the first thing he did when he came home, always. He took his shoes off. And that's all I was trying to do." He sniffed and sat up straight. "It was stupid. And it wouldn't have done him any good. But none of the other stupid things they tried did him any good, either, did they?"

I shook my head. "No."

"I know people are laughing at me. I hate it. I hate that school. I hate that football field. I hate that goalpost."

"So why don't you come to Tangerine with me?"

"It's too late now. I'm on the split shift."

"So get off the split shift. Get your dad up there. They're afraid of him. Believe me, they'll do anything he says."

Joey picked up his uniform and wiped his face in it. "What do you mean? Why are they afraid of him?"

I opened my eyes wide with surprise. It seemed so obvious to me. "Your dad's a lawyer. Your brother got killed on their property. In their care. They're afraid he'll sue them."

Joey looked at me dumbly, and I realized that the Costellos weren't thinking anything of the kind. They were mourning Mike, and that was all. I said, "Sorry. Bad idea. I'll shut up. But I could sure use some company at Tangerine."

"I'll bet you could. Anybody try to kill you yet?"

"No."

"Anybody mess with you at all?"

"Nobody who's still alive."

"Oh yeah. Right." Joey rolled up his uniform into a blue-and-white ball. "OK if I hop over your wall?"

"Sure."

"I just don't want to walk past..." He stopped and nodded toward the house.

"I don't blame you. How are you going to get to your house?"

"I'll go around to the guardhouse." Joey pulled himself to the top of the six-foot wall. He sat there for a minute before he said, "So Tangerine's not that tough?"

"I didn't say that."

"What about the soccer team?"

"They got some tough guys on that. Girls, too."

"Tough girls?"

"No. But they got girls. And they start."

"Wow. Any chance I'd start?"

"None. You'd stand next to me on the sideline."

Joey turned and looked over the wall to the other side. He said, "I'll think about it. See you." And he vaulted down into the mud of the perimeter road.

Friday, September 22

We played our first soccer game today, an away game against Palmetto Middle School.

After seventh period, Tino, Henry D., and I used the second-floor bathroom to change into our uniforms. We went out the back door to the bus lanes, where an old khaki green bus, with a noisy engine and no air-conditioning, was waiting.

I climbed up the steps and slid into an empty seat. Henry D. took the seat across the aisle. Nita and Maya sat together behind him. Victor and his boys were spread out across the back, but no one was talking. Shandra got on, and then Coach Bright, who hopped into the driver's seat. She looked in the rearview mirror and called, "Count 'em up, Victor."

Victor counted our heads and shouted, "Sixteen, Coach."

The coach closed the bus door, threw it in gear, and pulled away. We drove east, past small farms and dead citrus groves, past forests of scrubby-looking pine trees, past a sign that said, THE TURPENTINE CAPITAL OF THE WORLD.

After thirty minutes we reached a one-block downtown area. We rounded the corner and pulled into a school that looked very much like our own. It must have been built around the same time by the same people. We drove around back and parked in their bus lane, which was exactly like ours. They even had the same baseball diamond and the same green scoreboard. This one said, PALMETTO MIDDLE SCHOOL—HOME OF THE WHIPPOORWILLS.

Before she opened the bus door, the coach said, "Remember who you are. Remember who you represent. Victor, you lead them once around and then meet me at midfield. All right, everybody, let's look like a team."

Victor and his gang piled out of the bus and took off at a fast clip toward the field. The rest of us hurried to catch up.

I don't know why—maybe they were mad about having such a wimpy nickname—but these guys turned out to be really nasty. So did their fans.

The near side of the field was lined with people watching the Palmetto players warm up. There were middle school kids of course, but there were also many grown-ups, local people. They turned to us and started jeering as we began our lap around the field. I swear some of them spit at us before we made it to the turn and headed toward the far side, the visitors' side. We could still hear them yelling nasty stuff behind us.

I looked up at Victor. He was totally focused. He didn't seem to be listening to any of it. He led us at a sprint down the far sideline. Then we turned and cut a path through the green uniforms of the Palmetto players. They had some rude things to say to us, too, especially to the girls. We formed a circle around the coach at midfield.

Now I could see Victor's eyes. They were blazing with rage, and the muscles of his face were knotted like a fist. Betty Bright extended her long arm into the circle. Each player put a hand on top of hers. I squeezed in and did the same. She yelled, "Who are we?" and we yelled back, "War Eagles!"

"Who are we?"

"War Eagles!"

"Who are we?"

"War Eagles!"

Betty Bright pulled her arm back and stepped out of the circle. Victor picked up the chant, but all he was screaming was, "War! War! War!" We all started screaming with him, blocking out the catcalls from the Whippoorwills and their fans. "War! War! War!"—in a frenzy that drove away all the fear and intimidation that I felt from our opening lap.

Our circle broke up and the game began. There was only one referee, and he didn't seem like he knew too much about soccer. He seemed like a football guy. He lost control of the game in the opening minute, and he never got it back.

Of course, it wasn't really a game. It was a war. The Palmetto players got down and dirty right away, and their fans cheered them on. They tripped us, pulled our jerseys, got up in our faces, and pretended to throw punches. Their fans loved it. The longer the referee failed to blow his whistle, the bolder they got, and the more bloodthirsty their fans became.

I was standing on the sideline with Betty Bright and the other four kids who weren't playing. Directly behind us, about twenty yards away, was a line of trees. Some kids from the middle school had gathered handfuls of acorns from there. They started throwing them at us and then running back to get more. What could we do except duck?

The coach said to us, "You stand here by me, all of you. And stand up straight. Don't let some fool make you bow your head."

The Palmetto team had two big fullbacks who couldn't play soccer at all but who wiped out anybody who got near the goal. They were tripping, throwing elbows, getting away with murder back there.

I looked at my teammates, the victims of all of this, and was amazed at how calm their faces were. I was the only one who was freaking out. The rest of them had been through it before. They were acting like it was business as usual here at Palmetto Middle School—Home of the Whippoorwills.

So the War Eagles stayed focused and played their game. They controlled the ball. They passed to the open guy or girl. They got the ball to the people who knew how to score. Maya got off two excellent shots, hitting the goalpost once and just missing high with the other one. It was only a matter of time until she found the range and scored, in spite of those menacing fullbacks. Victor hadn't tried a shot yet. Maybe he was too caught up with being the enforcer for our side, with insulting the Whippoorwills' defenders and threatening their lives. Underneath all this ugliness was one fact: We were the better team. We had these guys dead. We played much better soccer, and we played it like a team.

Palmetto has a few individual players, but they don't

work together. Our fullbacks, Dolly Elias and a big guy they call Mano, were able to clear out every ball that came close. Shandra only touched the ball once, when Dolly kicked it back to her.

Of course, whenever you think things are as bad as they're going to get, they get worse. An afternoon storm came rumbling in. In a matter of minutes it got cold; then it got dark; then the rain started pouring down on the field, turning it into mud. That was good news for the big fullbacks from Palmetto. They could knock our players flying —Maya, Tino, Henry D., Hernando—all of them were flying through the mud at one time or another. And still the referee's whistle remained silent.

The half ended at 0–0. We all ran back to our bus to escape from the pelting of the rain. Betty Bright pulled out a brown bag and tossed everyone a tangerine. She spoke to us calmly, like she, too, had been through this before. "Maya, you find yourself a dry spot out there and stay in it. The rest of you, get the ball to Maya. I want to see her take twenty shots on goal this half. Victor, they're playing you for a fool out there. Forget about that bad-boy stuff and play ball." She waited until Victor responded with a disgusted snort. She continued, but not as calmly. "There's no way this team can beat you. You can only beat yourselves. And that's all I have to say. Let's go."

The coach opened the bus door. We all waited for Victor to get up and stalk to the front. He stopped on the bus steps and looked back at all of us. Then he jumped out into the rain and started running back toward the field, with the rest of us right behind.

Mercifully the rain let up in the second half. A Palmetto forward upended Tino right in front of our goal. Tino fell on top of the guy and started punching at his face. Betty Bright ran out on the field and pulled him off, his arms still punching away at the air. She dragged Tino to our sideline as the remaining Palmetto fans screamed for a foul. Suddenly the coach was looking straight at me. "Paul Fisher! Have you ever played anything but goal?"

I stared at her dumbly. I hadn't played, or even thought about playing, anything but goal for the past two years. But I heard myself saying, "Yes, ma'am. I've played soccer since I was six."

I guess that was good enough, because she said, "Get in there for Tino. Play center forward."

The referee responded to the fans. He awarded a penalty kick to Palmetto. A penalty kick is like a free throw in basketball, only better, because the coach picks the player who takes it. You really should make it 100 percent of the time. Your best kicker gets an unobstructed shot at the goalie from just twelve yards away.

Shandra got set, her heels on the goal line. She faced the kicker, the Palmetto captain. The kicker ran up and drove a low, hard shot to the left side. Shandra dove and got a piece of it, but it hit the inside of the goalpost and rolled in. The kicker threw his arms up into the air. The Palmetto players all came running up and jumped on him. They led 1–0.

It took a long time for them to get back into their positions. When they finally did, one of them wiped out Henry D. on the wing and then kicked the ball out of bounds. Some kids got a hold of it and kicked it even farther away, into the woods. Betty Bright yelled to the referee, "Time's out! Time's out on this play. Right?"

The referee himself wound up getting the ball. When he got back onto the field, he yelled over, "Five minutes left to play, Coach."

Dolly threw the ball in to Maya, who dribbled it all the way down the right sideline. I ran as hard as I could toward the goal. The defender took off after Maya, who looped the ball over him, right to me, in front of the goal.

I don't know what happened next. My brain got stuck

somewhere between *Shoot it now* and *Trap it first, then shoot it*. Anyway, I swung my leg back to kick, but the ball went rolling right under me, through my legs, to the other Palmetto defender, who cleared it away.

Victor was in my face immediately, his finger nearly stabbing through my chest. He screamed, "If we lose this game, you're dead!"

A minute later I got another chance to shoot the ball, but one Palmetto fullback knocked me down and the other kicked it away. I started to get up, but before I could, the fullback stretched out my goggles from my face, scooped up a handful of mud, and smeared it in my eyes. *In my eyes!* I went berserk!

Before he could get away, I scrambled up and jumped on his back. I brought him down and started punching at him blindly, the way I'd seen Tino do it. A whistle started blowing, and soon I felt the coach's big hands yanking me off him and dragging me away.

I stood next to the coach for the rest of the game, mud all over me, blood pouring out of my nose, tears pouring out of my eyes. I heard my teammates screaming, so I took off my goggles, cleaned them the best I could, and put them back on.

Through the blurry plastic lenses, I watched Victor take the ball through the Palmetto defenders like a wild bull. He fought off one nasty tackle, and then another. He lowered his shoulder at the fullback and crashed into him. The Palmetto goalie slid at him, but Victor was too quick. He pushed the ball to the right and vaulted over him. Then he kicked it into the open goal. It was 1–1.

Our players didn't celebrate. With one minute left, they lined up and started again. It was an open brawl out there now between some of our guys and some of theirs, but the referee did not blow his whistle. He just wanted to get this over with.

Victor called for the ball, and Shandra got it to him with a mighty heave. He fought his way out of a pack at midfield and sprinted straight for the Palmetto goal. Two defenders sandwiched him and threw him off balance, but his momentum carried him on. The fullback hit him with a forearm to the shoulder that sent him sprawling forward, sliding through the mud. Then the fullback kicked the ball back toward his own goaltender, who only had to cradle it and run out the clock.

But the ball never got to him. Victor somehow scrambled to his feet in the middle of his mudslide and lunged for it, flipping it with his foot. The ball flew up in an arc as Victor and the goaltender smacked heads. The ball bounced once and went in the goal. The referee threw up his arms, signaling the goal, and shouted, "That's it! The game's over!"

Victor staggered back to his feet and stood at the penalty line, the captain of the War Eagles, mud coating his entire body, blood streaming down from a cut over his eye. He held out his right fist and we all ran to him. We put our hands on his and jumped up and down, chanting, "War Eagles! War Eagles!" and "War! War! War!" in a frenzy. We ran in a pack, whooping and screaming and pounding on each other until we got back to the bus.

I looked out the window and saw that the acorn throwers had turned their attention to the referee, who was desperately trying to unlock his car. We heard some acorns hit the roof of the bus as the coach called out, "How many heads, Victor?"

Victor pulled off his shirt to tie it around his bleeding forehead. He scanned us quickly and yelled, "Sixteen, Coach!" and we pulled out of there, faster than the 5 M.P.H. sign allowed.

On the ride home, Victor smacked me on the back of the head and said, "Hey Fisher Man. I'm sorry I got on your case like that."

"No problem, Victor. You're right. I should have had it."

"Yeah, yeah. Shut up. I'm just saying I'm sorry. I know that playin' goal is your thing. I get pumped up, you know?"

"Yeah, I know. You were great out there."

"Sure I was. But I saw you playing hard out there, too. And I saw you get a piece of that fullback." Victor paused. When he continued he was no longer bragging. He was dead serious. "Listen, Fisher Man, here it is. If you're gonna play with us, then you're gonna play with us. Do you understand?" I nodded. "If you're a War Eagle, then you're a War Eagle. You got brothers to back you up. Nobody's gonna mess with you, not anyplace, not anytime. Do you know what I'm sayin'?"

I looked into Victor's fierce dark eyes and nodded some more.

Victor returned to the back of the bus, leaving me sitting in a kind of daze. Did I hear him? Oh yeah, I heard him all right. I heard his words clearer than any words I had ever heard before. And I do believe I know what he's saying.

Friday, September 22, *later*

Joey called me after dinner and announced, "I'm coming to your school on Monday."

"Whoa! What happened?"

"I took your advice. I went into the office with Dad. You were right. Mrs. Gates came out all smiles, you know? She shook Dad's hand. She said, 'Tell me what I can do for you.'"

"And what did you say?"

"I didn't say anything. My lawyer did all the talking. Basically, she did whatever we said."

"You said 'Jump' and she said 'How high?'"

121

"Exactly. She went in herself and got my folder out of the files. Dad asked her to put a note in there saying I should have all the same classes as you."

"She did that?"

"She said she was 'more than happy to.' Then we went to find Coach Walski to give him the uniform back."

"How was he?"

"Not cool. He started telling me that I shouldn't leave, that I won't be allowed to play at Tangerine Middle because I live in the Lake Windsor district. But Dad was ready for him. He cut him right off and said, 'We'll see about that. Wait here.'"

"He said that?"

"So we hustled back over to the office, right? Dad had Gates write out a letter giving me special permission to play soccer at Tangerine Middle School."

"All right!"

"Then we took it back to Walski. My dad stuck it under his nose and made him sign it."

"Awesome! What did he say?"

"Not a word. Not one word." Joey paused. Then he continued awkwardly, "So, uh, you think you'll be able to show me around on Monday?"

My mouth opened up to answer him, but I couldn't. I couldn't see myself leading Joey around the halls of Tangerine Middle School. That had to be somebody else's job. I said, "I'll tell you what you should do. When you get to the office, ask to see Dr. Johnson. Right? Then ask her to let Theresa Cruz take you around."

Joey repeated the name, like he was writing it down. "Theresa Cruz. Why? Is she cute or something?"

I hesitated. "Yeah, I guess she's kinda cute. But that's not it. She's connected. At Tangerine, it's all about being connected."

Joey said, "Uh-huh," but I don't think he understood.

Then he said, "What about the soccer team? What are those guys like?"

That was a good question. I didn't have an answer to it. Not yet. I finally said, "They're super-focused on the game, you know. On winning. It's like it's life or death for them."

Joey once again repeated my words. "Life or death. OK. I can handle that. I'll see you on Monday."

Saturday, September 23

Today was the first day of football season for the Lake Windsor High Seagulls. They played a home game against the Cypress Bay High Cardinals.

Dad was pretty hyper, like this was the most important day of his life or something. We got there at one o'clock for a two o'clock game, but I was glad we did. We barely managed to crowd into the home-side bleachers. We sat with the other Lake Windsor fans, and with the few Cypress Bay fans who remembered that half our bleachers had been condemned.

I hadn't seen the bleachers since the day of the sinkhole. There they sat, a big gray Erector set, now looped with yellow police ribbons that said DO NOT CROSS. Like a big VIP section reserved for people who were never going to show up.

By one-thirty the rest of the Cypress Bay fans had gotten the message: There was nowhere for them to sit. They were milling around both end zones, trying to find open places to stand and watch the game. Mom kept saying, "This isn't right. Didn't anybody plan for this?"

Finally a group of teenagers wearing red-and-white Cardinals shirts decided to do something about it. They walked around to the visitors' side, ducked under the yellow ribbon, and sat down in the front row. They then gestured back to the other Cypress Bay fans, like they were panto-miming, *See? We made it. It didn't collapse.*

Other fans started heading over there. Then suddenly we saw this fat guy in a gray suit go running across the field. Mom called out, "Look! That's Mr. Bridges!"

Sure enough. Mr. Bridges was yelling and waving at the Cypress Bay fans to go back, to get out of there, but they weren't listening. In fact more and more red-and-white shirts seemed willing to take a chance on the condemned bleachers.

A photographer in a *Tangerine Times* cap started bobbing in front of Mr. Bridges, taking pictures of him trying to turn the mob back. He finally gave up yelling and came stomping back across the grass, red faced, like he was about to have a heart attack.

It was past the time to start the game, but nothing was happening on the field. Mom spotted Erik in his uniform—light blue helmet, white pants, and light blue jersey with SEAGULLS written across the front. He had a white number 1 on his back. Arthur Bauer was standing next to him, of course. He was wearing number 4.

We continued to sit, baking in the sun, for nearly thirty minutes while nothing happened. Finally a squadron of police cruisers appeared on Seagull Way. They had their sirens sounding and their lights flashing. Right behind them came a square white truck with a big satellite dish on the top and CHANNEL 2 NEWS on the side.

They all pulled in behind the home bleachers. While the other cops spread out, two big sheriff's deputies marched across the field and confronted the Cypress Bay fans. It was all over in a minute. The fans weren't there to fight. They surrendered immediately, ducking back under the ribbons and finding places to stand along the far sideline. At last the referees and players took the field to start the game.

It turned out to be a pretty sloppy game, considering that

the *Tangerine Times* had picked both the Lake Windsor Seagulls and the Cypress Bay Cardinals as "Teams to Watch" in its preseason poll.

Erik kicked off for our side, driving the ball deep into the Cypress Bay end zone. But then he stood on the sideline for the rest of the half. Neither offense could get anything going. Each side would run three plays and then punt the ball away. Erik was the placekicker, but Antoine Thomas, in addition to everything else, did the punting. By the end of the first half, Antoine had run for about fifty yards, but nearly all of his passes had been dropped. The Seagulls had never gotten the ball close enough for Erik to try a field goal.

The Cypress Bay offense was no better. They had a big fullback who could pick up three yards through the middle, but that was about it. It was 0–0 at the half.

Tina, Paige, and the rest of the Lake Windsor cheerleaders (the Seagirls) took the field for a halftime dance routine.

The third quarter was as dull as the first two, but Cypress Bay's offense suddenly got it together in the final period. They drove eighty-five yards for a touchdown, most of those yards coming from that big fullback. The kick for the extra point was good, and Cypress Bay led 7–0.

Antoine responded with two short runs and then a beautiful forty-yard pass to Terry Donnelly, who was wide open down the left sideline. I could have caught that pass. My grandmother could have caught it, for that matter, but Terry Donnelly dropped it. Antoine had to punt again.

That's when I noticed the black clouds rolling in. That whole mess with the visitors' bleachers and Mr. Bridges and the cops had pushed the game past the four o'clock barrier. In a matter of minutes we went from sunny skies to *kaboom!* And then down it came, a hard, cold rain. Most of the fans climbed down from the bleachers and ran for their cars. Mom yelled, "Come on, you two!" but Dad said, "No, you go ahead. I'm staying," so I said, "I'm staying, too."

Mom was already on the ground. She yelled back, "Fine. Stay. I hope neither of you gets killed." She ran back to the Volvo, leaving us to get soaked. Or worse.

The rain turned out to be a blessing for Lake Windsor. The offensive line started pushing Cypress Bay back, letting Antoine move the ball steadily down the field—five yards, six yards, five yards, seven yards. With two minutes to play, the Seagulls were all the way down to the Cypress Bay five-yard line. Antoine faked a run to the right and lofted a pass into the left corner of the end zone that some mud-covered Seagull receiver caught for the touchdown. A soggy cheer went up from the few fans left in the bleachers. The score was 7–6, and Erik's big moment had arrived.

He came running onto the field in his perfectly clean, mud-free uniform to kick the extra point that would tie the game. Erik had never missed an extra point. Never. I was expecting to see Arthur Bauer trotting out with him, but number 4 was still standing there on the sideline with the other clean uniforms.

The two muddy teams lined up. Erik got into his kicking stance, and Antoine Thomas crouched down in front of him to hold the ball. I said, "Check it out, Dad. Antoine's the holder."

"I see," he said grimly. "Erik told me that Arthur would be his holder. I don't think it's such a good idea to throw a surprise like this at your kicker."

Dad, and Erik, and I, and everybody else figured that Arthur had taken over Mike Costello's job. But no. There was Antoine, in the crouch, getting ready to spin the laces and set the ball down for Erik.

The referee blew his whistle, the clock started to tick, and Lake Windsor's big center snapped the ball. Erik, his head down in total concentration, took two steps forward, like he's rehearsed a million times. His foot started toward the ball in a powerful arc, and then—the most incredible thing happened. Antoine whipped the ball away at the last second, like Lucy does with Charlie Brown. He took off running around the right side and crossed the goal line, untouched, for a two-point conversion. Seagulls led 8–7.

At the same moment, Erik, who clearly did not expect Antoine to pull the ball away, kicked at nothing but the air. His left foot went flying off in one direction, his right foot in another. For a split second he was a parallel line three feet above the ground. Then he made a perfect banana-peel back-flop landing in the mud. The people around us started laughing, hooting, and cheering, all at the same time. Antoine spiked the ball in the end zone, and all the Lake Windsor players, except Erik, ran over and jumped on him. All the Lake Windsor players on the sideline, except Arthur, started jumping up and down, too.

Erik finally got up and walked to the sideline to get his kicking tee. His front was still clean and white, but his back was now filthy. He kicked the ball back to the Cardinals, but they fumbled it away, and that's how it ended. Lake Windsor 8, Cypress Bay 7.

When we got back to the car, Mom just said, "From here, it sounded like we won."

I wanted to tell her all about Erik's banana-peel back-flop special, but Dad cut in right away. "Yes. We won on a fake kick. They sent Erik out to fake the kick for the extra point. That drew the offense to him, and it cleared the way for Antoine to run it in for two points."

Mom thought for a minute. "So Erik did something that helped to win the game."

"Most definitely," Dad said. "It's not something that shows up in the stats in the newspaper. It's not something people will remember. But it helped win the game."

I thought to myself, *Not remember? You've got to be kidding. Erik's flying banana-peel back-flop in the mud is the one thing about this game that* everybody *is going to remember.*

Dad continued talking in this manner throughout dinner, pounding home his theme to Erik—that Erik had contributed big-time to the victory, that Erik had actually made victory possible by being the decoy. I don't think Erik was even listening. He was just sitting there, looking down, twisting his varsity ring around and around on his finger.

After dinner Dad flipped on the TV so we could all watch the local news. The lead story on channel 2 was the revolt of the Cypress Bay fans and their brief takeover of the condemned visitors' bleachers.

About two-thirds of the way through the broadcast came "The Saturday Sports Roundup." The sports anchorman went through the professional baseball and football stuff, then the college football scores, and then the high school scores. "Lake Windsor 8, Cypress Bay 7."

The broadcast ended with a feature called "The Weak in Sports." It was a collection of sports bloopers, and guess who they saved for last.

The anchorman said something like, "Finally, a play that looks like it was drawn up by the Three Stooges. Watch closely." And there it was. A ground-level view of the ball being snapped to Antoine, of Erik striding forward confidently, and *Whooo!* Up in the air he flew! It was even more comical than I had remembered. Erik went splashing down into the mud, but he didn't stay there. They rewound the tape so that he popped back up, flopped again, popped back up, and flopped again. Finally, the camera turned toward the end zone to catch Antoine spiking the ball. It zoomed in on his face. Antoine was laughing and pointing his finger at that big center, who was pointing back at him.

When the anchorman came back on, he was cracking up. So were all the other news people. The credits started rolling, and they started saying stuff like, "Does that school have a diving team?" and "I hear those mud baths are good for wrinkles."

Dad got up and snapped off the TV. The four of us sat there in stony silence.

I was thinking that if I were at somebody else's house, we'd be rolling on the floor and laughing at this. I was thinking that kids all over Florida were rolling on the floor and laughing at this, at Erik Fisher the Flying Placekicker. But this isn't somebody else's house. This is the house built on the Erik Fisher Football Dream.

Finally Dad said to Erik, "Hey! All you can do is laugh it off."

Mom agreed. "That's right. You just leave it behind you. That's all you can do. You leave it behind you, and it's over with."

The four of us got up and went our separate ways—me up to my room.

I stared out my window at the back wall. *Forget it, Dad. Forget it, Mom. Erik can't laugh this off. Erik can't leave this humiliation behind him. Someone has to pay for this. I'm not sure why I'm sure. But I am. Someone has to pay for this.*

Tuesday, September 26

Today was our second game of the season, and our first home game at Tangerine Middle. The opponents were from Kinnow Middle School. They wear black uniforms with silver letters. Pretty sharp. Henry D. told me they beat us last year.

We had an impressive turnout of fans. In fact I've never seen so many fans at a kids' soccer game. Some of them are obviously regulars, because they brought along water and tangerines for the team. I recognized Theresa and Luis Cruz. They were standing with a man who looked like he could be their father. Was he the Tomas whose name was written on the truck? There were a lot of mothers with little kids.

A couple of ladies had lawn chairs, but everybody else—and there must have been a hundred kids and grown-ups—stood for the entire game.

I saw Shandra talking to a lady, and I overheard somebody say, "That's Shandra's mother with her."

That got me wondering. *Why isn't my mother here? Or my father? They could be watching this game. So could Joey's parents. If we were playing football, they'd all be here.*

We were all more relaxed before this game, except for Victor. He was already talking trash to some of the Kinnow players, reminding them about something that had happened last year. They were giving it right back to him, saying stuff like, "Hey, Guzman, why are you on the girls' team? Couldn't you make the boys' team?"

We started with the same lineup, with me on the sideline. This time, though, I was standing next to Joey. He's now wearing number 19 for the War Eagles.

The referee was clearly a cut above the last one we had. A Kinnow defender took Maya down in the penalty area, and he blew the whistle right away. Maya drilled the penalty kick, upper right, into the net, and we were up 1–0 in the first minute. But these were not the Palmetto Whippoorwills. They had a good offense. They were fast, and they knew how to move the ball.

Shandra was very busy in the goal. She looked sharp out there, really on her game. That's what I think when I watch Shandra in goal—how sharp she looks, how big she looks, like one of those American Gladiators. What must people think when they see me in goal? How small I look? How goofy I look in my goggles?

Dolly and Mano sandwiched a guy in front of our goal and got whistled for it. Penalty kick. Shandra never got a hand on the ball, and it was suddenly 1–1. I wouldn't have gotten a hand on it, either. At least I don't think I would have.

Standing on the sideline for this game was a pleasure after that awful time we had at Palmetto. These are two teams who know how to play soccer. Some highlights: Maya stopped on a dime and passed the ball back to Tino, who drove it into the goal. Then they came back and scored. Henry D. lifted a beautiful corner kick in to Victor, who leaped up and headed it into the goal. Then they came back and scored. At halftime it was 3–3, and there hadn't been one fight.

We all gathered in a circle on the sideline to eat our tangerines. The coach said "Good game" to a couple of players, then spent the rest of her time talking to Shandra about the three goals—how she shouldn't think anymore about them; how she should adjust for the second half. Finally she looked over at Victor. "Captain? Do you have anything to say?"

We all turned toward Victor, and we saw why he hadn't been talking or drawing any attention to himself. He had his hand pressed against his forehead, trying to stop a trickle of blood from running down his face. It was in the same spot where he had smacked heads with the Palmetto goalie. The head ball that he put into the net must have reopened the cut, because it was sure bleeding now. He said, "No, I got nothing to say here. I'll do my talking out there."

Betty Bright walked over and pulled his hand down from the cut. She shook her head and said, "Is your mother here today?"

He snarled, "My mother? No, my mother's not here. What are you talking about?"

"Tino, please ask your father if he'll drive Victor to the emergency room." She turned back to Victor. "I'm sorry. I should have had this stitched up when it happened. It's never going to heal like this. I hope Mr. Cruz can take you now."

"No way! I'm not going to any emergency room. I got a game to play!"

The coach said, "Not this game, Victor. You get yourself together for the next game. We'll have to win this one without you." Then, without even thinking about it, she turned to me and said, "Paul Fisher, you're in for Victor."

Victor continued to protest. "It's not even bleeding anymore."

"Yes, it is bleeding. You should see your shirt."

"I can play this half and then go."

"You're already gone, Victor. Now deal with that."

Victor looked at me for a few long seconds. Then he turned to address us all. "Who wants to win this game?"

Everybody in the circle looked back at him, not knowing what to do.

Victor shouted, "Do you want to win this game?" and we started yelling, "Yeah! Yeah!"

"Do you want to win this game?"

"Yeah! Yeah!"

Victor reached out and fixed his clenched fist in the middle of the circle. We all leaped up and put our hands on his as he started the chant—"War Eagles! War Eagles!" We started moving our hands in unison, up and down, changing the chant into the frenzied cry of "War! War! War!"

We opened the second half with fire in our eyes, even though we had me in instead of Victor. This time it was the defense that sparked the rally. They wouldn't let the Kinnow players cross the midfield line with the ball. Mano, Dolly, Hernando—they kept pounding the ball upfield to the strikers.

Maya was getting the ball a lot, more than in the first half, and she was making things happen. She beat her defender to the outside and then crossed the ball in to Tino, who scored the first goal of the half. We didn't celebrate. We came right back at them. Maya hit one in herself, a beautiful, looping shot into the upper right corner of the goal. The Kinnow goaltender never even saw it coming.

The defense got the ball back upfield immediately. Maya dribbled right, and three defenders went after her. She lobbed the ball back over their heads, and guess who was standing there, all alone, in front of the goal? This time I didn't stop to think. I kicked the ball as hard I could. It glanced off the goalie's left hand and carried into the net.

I had scored a goal! Had this ever happened before? I just stood there, staring at the net, until I realized that my teammates were hurrying to line up again.

I was still trying to remember any time when I had ever scored a goal when Maya got another one on a long cross pass from Nita. She raised her foot, knee-high, and smacked the ball right out of the air into the net. Suddenly this tight game was a 7–3 blowout.

The coach started sending in other subs. She sent Joey in for Hernando. She sent one of the sixth graders in for Maya, who got a loud ovation from the fans.

The Kinnow players never recovered from that assault, although they did manage to move the ball into our end of the field. It turns out that Joey's a pretty terrible soccer player. They had no trouble beating him again and again. Shandra had to make a few tough saves near the end, but that's probably what Betty Bright wanted. The final score was Tangerine 7, Kinnow 3.

Mr. Cruz and Victor came back right at the end. Victor had a line of black stitches going up his forehead, like Frankenstein. He fell on his knees in thanks when he found out the score. Then he started high-fiving with the starters.

He called over to me, "Hey Fisher Man! You were *me* out there, right? How many goals did I score?"

I shrugged. "Sorry, Victor. I could only get you one."

Victor looked at Tino to confirm this, and Tino nodded.

Victor stepped toward me and held up his hand. I high-fived it for all I was worth.

Tuesday, September 26, *later*

The portable phone rang just as I walked past it in the great room. I heard my grandmother's no-nonsense voice. "Hello, Paul. How are you?"

"I'm fine, Grandmom."

"You didn't get hurt in all that sinkhole business?"

"Oh no. No. I got pretty dirty, but not hurt."

"And how are you otherwise?"

Mom walked in and mouthed the words "Who is it?"

I said out loud, "Grandmom," and she reached out for the phone.

I signed off. "I'm all right, Grandmom. Here's Mom."

Mom always seems eager to get on the phone with Grandmom and Grandpop. Dad and Erik certainly don't. They make themselves scarce. Mom began to tell her mother about the sinkhole and the emergency relocation plan, so I made my way upstairs. It sounded like she was going to be on for a long time, which is why I was surprised a few minutes later when she opened my door and held out the portable toward me.

I mouthed the word "Grandmom?"

She whispered back, "No, a girl," and left.

Puzzled, I said, "Hello."

"Paul? Hi. It's Cara Clifton. From Lake Windsor Middle? Do you remember me?"

"Yeah."

"How's it going?"

I couldn't think of a thing to say, so she continued. "I just wanted to find out how you liked Tangerine Middle.

134

Joey says it's really different. I don't know what he means by that."

"Neither do I. Uh, maybe he just means that it's a tougher place."

"Yeah? So what are the kids like?"

"Some of them are pretty tough. They have gangs and stuff. But the kids I'm with are cool."

"Yeah? So ... are you going out with anybody from there?"

I was shocked. No one had ever asked me that question before. I said, "What do you mean?"

"Joey said he thought you might be going with some girl from there."

"He did? No. No, I'm not."

"Uh-huh. Oh, do you remember Kerri? My friend Kerri Gardner?"

"Yeah. Sure."

"I almost forgot. I told her I was gonna call you, and she said to say hi."

"Oh. OK. Well, tell her I said hi."

"Yeah? You want me to tell her you said hi?"

"Sure. Yeah."

"So you kinda like her, then?"

I froze. I suddenly felt like someone was looking at me through one of those two-way mirrors. I didn't say anything else, so Cara finally said, "OK, then. It's just that she's a friend of mine, and she asked me to say hi, so I wanted to make sure I did."

"OK."

"Let me get off now. Maybe I'll be seeing you around sometime with Joey."

"OK. Bye."

"Bye."

I sat there for a minute, stunned. Then I turned the phone

back on and called Joey. "Hey, your girlfriend just called me. Cara?"

"Yeah? What does she want with you?"

"She started asking me if I like Kerri Gardner."

"Oh. OK. Say no more. You know what they were doing, right?"

"What?"

"They were scamming you. Girls scam guys all the time with that. Kerri was listening in on the extension."

"No!"

"Yeah. That's how it works. She has her friend call you up and find out what you have to say about her. It's kinda like a hidden-camera interview."

"Yeah! Yeah, that's exactly what it felt like. So Kerri was on the other end?"

"Yup."

"So what do I do next?"

"About what?"

"About Kerri."

"Well, if you want to talk to her, you call her up."

"OK. But what if I don't call her? Am I going to be hurting her feelings or anything like that?"

"Nah! You're taking all this stuff too seriously. They're probably calling up half a dozen guys tonight and asking them the same thing. It's like a phone survey."

"Uh-huh. So what about that Adam guy? The one from the carnival? Is he still going out with her?"

"Hey, what am I? *People* magazine? I don't know. I don't even see those guys anymore."

"Uh-huh. Well, maybe if you hear something, you can let me know."

"Yeah, yeah. OK. I gotta go eat."

"All right. I'll see you tomorrow."

"Right."

He hung up, and I took a deep breath. I held on to the

phone for a long time. I thought about the situation from all different angles and in all different ways. No matter how I looked at it, my conclusion came out the same. One inescapable conclusion: Kerri Gardner knows about my glasses, but she doesn't think there's anything wrong with me.

Wednesday, September 27

The coach wouldn't let Victor practice today because of his stitches. He stomped away, threatening to go home and pull them out himself. Once again I got put in in his place. I had a couple of opportunities to score against Shandra, but I didn't.

Victor returned near the end of practice carrying a Super Big Gulp from the 7-Eleven. He stood down in the far goal, where I usually stand, and, as usual, the ball never went there. He started to get on Joey's case, telling him to stop standing around doing nothing. But the coach soon noticed him and told him to get out of there.

After practice I got my bag and started walking with Joey when Victor fell into step behind us. His boys, of course, were right behind him.

"Hey, Fisher Man. Since you're *me* now, do you want a drink of my Big Gulp?"

"No, thank you, Victor."

"What? You too good to drink outta my Big Gulp?"

"Yes. I am."

Tino, Hernando, and Mano started laughing. Victor smiled and continued. "Hey, Fisher Man, why's this boy always following you around?"

I glanced at Joey. He was looking straight ahead. "I don't know, Victor. Why don't you ask him?"

Victor tapped Joey on the shoulder with his cup. "Hey! Yo! Why are you following Fisher Man around all the time?"

Joey looked upset. He didn't know how to handle this. I smiled to show him that Victor was just messing around, but he wouldn't even look at me. And he wouldn't answer. I knew that things were about to get worse.

Victor tapped him again, a little harder. His voice got a little louder. "Yo! I said, 'Why are you following Fisher Man around all the time?' You his boyfriend or somethin'?"

Joey turned toward him angrily. "No. I'm not."

Victor ignored him and started on me. "Fisher Man, you can't take two steps without this boy followin' you. What's up with that? Is he some kinda fish, maybe? Does he hope you're gonna catch him?"

The boys behind Victor were getting into it now. Victor turned to Tino and said, "Who's that fish your daddy has the picture of? You know, that fish picture that's hangin' up in the hut?"

Tino shook his head. "What are you talking about?"

"Your daddy has that old magazine ad on the wall, makin' fun of Tio Carlos."

Tino thought about it and then yelled out, "Sorry, Charlie!"

"Yeah! Yeah, that's the dude. Sorry, Charlie! Charlie the Tuna. He's always trying to get caught. He's always hanging around trying to get on that hook, right?" He poked Joey again. "Is that you? Are you Charlie the Tuna?"

The boys were laughing wildly now. I spoke in a calm voice to Joey: "Just chill out." But he wouldn't chill out. He was letting it get to him.

Victor kept after him. "Starkist don't want tunas with good taste, Charlie. They want tunas that taste good." The boys were laughing like maniacs now and slapping hands. "Do you understand the difference, my man?"

Joey continued to stare straight ahead, his face red, his jaw clenched. We all reached the green pickup truck, and the boys piled into the back, still laughing about Joey. We continued on through the school. He didn't say a word until we were standing out at the curb.

"So what was that supposed to be? Some kind of initiation or something?"

"Yeah. Yeah, don't take it so seriously. That's just Victor."

"Did he ever mess with you like that?"

"Sure—on the first day I went out for the team."

"And then he stopped?"

"Yeah. Yeah, sure. He stopped."

Joey stared down the street, looking for Mom's car. I didn't have the heart to tell him the rest of it—Victor might stop messing with him, but his name will be Charlie the Tuna from here on out.

Mom pulled up, and Joey hopped into the backseat without a word. I got in the front and noticed that Mom was staring at something ahead of us. She pulled up ten more yards, to where Maya and Nita were standing. She rolled down the window, smiled, and said, "Hello, girls."

Maya smiled back. "Hello. How are you?"

There was an awkward silence until Mom said, "So . . . how is it playing against these boys?"

I'm not sure Maya understood the question. She answered, "Oh yes. Some of them are quite good players."

"I think it's great that you have a co-ed team. I really do."

"Thank you."

Mom rolled the window back up and pulled away. I said, "What was that all about?"

"I just wanted to encourage those girls a little."

No wonder Maya seemed confused. I said, "Mom, Maya doesn't need too much encouragement. She's the top scorer in the county. Numero uno. She'll make the All-County Team for sure."

Mom's jaw dropped. "Are you serious? That tall girl— she'll be on the All-County Boys' Team?"

"Yes. So will Shandra, if she doesn't get hurt."

"That's fantastic! Does Mr. Donnelly know about this?"

"Mr. Donnelly?"

"Mr. Donnelly from the *Tangerine Times*. This should be in the newspaper. Don't you think so, Joey?"

Joey was sulking pretty heavily in the back. I don't think he even heard her. We drove the rest of the way in silence. We turned into the entranceway to Lake Windsor Downs and then onto Joey's street. It was a weird sight. The houses on either side of his were completely covered by huge, bright blue tents. They had signs posted all around them: DANGER—POISON GAS.

Mom tried to make eye contact with him in the rearview mirror. "Joey, why are your neighbors getting their houses tented?"

"They gotta get fumigated," he said. "Fumigated for bugs. We've all got bugs."

"You all do? Your house, too?"

"Yeah. The whole street, I think."

"What kind of bugs?"

"I don't know. Roaches. Termites."

"So are you getting one of these tents put over your house?"

"Yeah. Next week, I think." We pulled into Joey's driveway. I could see the tents better now. They were really big pieces of blue canvas, tied together with ropes to hold in the poison fumes.

Mom said, "How long do you have to stay away when they fumigate?"

"Two days."

"Well, you're welcome to stay with us. You and Paul do everything else together. You may as well sleep together. Right, Paul?"

I thought to myself, *Perfect, Mom. The perfect thing to say under the circumstances.*

Joey got that upset look on his face again. He muttered, "I don't think so," and went inside.

Mom turned to me. "What's with him? Why wouldn't he want to come to our house?"

I shrugged and said, "I don't know."

But of course I do know. Joey hasn't set foot in our house since the day he met up with Erik and Arthur. He will probably never set foot in it again. But Mom could never understand that. For Joey, our house may as well be covered with canvas and bound by ropes, because it's filled with poison.

Friday, September 29

Joey didn't show up for practice yesterday, but someone else did.

We had been loosening up for about ten minutes. The starters, including Victor, were taking shots at Shandra in the goal. The subs, including me, were kicking a ball around in a circle.

I looked over toward the bus lanes and saw a white van pulling in. It had two high-tech-looking antennas on top—one on the back that looked like a corkscrew, and one in the middle that swiveled.

Anyway, this van kept driving, right off the blacktop and over the grass toward our field. When it got closer, I could see that TANGERINE TIMES was printed on the side. I suddenly got a sick feeling. Mom had actually done it. She had called Mr. Donnelly about our team—or at least about the girls on our team.

The van pulled up next to Betty Bright's car, her 1967 yellow-and-white Mustang. A young guy with long hair and a big camera hanging around his neck jumped out of the driver's side. He set a black leather case down on the back of the Mustang. Mr. Donnelly got out of the other side. He had on a blue suit and carried a small notebook. He walked straight up to the coach, who was on the sideline talking to Dolly. I drifted toward them to hear what they would say.

It was obvious that Mr. Donnelly and Betty Bright knew each other. She shook hands with him and gave him a big smile. She stopped smiling pretty fast, though, when she saw the long-haired guy's case on her car. She started walking over there just as the photographer closed in on Nita and Maya and started taking pictures.

Mr. Donnelly walked with her, opening his notebook. He said, "I understand that you have a couple of pretty special players on your team this year."

The coach took the photographer's bag and dumped it on the ground. She said, "Uh-huh. And who would that be?"

Mr. Donnelly flipped back a few pages in his notebook. "A girl named Maya and a girl named Shandra? They're both supposed to make the All-County Boys' Team?"

When Dolly heard this she yelled over, "Hey, Shandra! They want to talk to you, girl!"

Shandra had been focused on the shooters all this time. When she heard Dolly she looked over, puzzled. Then she spotted the *Tangerine Times* van and the long-haired guy with his camera. A look of terror came over her face. She spun around on her heels and sprinted away—right out of the goal, across the field, across the bus lanes, and into the school. Everybody stopped what they were doing and watched her go.

Now that there was no one in goal, Victor walked up to the photographer and announced, "You must be here to interview me. I'm Victor Guzman, the captain of the first-place Tangerine Middle School War Eagles. How do you do?"

The guy looked over at Mr. Donnelly. Then he said, "Excuse me," and tried to get around Victor. But Victor blocked him and added, "You'll probably want to get some action shots of me before you do anything else."

The photographer stared at him dumbly. Then he stepped back and lined up a picture of Victor, who struck a pose and smiled. The camera flashed, and Victor added, "That's Victor Guzman. You know how to spell that? G-U-Z-M-A-N. Don't you go spelling my name wrong, or I'll have to mess you up."

Hernando, Tino, and Mano crowded in front of the photographer next, telling him their names and demanding that he take their pictures. The guy looked over at Mr. Donnelly, who signaled at him to go ahead and do it. Mr. Donnelly said, "Look, Betty, I'm sorry for disrupting your practice. Can I just get the last names of the girls?"

The coach still wasn't looking at him. And she still was not happy. "This is more disruptive than you could know, Mr. Donnelly. If you want to run a picture of our team, you should show Victor. He's our captain."

Mr. Donnelly replied, "But he's not news, Coach. Having girls on your team is news."

"Not really. I've had girls on this team for five years. Why is it suddenly news?"

Mr. Donnelly held up his hands to explain, and the coach looked at them. "You're the first-place team in the county. You have the top scorer in the county. And she's a girl."

The coach nodded. "All right. Fair enough. Her name is Maya Pandhi. P-A-N-D-H-I."

He wrote this down. "Great. And what about Shandra?"

"You never mind about Shandra. She doesn't want any part of newspapers or publicity, so that's the way it's gonna be."

Mr. Donnelly nodded. "OK. I'll certainly respect her wishes."

They shook hands again. The guy with the long hair saw

this and broke away from the boys. He grabbed his bag, climbed up into the driver's seat of the van, and the two of them drove back the way they came.

Betty Bright watched them go, then walked slowly across the field and into the school. Victor sat down, so the rest of us did, too. Finally the coach and Shandra came walking out. By the time Shandra was back in goal to start the scrimmage, we had lost about twenty minutes of practice time.

Like I said, that all happened yesterday. This morning I looked in the *Tangerine Times*, in the back of the sports section. There was no article about our team, but there was a photo. The wrong photo. It was a photo of Nita Shirali with the caption, "Maya Pandhi Leads All Scorers in Tangerine County."

Good going, Mom.

Monday, October 2

I'm in classes with Theresa, Tino, Maya, Nita, and Henry D. all day. Now Joey has joined that group.

The first and last periods of the day, science and language arts, do cross-curricular projects together. That means that we do a science-type project in science class, and we write about it in language arts class. I came in at the tail end of the last project, so all I could do was sit and listen to kids read their reports. They were really good.

Now we're starting a new cross-curricular project. Mrs. Potter passed out a project sheet that describes what we're supposed to do, how we're supposed to do it, and how we're supposed to present it to the class. At the top of the project sheet, it says:

Science/Language Arts Cross-Curricular Project
Broad topic—Florida agriculture

Narrow topic—an agricultural product that is native
   to this area of Florida
Your topic—??????

Mrs. Potter gave us twenty-four hours to form our own groups of four to six kids. After that she would form new groups out of "the leftovers," as she called them.

I was looking over the project sheet with Joey when I saw Tino walking back toward us. He stopped at Henry D.'s desk and said, "Yo, Henry D. You want to be in a group with Theresa and me? We got a hot idea."

Henry D., whose real name is Henry Dilkes, is a quiet country boy, always polite. He said, "Thank you. I'd be pleased to."

Tino bumped his fist down on top of Henry's and started back toward his desk. I called out to him, "Hey, Tino! What about me and Joey? Can we be in your group?"

Tino stopped and looked at me, surprised. He thought a minute and said, "Yeah. Why not? But it's our group. You got that?"

"Yeah. Yeah, sure."

He returned to his seat and Joey said to me, "What did you do that for?"

"Do what? We gotta get in a group, right? I don't want to be a leftover."

"So why don't we form our own group?"

"With who? We need four to six people."

"With anybody. Anybody but him." He shot an angry look at Tino.

"C'mon, man. Henry's nice. Super nice. So is Theresa. And Tino's OK, when he's by himself."

Joey shook his head. He didn't believe me. "That guy's bad news. I don't need this. I don't need this at all."

"Hey, this isn't soccer practice, it's science class. You're an ace in science, right?"

Joey glared at me. "What are you saying, that I stink in soccer?"

"No. I'm not saying that. I'm just saying that this is different. This is something that you're really good at."

Joey finally agreed, doubtfully. "All right. All right."

"Good. This'll give you another kind of chance with people. You know? A chance to get in with some of the people from the team."

There was a strange pause. Joey finally said, "I'm not on the team anymore."

I couldn't believe what I was hearing. "Since when?"

"I turned in my uniform this morning."

I looked at him, but he wouldn't look back. I finally said, "That's it? You're just not on the team anymore, and that's it?"

Joey tightened up. "Yeah. That's it. So what? What's it to you?"

"It's nothing to me. I just don't understand. I thought you wanted to play soccer."

"Well, I don't. Not here, anyway." He finally looked at me. "Not anywhere. I'm gonna play football when I get to high school. You understand that?"

I understood. I said, "OK," and I was willing to leave it right there.

But Joey wasn't. He was practically snarling now. "I can't believe I let you talk me into this," and he gestured around the room. "I let you talk me into coming to this dump." I suddenly became aware of the other kids around us as he went on. "This place is like darkest Africa. Like the Amazon jungle. Like we're learning to live among the natives here."

I took in the ugliness of Joey's words, and I saw, for the first time, how different he was from me—different parents, different friends, different brother. The speaker came on, and the gong sounded. I had to say something, so I muttered, "I'm sorry you feel like that," and headed out, without him, into the crowded hallway.

Tuesday, October 3

There's something I forgot to record here about Joey's first day at Tangerine Middle School. Or maybe I didn't forget. Maybe I just wanted to block it out. But after what he said yesterday, I can't. The scene came back to me today on the way home.

It was last Monday. I was sitting in homeroom. Suddenly Joey walked in and handed Ms. Pollard a pass. He was all by himself—no Theresa to show him around, like I had hoped. Ms. Pollard told him to take a seat, so he came back and sat next to me. He was all smiles, and he said something like, "Hey! So far, so good."

I said, "Where's Theresa?"

"Who?"

"Theresa. Theresa Cruz. I told you to ask for her as a guide."

"Oh yeah. She's back in the office. I saw her there."

"What? Is she guiding somebody else today?"

"Nah. I just said I didn't need it. What do I need a guide dog for?"

"A guide dog? You're calling Theresa a guide dog?"

Joey laughed. "C'mon, man. Lighten up. What?—Do you think she's good-looking?"

I thought about that. "Yeah. I guess I do."

Joey still had that cocky smile plastered on his face. "Then you've been here too long."

I couldn't believe what I was hearing. I just shook my head. I finally said, "I gotta tell you, you're comin' in here with the wrong attitude."

"Hey, what's the big deal? I got here OK without a guide, right? You'd have to be blind to get lost in this place."

"Oh, is that right? So now you're calling me blind?"

"No, I'm not calling you blind—"

"You're calling Theresa a dog?"

"No, I'm just pointing out that she's not my type."

The bell rang for first period. All I had time to say was, "Don't do this. Don't come in here with attitude."

Like I said, that scene came back to me today. We had our first meeting for the science project. Each group of kids pulled their desks together; the leftover kids then got put into their own groups. Joey and I pulled our desks into a circle with Henry D., Theresa, and Tino. I was surprised when Theresa, not Tino, took charge of the meeting. And it was obvious that she had done this sort of thing before.

Theresa began by reading the assignment aloud: "To research and present information about an agricultural product that is native to this area of Florida." Then she passed out a glossy one-page ad with a picture of a citrus tree laden with fruit. "When we heard this assignment, Tino and I knew right away what we were going to write about. I just gave you all an advertisement for an agricultural product that was developed by our brother, Luis. It's a new variety of citrus that he has named the Golden Dawn tangerine.

"This tangerine is seedless, very juicy, and very resistant to cold weather, which makes it perfect for this area. Luis thinks it could even return this area to its former prominence as the tangerine capital of the world. He just got it registered with the state this year as a new variety. Now he is starting to market it to citrus growers in Florida, California, and Mexico. So our report is going to be called 'The Golden Dawn Tangerine.'"

Theresa passed out sheets of paper that had our report title typed across the top. She said, "What we want to do today is divide up the research part of the project. Tino and I will concentrate on Luis's invention and what he had to do to register it with the state. Somebody else can do the history of the citrus industry in this area. Henry, we thought you could do that part. You know—When did citrus growing start here? What are the types of trees that grow best here? That kind of thing." Henry D. nodded and jotted something down. Then Theresa turned to me. "Somebody else could do basic research on what a tangerine is and how it is grown. We thought that you and your friend could handle that." I nodded. Theresa added, "Any questions?"

Henry D. said, "Excuse me. How long did it take for your brother to invent this tangerine?"

Tino answered. "His whole life. I can't remember a time when Luis wasn't working on this. And I don't know if Theresa made this clear or not, but this is really a big deal. It's like inventing a new kind of medicine or something. Luis is going to be famous for doing this."

Theresa said, "Luis is real interested in helping us, too. He'll answer questions and he'll show us how it's all done. We figure we'll get all this research in. Then we'll have an organizational meeting, probably with Luis. Then each group can write its section of the report, and give it to me, and I'll type it all up."

Joey interrupted her. "Just put it all on a disk and give it to me. I'll run it off on the laserjet at home."

Theresa looked away. She seemed flustered. She said, "We don't have a computer. We use a typewriter."

Tino snapped at him, "You got a problem with that, Tuna?"

Joey stared him down. "No, I don't have a problem with that. I guess I got a problem with you."

"Yeah? You gonna have a big problem with me! Bigger than you know, chump."

I felt I had to head this off, so I said, "C'mon, you guys. Forget this."

"Shut up!" Tino snarled, his eyes still locked on Joey's.

"Joey," I said. "It's Tino's group, right? We agreed to that when we joined."

Joey stood up and moved his desk back. He looked at me with disgust. "*You* agreed to that. You'd agree to anything. Not me. I'm joining another group." He started to drag his desk away, but then he stopped and looked at Tino, adding sarcastically, "Not that your brother and his new type of banana aren't fascinating."

Tino jumped up and lunged at him, but Joey was too fast. He leaned back, and Tino flew past him, landing on the desks of the next group. Mrs. Potter was there before he could recover. She got a grip on Tino's arm and hustled him out into the hallway.

Joey turned on me. "This is how you get by here, right? You kiss up to these guys? You're scared of these guys?"

"What are you talking about? I'm not scared."

"You're a gutless wonder, Fisher. You're afraid of girls. You're afraid of your own brother. Now you're afraid of these lowlifes. They treat you like a dog, and you take it! Take it? You like it! You think they're your friends!"

Everyone's eyes were on Joey. He was red faced and angry. "Let me tell you something. You're bigger than this little punk. You know that? And I'm bigger than you. If he ever messes with me again, I don't care where it is, I'm gonna punch him out!"

Mrs. Potter stepped back into the classroom and signaled for Joey to join her in the hall. He walked out, and everybody's eyes turned to me. I had no clue what to do. I just stood there.

Finally Theresa broke the tension. "So are you joining another group, or what?"

I answered immediately. "No. I want to stay here."

Theresa spoke to the class. "Then let's all sit down."

I spent the rest of the period staring at a blank piece of paper, trying to sort out what had happened. Joey came back at the end of the period and sat down with the leftover group behind me. Tino didn't come back at all. The word at practice was that he had been suspended for three days.

Wednesday, October 4

I type these journal entries, and my homework assignments, on the little PC clone up in my bedroom. For anything major, like a school report, I use Dad's big IBM, which is down in an alcove off the great room. Dad has a CD-ROM encyclopedia, a fax modem, and a Web navigator that gets hundreds of information services. I can find out anything about anything without ever leaving the chair.

Tonight I was down in the alcove searching for information on tangerines when Mom announced, "I've got people coming over tonight, Paul. You might want to work upstairs."

"Who's coming?"

"It's a meeting of the Homeowners' Association. I think it's going to be a loud one."

"Why's that?"

"Mr. Costello has been getting a lot of phone calls about a lot of different things. There's the termite problem. And there have been break-ins over on his side of the development."

"Robberies?"

"Yes. People are talking about organizing a neighborhood watch patrol or even hiring a real guard to sit in the guardhouse." She stopped and looked at me. "You haven't heard anything about break-ins, have you? Are kids involved?"

"I haven't heard a thing."

"Joey hasn't said anything to you?"

"No."

The doorbell rang. I went back to my search as the home-owners started to arrive. I could hear them file in behind me—the yellow Tudor, the York with the three-car garage, and a loud group from Joey's street, the street where all the houses are getting blue tents put over them.

I stopped working when Mr. Costello came in. I rolled my chair to the entrance of the alcove so he could see me.

"Hi, Paul. How's it going?"

"Fine, Mr. Costello."

Mr. Costello's face has looked lined and tired ever since Mike got killed. He carried a thick black appointment book in one hand. He walked to the kitchen end of the great room and said quietly, "All right, let's get started."

The meeting began like the town meetings we used to have in social studies class—treasurer's report, old business, new business; "I move"; "I second the motion." I had turned my attention back to the computer screen when I heard a man call out, "What's with Donnelly's house? It looks like something that landed from outer space!"

I rolled my chair back and watched Mr. Costello. He checked his notes and said, "All right. Mr. Donnelly applied for permission to install a lightning rod on the roof of his house. The Architectural Committee, because of his unique problem, did approve that addition. But then, for some reason, Mr. Donnelly went and installed a series of ten lightning rods across the top of his roof. It does look odd."

"It looks like hell."

Mom spoke up. "The Architectural Committee has sent Mr. Donnelly a strongly worded letter about it. I think he clearly took advantage of us."

"What are you going to do about it?"

"As I just said, we sent him a letter. I had hoped he

152

would show up tonight so we could work this out. If he doesn't respond, we will take further action."

Another homeowner stood up. "I've been keeping track of our fish population, what there is of it, and I'd like to announce that it is now down to zero. As far as I can tell, we have zero fish left in that pond."

Mr. Costello nodded grimly and flipped to another page. "You're probably right, Ralph. The koi appear to be all gone. We're not sure why, but we think someone may have stolen them."

I thought, *Think again, Mr. Costello. Your koi are a gourmet meal for the ospreys out on Route 89.*

Another voice called out, "What about the muck fire?"

Mr. Costello knew right where to flip for this one. "All right. We've certainly heard your complaints about the muck fire, and we certainly share your . . . distaste for it. Since our last meeting, Mr. Porter and I have contacted the Tangerine Fire Department on three different occasions."

Mr. Costello began to read directly from his notes: "The captain there basically told us that he can't do anything about it. We said, 'Why don't you pour water on it until it goes out?' and he said, 'Why don't you?' So we did."

Mr. Costello slammed his book closed with one hand. "We hired a contractor to sink four wells in the muck-fire field. We rented pumps and spraying equipment and started saturating the area last month. To make a long story short, the muck fire is still burning, and now we have swarms of mosquitoes breeding in the swamp that we created out there."

I heard Mom speak up again. "These mosquitoes carry encephalitis. Two children died in Tangerine last year after they were bitten by mosquitoes."

Mr. Costello nodded gravely. "Right. We've already contacted the county about it. They have a spray truck that is for hire. Starting tomorrow night, they will drive through our development spraying a cloud of insecticide *every other evening* until the mosquito problem is under control. Do not—I repeat—do not allow your kids to ride their bikes behind the spray truck. They'd be inhaling a powerful pesticide. Also, you should keep your pets inside, and you should move any delicate plants from your porches, patios, whatever, into the house."

Everyone got quiet at the thought of the spray truck spewing insecticide every other night. Finally the man who had asked about Mr. Donnelly's house said, "OK, what about all the robberies?"

Mr. Costello opened his book once again and addressed the man. "The Sheriff's Department has assigned someone to our case, Sergeant Edwards." He looked at the rest of the homeowners. "For those of you who don't know, five of the houses that were tented for bugs have been robbed of jewelry, watches, and other valuables."

The man interrupted. "My lawyer tells me that the exterminator is required by law to either post a guard or to arrange for guards to patrol around the houses that are tented."

"That may be true, Dan. But our local guy says he was not aware of that law."

"He shoulda been. It's his business."

"Maybe so. But I've talked to the guy, and his attitude is that you'd have to be crazy to go into a house that's been pumped full of deadly poison. Therefore there's no real threat of anyone doing it."

"But somebody *is* doing it. Somebody busted in my patio doors with a baseball bat, too. And whether his attitude likes it or not, he's liable for that and for my missing property."

Mr. Costello turned his palms upward. He answered patiently, "If you think you have a case against him, then by all means, pursue it. But is it really worth your time and money to hire a lawyer and go to court just to take some guy's dilapidated pickup truck away? Because that's what it'll come down to. That's just the way it is around here."

The homeowners just sat there glumly until Mr. Costello said, "OK. Somebody move to adjourn."

I turned back to the computer as the meeting broke up. I took out the disk and got into Dad's personal library, looking for another information service.

I saw a file listing that had definitely not been there before. I would never have missed seeing this. *"Erik— Scholarship Offers."*

I looked around for Dad. He and Mom were saying good-bye to people in the foyer, so I clicked on "Erik— Scholarship Offers."

The file was two pages long. It was carefully designed, like someone had spent a lot of time thinking about it. Each page was filled with rectangular boxes stacked on top of each other. But get this: The boxes were light green football fields, with white grid lines at ten-yard intervals. Over the green-and-white fields, printed in red, were vital statistics. Each box contained the name of a university, its address and phone number, and the name of its head football coach. The top three boxes on page 1 were set up for the University of Florida, Florida State University, and the University of Miami. Ohio State had a box on page 1. So did Notre Dame, Penn State, and the University of Nebraska.

It didn't look like any of these schools had expressed any interest in Erik. Not yet. I scrolled to page 2 and found some that had. Rice University, Baylor University, and the University of Houston had sent letters to Erik. From the dates of the letters, they must all have contacted him at the same time—right after his junior-year season in Houston. Dad, apparently, had not written back to any of them.

I heard the front door close, so I quickly clicked out of the file.

But I'll be back.

Thursday, October 5

Joey didn't come to school today. I wasn't surprised. I know exactly where he was. He was in the office at Lake Windsor Middle School, re-enrolling. It's the right thing for him to do. It's the right place for him to be.

I never should have talked Joey into coming to Tangerine. He doesn't fit in here. I should have seen that. Joey's not me. Joey fits in with his family; he fits in with his friends; he fits in with Lake Windsor Downs. That's where he belongs. That's where he is now. And that's all there is to say about it.

Right before science class began, I went up to Theresa and handed her six pages of research. She seemed pleasantly surprised. I said, "So what's up with Tino?"

She said, "Not much," and started to look at my papers.

"Does the coach know that he got suspended?"

"Yeah. I guess so. Everybody else knows."

"Is he gonna miss tomorrow's game?"

"No. He's coming back tomorrow."

"Yeah? I heard he got three days."

"Luis went in and talked to Dr. Johnson. She said that since Tino didn't actually hit anybody she'd reduce his time out to one day."

"Oh? That's cool."

Theresa stopped thumbing through my report. She looked me right in the eye, like she never had before. "Yeah. Look, uh, Paul Fisher. You got to understand one thing. You can't come in here and start talking about Luis any way that you like. Luis means too much to us."

I nodded quickly. "Yeah. Yeah, I understand."

"Tino and Victor, they don't play that kinda stuff. I told

them last night that they should leave you alone—but you better tell your friend to keep out of their way."

I thought about that. "I don't think he goes to school here anymore. And I don't think he counts me as his friend. Not anymore."

"Well, I don't know anything about that. I'm just tellin' you what I'm tellin' you." She pulled a piece of white paper out of her back pocket. "Here. This is a map to our house. Henry's coming over after practice to meet Luis. If you want to meet him, you can come, too."

I stared at the map, and at the large black X marking their house. As coolly as I could, I said, "So what about Tino?"

"What do you mean?"

"He won't be mad if I come?"

"No. Why should he?"

I shrugged. "You know. The stuff with Joey . . ."

"You're not Joey. Are you?"

"No. But is he mad about getting suspended?"

"You're not the one who got him suspended. Are you?"

I shook my head and said, "No." But I thought to myself, *Not this time, anyway.*

I went over to talk to Henry D., and we wound up working out a great plan. Henry's brother was going to drive him from Tangerine Middle School to Theresa's house, come back to get him, and then drive over to Lake Windsor Downs to do a job. Henry said that he and his brother "would be pleased" to drop me off right at my door. I called Mom and explained the plan. She sounded doubtful, but she agreed to let me do it.

At practice the coach put me in at Tino's position. I played poorly, but nobody seemed to care. It was just temporary; Tino would be back tomorrow. After practice I followed Henry D. to the parking lot. We walked up to a small blue pickup truck and climbed in. Henry said, "This is Paul. This is my brother, Wayne."

Wayne Dilkes! I knew him right away—the fireman! The young guy who had come to our house about the muck fire. He gave me a friendly "Hi," but I don't think he recognized me. Anyway, he didn't say anything as we drove east toward the groves, listening to a country music station.

Soon we were flying past perfect rows of citrus trees, and that glorious scent was in the air.

I saw a large wooden sign that said TOMAS CRUZ GROVES/ NURSERY. Wayne slowed to five miles per hour and turned right onto a dirt road. We bumped along past an oblong pond fifty yards across, ringed all around with tall cattails. Behind the pond, on higher ground, was a grove of trees, hundreds of them, all about ten feet high and six feet wide. Water sprinklers rose tall among the green trees like skinny metal weeds. We bumped to the left, toward several buildings—a house; a separate garage; a small shed; and another, strange-looking building.

The house was large—two stories high, with old shade trees around it. It appeared to be built of cement blocks covered with a kind of mustard-colored stucco. We rolled in a cloud of dust past the house, pulled up next to the classic green Ford, and climbed out in front of that other building.

Wayne said, "I'll see y'all in an hour," and backed out, leaving us standing before one of the strangest structures I have ever seen. It looked like a gigantic tin can that had been cut in half, lengthwise, and then pressed down into the ground. I asked Henry, "What is this thing?"

"It's a Quonset hut. They had a lot of them left over after World War II. Some of the citrus farmers bought 'em up cheap, as war surplus."

"Yeah? Did you find that out in your research?"

"Yes, I did." Henry knocked on the wooden door of the Quonset hut. I looked up and figured that the door was six feet tall, and the hut was twelve feet tall at its highest point. At its lowest points, the ends stuck right into the ground.

Tino opened the door and said, "Yo, Henry D." Then he turned back inside without acknowledging me.

I followed Henry and Tino to the far end of the Quonset hut, about twenty yards down through the cool, dark, windowless building. The sides, where the metal ceiling curved down to the cement floor, were jammed with wooden crates, sprinkler heads, wheelbarrows, and all kinds of equipment.

We joined Theresa and Luis at the rear door. Theresa pointed at us and said to him, "That one's Henry D.; that other one's Paul Fisher."

Luis smiled. He had large teeth inside a large head. He had a strange shape, too—bony and muscular at the same time. His arms, his legs, his whole body were like thick rope.

Luis said, "Good to see you guys." His voice was soft and seemed accented more than Tino's or Theresa's. He walked ahead of us, limping as if his left knee would not bend. He led us out of the Quonset hut toward the weather-beaten trees on a hill north of the house.

Luis stopped about five rows in, pointed around him, and said, "This is a grove. We grow a fruit here called the Cleopatra tangerine, and we sell it to citrus packers and juice companies. Our family has done that for forty-five years now."

Luis doubled back, and we followed. We turned left at the hut and soon came to an open space, as long as a soccer field, but square in shape. Here the trees were like babies— only a foot and a half high—and spaced not much more than a foot apart. There must have been a thousand of them.

Luis sat down next to one of the baby trees, so we all copied him. He said, "Look around you. This is a nursery. The purpose of a nursery is not to grow fruit, it is to grow trees. We then sell these trees to fruit growers." Luis placed a long finger at the base of the baby tree. "This part of the tree is called the rootstock. It is the root and trunk of a rough lemon tree. Believe it or not, every type of tree that we produce here begins its life as a rough lemon tree." His finger rose six inches to the knobby beginning of a branch. "At this spot, we cut a slit into the rough lemon tree, set a new type of bud inside, and close the slit up with tape. Now we have turned the tree into something else—perhaps a Valencia orange tree or a Red Ruby grapefruit tree. The new bud that we grafted onto the rootstock is called a scion. The word *scion* means, like, a child or a descendent of the tree."

Luis pointed his arm back to the tall trees. "Check this out: A scion can be any kind of citrus that you want—orange, grapefruit, lemon, lime—and they can all be growing on the same tree at the same time! That means that on one little tree, you could have a branch of white grapefruit, a branch of red kumquats, and a branch of green limes, like some kind of Frankenstein fruit tree, all stitched together." He caressed the trunk of the baby tree. "The rough lemon is totally worthless in the supermarket, and yet there is no more valuable tree out here in the nursery."

Luis got to his feet, flushed with feeling. He pointed to the thousand baby trees before us. "If you look out here, you'll see that all of these trees are the same. On each there is one scion grafted onto a rough lemon rootstock. That scion is a new type of tangerine called the Golden Dawn."

Luis stared with us at the field that he had created. Then he turned and led us back through the rows of adult trees. He pointed out different types of citrus trees, including some Frankenstein experiments of his own. He answered many questions for our report.

All too quickly we were back at the Quonset hut. Henry D. looked out the door and announced, "Wayne's waiting."

I walked up to Luis and offered my hand to shake. He took it in a powerful, ropelike grip. I said, "Thank you. I'm really interested in this stuff."

He answered, "Then you should come again."

I said, "I'd definitely like to." I turned toward Theresa and Tino. "See you guys later."

Theresa waved; Tino acted like he didn't hear. I followed Henry D. through the door and then stopped short. There, attached to the back of Wayne's pickup truck, was a short trailer. It had a fat, heavy generator mounted on it, with a large fan and a spray nozzle on either side. I said, "What on earth's that?"

Wayne answered cheerfully. "It's a sprayer for y'all's mosquitoes."

We bumped along with the sprayer behind us, all the way to Lake Windsor Downs. As soon as we turned into the entrance, Wayne spotted the blue tents along Joey's street. "Look at that, now," he said. "Y'all are having a regular nine plagues of Egypt over here, aren't you?"

"Yeah," I said. "Nine and counting."

"How many houses got termites?"

"It looks like that whole street has them, all along the west side."

"Then that's where they buried the citrus trees," he said. "This was a grove, you know."

"Yeah. So I've heard."

"It was all groves around here. When they cleared this land for houses, they just set fire to all the trees and plowed them under. You see how that whole blue-tent street seems to be on a hill?"

"Yeah."

"That hill's made of dead trees—dead tangerine trees. Termites live in all that wood under the ground, but they got to come up to the surface to get water. That's where your problems start. If the wood in your house is in their way, they start eating that."

I said, "You can stop them, though. Right? You can kill them? You can call the Orkin army or something?"

Wayne shook his head. "You can't stop 'em. You can put a barrier around your house. That's about it. But you can't stop 'em from eatin' wood any more than you can stop that muck fire from burning or them mosquitoes from suckin' blood."

We were at the house. I said, "Here it is." I got out and looked at the spraying rig. "You guys gonna turn this thing on now?"

Wayne smiled. "Yeah. We're gonna let her rip. We'll kill some of them skeeters for you, anyway."

I said, "Thanks for the ride, Wayne. See you, Henry."

Wayne waved. He reached under his seat and handed something to Henry. Then, in the same motion, they both pulled black rubber gas masks on over their faces. They sat there for a minute, looking like a pair of ant-men who had stolen a truck. Then Wayne got out, walked back, and pulled the starter cord on the generator. I watched as the rig coughed and sputtered to life. Then I backed away and hurried inside.

I dropped my stuff in the alcove and went into the kitchen for a drink. Out of the corner of my eye I detected two people in motion, and I heard the *Poomph-poomph-poomph* sound. I knew that Erik and Arthur were practicing in the back. Would they stop when they smelled the insecticide?

I got a soda and stood at the breakfast bar, waiting to see what they would do. I saw a billowing white cloud enter the backyard, like an angel of death. It came from the right to the left, in white waves, and quickly filled up the whole yard. But as I watched the scene, it happened again. Just like in Houston. Just like at the gray wall. A feeling came over me, overpowering me. Like I had to remember something, whether I wanted to or not.

I stared hard into the backyard. First I could see Erik and

Arthur. Then I couldn't see them. Then I could see them. Then I couldn't. And I remembered:

Our backyard in Huntsville. Mom and Dad were standing in front of me. Dad was directing Erik to move in a circle, around and behind me. Dad was saying, "OK, Erik. Pretend that Paul is in the center of an imaginary clock, and that I am standing here at the six o'clock position. I want you to stand at the twelve o'clock position, right behind him. Good. Now move to the eleven o'clock position."

Then he said to me, "Paul? Can you see Erik?"

I said, "No. I can't see him."

"OK, Erik. Move to ten o'clock. Paul? Can you see him?"

"No. I can't see him."

"Move to nine o'clock."

"I can't see him! I can't see him!"

Mom broke in. "It's OK, honey. It's OK." She said to Dad, "There. I told you. The problem is with his peripheral vision."

Suddenly I felt the hot breath of a predator on my neck. I screamed in terror. Erik laughed and ran over to Mom and Dad. He had snuck up on me from behind, from somewhere back around ten o'clock.

Dad snapped at him, "Erik! Cut that out! Are you here to help us or not?"

I remember that I started to cry, in the middle of that pretend clock, but Mom and Dad did not notice. They were arguing about my eyes, or about my glasses. Mom finally said, "Well, it won't hurt to try. Will it? I'm taking him back there tomorrow to see what they can do."

And she did. That was when I got my new glasses. That was when I started to see better. From that day on, I could see things that they could not. I could see Erik posing in front of them, in the shining light of the Football Dream. And I could see Erik lurking behind me, in the shadows of the clock.

Thursday, November 2

I used to be aware of every hour in every day. But now, with soccer games, and football games, and school, and cross-curricular projects, whole chunks of time fly by and I'm amazed at what hour it is. Sometimes I'm amazed at what day it is.

The last four weeks have been like that. They have gone by in a blur. And it's not just me. Each member of our family is now so busy that we don't even eat meals together anymore. But I'm not complaining. I guess none of us are. We are all doing what we expected to do in Tangerine. We are all becoming big fish in this little pond.

Dad is now firmly in command as the Director of Civil Engineering for Tangerine County. Old Charley Burns didn't survive the avalanche of bad publicity, lawsuits, and criminal charges being hurled at him. He died of a heart attack in his lawyer's office. Dad didn't even go to his funeral.

Mom is now the head of the Architectural Committee, a block captain for the Neighborhood Watch patrol, and the person most likely to succeed Mr. Costello as president of the Homeowners' Association. No surprises there. Mom knows what she wants for Lake Windsor Downs.

What of the news in football? Erik Fisher's fortunes have changed. Big time. In four weeks he has gone from local joke to local hero as the placekicker for the Lake Windsor High Seagulls. He is now always surrounded by kids who, I suppose, look up to him. I guess people see what they want to see. Erik kicked field goals of 12 and 25 yards in a 20–0 win over Crystal River. Then he made one from 37 yards to win the Gulf County game 10–7. The following week he was on the front page of the *Tangerine Times* sports section for making kicks of 40 and 45 yards to beat Flagler

6–0. Yesterday he missed from 50 yards, but he hit from 30 and 38 in a 20–14 win over Suwannee. Everyone in Tangerine County knows him now. Or they think they do.

And what about the other member of the family? The other athlete in the family? The Tangerine Middle School War Eagles have won seven games in a row, and I have played in all seven games. I even started two games at fullback after Shandra collided with Dolly in practice and wrenched Dolly's back. I played all ninety minutes. In the other five games I went in as a sub for either Victor or Maya in the second half. By then we already had enough goals to beat most of our opponents: 10–0 over St. Anthony's, 8–0 over Heritage Baptist, 3–0 over De Leon, 4–0 over Seminole, 7–0 over Highland Park, 4–0 over Cortes, and 7–0 over Palmetto in a rematch at our home field.

Those are the statistics of this soccer season. But I have to describe the feeling that this has given me. It's not enough to say that we have won seven soccer games in a row. It's *how* we've done it that is so extraordinary. The War Eagles have set out on a bloody rampage through the county. We have destroyed every enemy. We have laid waste to their fields and their fans. There is fear in their eyes when we come charging off our bus, whooping our war cry. They are beaten by their own fear before the game even begins. This is a feeling that I have never known before. Anyway, I have never known it from *this side* of the fear. Maybe I am just a sub, maybe I am just along for the ride, but this is the greatest thing that has ever happened to me.

Saturday, November 4

Back in October, when we all visited the tangerine nursery, Luis definitely said to me, "You should come again." I think he meant it. I know *I* meant it when I said I wanted to. But since that day, Theresa and Tino have held all of our project meetings in class. Anyway, I decided to take charge of the situation. I wanted to go back to the nursery, and so I did.

Mom drove me through Tangerine on a sleepy Saturday morning. I had no problem remembering the way—out through the groves, down the long driveway, past the house, to the Quonset hut. She said, "Are you sure these people are expecting you?"

"Yeah."

"What kind of building is that?"

"It's called a Quonset hut."

"Is it safe?"

"Mom, it's built by the army. It'll withstand a direct hit by a twenty-megaton bomb."

"What goes on in there? Is that their office?"

"It's more like Dr. Frankenstein's laboratory."

"Please, Paul. Give me a break. I'm worried about you out here."

"Mom. It's a citrus tree nursery. The worst thing that could happen to me is I'd overdose on vitamin C."

"Just don't touch anything rusty. You haven't had your booster shot."

"OK."

"What time should I come back?"

"I'll call you."

"All right. Be careful."

Mom pulled away. I walked up to the door of the Quonset hut and knocked. There was no answer. Then from behind me I heard, "Fisher Man? What're you doin' here?"

It wasn't a friendly greeting. I turned and saw Tino and Luis coming out of the house with coils of thin black hose wrapped around their shoulders, like bandolera ammo belts.

Tino and I get along OK on the soccer team, as long as I know my place and stay in it. But he has little use for me away from the team, and he has no use for me at all in science class. I swallowed and said, "I wanted to find out more about the nursery. Luis said to come back sometime, so I did."

"What? You don't have phones in Lake Windsor Downs?"

Luis said, "It's all right, Tino. I invited him to come back and he's come." He pointed to a pile of black hoses on the ground. "You can grab some of those and work with us."

I wrapped a bandolera of hose around my shoulder and followed them. We walked around the Quonset hut, through the rows of adult trees, and out to the baby trees—the Golden Dawn tangerines. We laid out all of Luis's hose, then all of Tino's, then all of mine, up and down the rows of little trees. Then we went back and loaded up again from the pile. We continued to haul and lay out hose for three hours, until every row had a black rubber stripe running down it.

We walked back again through the adult grove, but this time Tino sat down on a crate between two large trees. Luis pointed to two more crates, which I hauled between the trees for us to sit on. He reached up, pulled off a tangerine, and tossed it to Tino. Then he tossed one to me. We all sucked them down hungrily, and Luis pulled down three more. I hadn't said a word for hours until Luis asked me, "So how do you like the tangerine business?"

"I like it a lot."

Tino snorted. "Is that right? What do you like about it?"

I knew the answer to that right away. "The way it smells. I like how it smells out here." I held up my tangerine. "I guess I like how these taste, too."

Luis smiled. I asked him, "What's the best thing about it for you?"

Luis stood up to get us three more. When he sat down, he answered, "Just like you said. The way it smells out here. That scent. It's like nothing else in the world." Luis looked at me intensely, but he spoke softly, almost musically, almost tearfully. "You know, I walk out here in the mornings sometimes, and I fall on my knees, and I weep, right into the ground. I'm overcome by the beauty of it all. I've tried to describe that scent, all around, in the air. I've tried to give it a name. But the closest I can come is . . . It's the scent of a golden dawn."

Luis looked away. Tino was staring at him with reverence, with no trace of the hard-guy face he usually carries around.

We rested for five more minutes and then went back to the baby trees. Luis gave each of us a small, sharp hand clipper, which he called a tangerine clipper. We proceeded to crawl up and down the rows, slicing a hole in the black hose next to each tree. It was back-breaking, knee-scraping, glasses-fogging work. I could feel the sun doing damage to the back of my neck and to the backs of my legs.

We didn't break again until we had sliced a thousand holes in a thousand spots. Then we sprawled out again between the trees with our tangerines. Luis and Tino were hot and tired, but I was more like in critical condition. Luis said, "I think that's all for you today."

Tino added, "Yeah, Fisher Man. You don't look too good. You look like a lobster special."

Luis pointed at the Quonset hut. "Take him inside, Tino. Get him some of that first-aid spray."

Tino actually took my arm, helped me up, and guided me into the hut. He found a purple aerosol can, shook it, and said, "Close your eyes." He sprayed a cold white foam on the back of my neck, my arms, and my knees. I sat carefully on the top of the desk and said, "Thanks. Can I use this telephone?"

"Yeah. Go ahead."

Mom answered the phone after one ring. I said, "Mom, I'm ready to be picked up."

"Are you all right, Paul?"

"Yeah."

"You sound hurt."

"No."

"I'll be there in fifteen minutes."

I hung up and said to Tino, "So where's Theresa today?"

"She's out with our daddy. She's helping him fill out some paperwork at the county building."

"Oh yeah?"

"Yeah. She's gettin' more into that now. She's learnin' how to run the family business." Tino paused. "You know, I was thinking... Theresa is real busy with that stuff, so maybe you should do the final report for the science group. You know, on a computer." He nodded, like he was agreeing with himself. "Theresa thinks so, too. In fact, it's her idea."

"Sure. I can do that." I waited for Tino to look at me. "We could have a project meeting at my house if you like. I can show you the types of graphics that we have on my dad's computer. You know, pie charts and stuff. We could design the whole thing."

"Yeah, well, let me talk to Theresa about that."

I slid off the desk and started to walk awkwardly toward the front door. It felt like my skin was too tight for my body. Tino laughed. "That's hard work, huh?"

"Yeah. I don't know how people can work out in the sun all day. I wouldn't make it as a fruit picker. I'd be dead."

Tino nodded. "Yeah, well, you do what you gotta do. I never did that, 'cause I never had to." He started to follow me down the length of the hut. "My daddy had to. Luis did it, too. But he did it 'cause he wanted to. He used to beg to go on trips with daddy and Tio Carlos. He picked oranges down in Orlando; he picked tangerines over on Merritt Island. That's how his knee got messed up."

I opened up the front door enough to look out for Mom. Tino went on, "You don't pick tangerines, you clip them, with one of those clippers. Luis was doin' that when he fell out of a tree. He was twelve years old back then. He landed on his kneecap, cracked it, and stabbed himself in the hand with the clippers. Daddy picked him up and drove him to the hospital. They bandaged up his hand, right? But Luis didn't say anything about his knee 'cause it wasn't looking too bad, and he was afraid that our mama wouldn't let him go along to pick anymore. The next morning his knee looked like a soccer ball. He had messed up his cartilage so bad that they had to operate. They had to put a pin in there, too. He couldn't walk at all for about two months. And he was right about Mama—Mama told him he could never go out picking again." Tino nodded slowly, remembering. "Anyway, after Mama died, Luis couldn't go anywhere. He had to stay at home with Theresa and me."

Tino pushed past me through the door. I followed him outside. He said, "It worked out OK for Luis, though. He became a genius at horticulture. There's nobody better in Florida."

I waited to see if that was all that he had to say. It wasn't. "Luis played soccer, you know. At Tangerine Middle School. At the high school, too."

"No kidding."

"Yeah. He was good. We used to go watch him."

"What position did he play?"

Tino looked surprised at the question. "What else could he play? He was the goalie."

"The goalie?"

"Yeah. They had to put him in there 'cause he was handicapped."

I looked at Tino to see if he was mocking me. He wasn't. He was just making conversation. He was in the nicest mood that I had ever seen him in. I figured it was my chance to clear my conscience once and for all. I said, "Hey? Do you remember when you guys got busted at the carnival?"

"Yeah. What about it?"

"Well, I'm the one who ratted you out. They accused some of the Lake Windsor soccer players of wrecking that exhibit. The Ax Man? I'm the one who told them that it was Tangerine Middle soccer players."

Tino nodded slowly. Then he said, "Turn around."

"What?"

"Turn around. Look over there."

I turned around and looked out toward the house. Suddenly I felt a swift kick in my backside. It made me hop forward about a foot. I turned back and looked at Tino. He had a sly smile on his face. He said, "If any of your Lake Windsor homeboys ever ask you what happened when I found out, you tell them about that."

Mom's car appeared around the corner. She drove through the shade of the house, into the sunlight, and up to where we were standing. She waved to Tino as I climbed in. Tino returned her wave and then walked around the Quonset hut to go back to work.

Sunday, November 5

Mr. Donnelly called Dad last night, which is funny because Mr. Donnelly has never returned Mom's phone calls or responded to her letter about the row of lightning rods on his roof. Anyway, he called Dad and invited us all over there tonight.

Mr. Donnelly, aside from being an outlaw wanted by the Architectural Committee, is a big University of Florida football booster. He has season tickets. He knows the coach. He even travels to games as far away as Tennessee. Dad has been after him ever since we moved here to come and see Erik kick. Now that Erik is starting to live up to Dad's bragging, Mr. Donnelly has taken notice. After the field goals of

40 and 45 yards in the game against Flagler, he showed up at the practice field and watched Erik make three fifty-yarders in a row. He was impressed.

So we're all invited over there to meet two other Florida football guys from this area. Dad says, "I want coaches from Florida, FSU, and Miami to start hearing about this kid from Lake Windsor High."

The kid from Lake Windsor High agrees. Erik is now as famous in these parts as Antoine Thomas. There are even those who say that Erik is more important to the team. This hasn't sat well with Antoine and some of the other players. Some of them obviously don't like Erik, but it seems that most of them do. Erik and his flunky, Arthur, are always in demand. They're in big demand this evening. Arthur picked Erik up about two hours ago to go somewhere (we never know where), and they'll be going somewhere *else* right after Mr. Donnelly's.

You can just imagine Mom's reaction to this visit tonight. She told Dad, "I don't care if this is supposed to be about football. He's going to tell me why he won't answer the letter and the phone calls from the Architectural Committee."

Dad said, "Please. Tonight is not about that. Tonight is only about Erik."

Mom, Dad, and I decided to walk to Mr. Donnelly's. We turned the corner at Kew Gardens Drive just as the sun was setting. The row of lightning rods in the red sky looked like some weird science experiment, like NASA's model home on Mars. Complete with a For Sale sign.

Arthur Bauer's muddy Land Cruiser was parked out on the street, in front of the house, ready for a quick get-away. I wondered if Erik and Arthur were sitting in there. I stared hard at the tinted glass, but I couldn't see anything inside.

Dad must have been wondering the same thing. He

started to walk up to the passenger-side door, but he never got there. That was when the mosquitoes attacked. I looked up into the setting sun. Mosquitoes completely filled the air above us, hovering there, skinny, black, and silent. They glided down onto us like tiny, bloodsucking men in parachutes. We all started to slap at ourselves as we felt the first bites. I watched one land on Mom's cheek. She screamed and started to run. Dad and I hurried after her. At the front door, we brushed at each other frantically until Terry Donnelly opened it.

We dove through the door, nearly capsizing a glass trophy case in the foyer. Around the corner, in the great room, a videotape of a Florida Gators football game was playing on a big-screen TV. And there sat Erik—composed, casual, wearing his football-hero smile. He was on a long couch with Mr. Donnelly and two other men, who Mr. Donnelly introduced as Larry and Frank. Erik stood up when the others did, like a gentleman would. Everything seemed to be going exactly as planned. Larry and Frank were smiling. They seemed to like Erik; to be impressed with him; to be ready to support the Erik Fisher Football Dream in any way they could.

Mom looked around and said, "So where is Arthur?"

Erik seemed genuinely surprised by the question. He said, "Arthur? He's out in the truck," as if to say, *Where else would he be?*

But Mr. Donnelly called over to his son, "Terry! Go outside and tell that boy to come in."

Erik waved at Terry Donnelly and said, "Nah. Nah. He doesn't want to come in. He smells too much like bug spray."

Mom sniffed. "Now that you mention it, so do you."

Erik pulled his shirt up to his nose and sniffed, too. "Bauer always has bug spray in the truck. In case we want to go mud runnin'."

Mr. Donnelly said, "Yeah. Those swamp skeeters'll eat you alive."

The conversation went on like that for a while. Erik remained charming. Larry and Frank remained impressed. Arthur Bauer remained in the truck.

Mr. Donnelly turned out to be a nice guy. And a good host. He didn't sit there listening to Erik all night. He talked to Dad about Old Charley Burns and the parties he used to have in his skybox. Then he talked to Mom about the concerns of the Architectural Committee.

I drifted back over to that glass trophy case to examine its contents. A lot of it seemed to be rinky-dink stuff that Terry Donnelly won as a kid. But there were a couple of old things that belonged to Mr. Donnelly. Suddenly he was at my elbow, saying, "I keep my Heisman Trophy out in the garage." I laughed, and he continued. "Now, what about you, Paul? Are you a kicker, too?"

"I play soccer, sir."

"Ah, then I suppose you *are* a kicker. Do you play for Lake Windsor Middle?"

"No, sir. I play for the War Eagles—Tangerine Middle School."

He opened his eyes wide. "I remember! Betty Bright's team! You have those all-star girls playing for you, right?"

"Yes, sir."

"How is your season going?"

"We're number one. We're undefeated. We're breaking all county scoring records."

Mr. Donnelly looked at me with increasing interest. "And you're doing all that with a mixed boy-girl team?"

"Yes, sir."

He nodded. "I've known your coach for a long time. She's an extraordinary person. Does she ever talk about her track career?"

"No, sir."

"No? Well, let me tell you, Betty Bright is the greatest track and field athlete ever to come out of this area. She ran the hundred-meter dash and the hundred-meter hurdles; she threw the discus and the javelin; she did the high jump and the broad jump. She did it all, right over at Tangerine High."

"Did she ever play soccer?"

"No. Not to my knowledge. She became famous as a hurdler. I mean really famous. The *Times* started a fund to send her to the U.S. Olympic trials back in 1978. She made the team, too! She competed in the Pan Am Games in Buenos Aires the next year." Here Mr. Donnelly turned to the men who were watching football. "Do you guys remember that fund drive we had for Betty Bright?"

Larry got up and joined us. "Sure. She's the runner."

"The hurdler," Mr. Donnelly corrected him. He turned back to me. "I remember Larry and a bunch of us at the newspaper office one Saturday afternoon watching Betty Bright on *ABC's Wide World of Sports*. You know—the thrill of victory, the agony of defeat. And there she was! It was a great feeling. Our paper had gotten behind her cause, and now there she was!"

Larry interjected, "She got punched or something, right?"

"Right. The East German hit her in the eye going over the first hurdle. Betty finished fourth in her heat and didn't qualify to go on."

Larry reached his fist over to demonstrate next to my face. "This German punched her right here. Knocked her off her balance. You could see it on the replay."

Mr. Donnelly picked up the story. "The U.S. coach protested, but nothing came of it. That was it. She was out of the competition."

Larry said, "Yeah. It was a bad break. And then she ran into the boycott."

"Right." Mr. Donnelly explained for my benefit. "Two

years later the U.S. boycotted the Olympic games in Moscow, so *none* of our athletes got to go." He stopped and stuck a finger into the middle of my chest. "But all that aside, Betty Bright was great, and she had a great amateur career. We were proud to have sponsored her. She got a free ride through college out of it. She got scholarship offers from all the big schools. She chose Florida A & M so she could stay close to her family."

Mom, Dad, and Erik walked up behind Mr. Donnelly. He turned and said, "What? You're leaving so soon?"

Mom smiled. "I'm afraid so. Busy, busy, busy."

"Hey, it was great to meet you, Erik." Mom, Dad, and Erik smiled. "And it was great to meet you, too, Paul." Mom, Dad, and Erik all pulled back at once, as if in group shock, as if that was the craziest thing they had ever heard. We said a couple more good-byes and hustled outside, ready to run in case the mosquitoes were still there. They weren't.

Erik walked up and opened the passenger-side door of the Land Cruiser. I don't think Arthur expected that. He looked up quickly, his eyes wide and startled in the dome light. He scooped something shiny from the dashboard into a plastic bag as Erik closed the door. Then all was dark inside again. The Land Cruiser's engine roared to life, and they pulled away.

Mom, Dad, and I walked home through the smoky air. We all had come up with things to say to Mr. Donnelly, bright and clever things. But we had nothing left to say to each other.

When we got to our house, Dad unlocked his car, reached in, and pressed the garage-door opener. The door slid up for us just as we reached it. We all ducked inside quickly, but I stopped myself at the kitchen door. I had to stop, and I had to look back, because something was nagging at me. Troubling me. A memory?

Mom called back to me, "Will you get the garage-door button, please?"

One of them must have turned on the message machine, because I suddenly heard my grandmother's voice. She said, "Caroline, your father and I are talking about taking some vacation time down in Florida..."

I heard those few words spoken in Grandmom's flat voice. I heard them deep inside me. I never heard the rest of her message. I stood still in that garage, staring back out at that driveway. And I remembered:

Standing in our garage in Huntsville, staring out at the driveway. Grandmom and Grandpop came walking up. They each carried an overnight bag in one hand. Erik suddenly appeared on the driveway, so they stopped to say hello to him.

Mom was standing next to me. I remember her bending over and whispering, "Paul, darling, don't say anything bad to Grandmom and Grandpop."

They resumed walking up to where we stood. Grandmom looked at me and then leaned back, as if to see me better, as if she couldn't believe what she was seeing. Grandpop leaned the other way. He bent right over, right in my face, and said, "What the hell happened to your eyes?"

Mom told them, "We can talk about it inside. The important thing is that he's going to be OK."

I remember them all going in, leaving me staring out at that driveway. Leaving me to stare out at Erik, who was staring back in at me.

Tuesday, November 7

We had our last home game today, against Manatee Middle. They hadn't won a game all year, and they had been recently trounced 8–0 by Lake Windsor Middle. They looked terrified to be on the same field as the fearsome War Eagles. I got to start the game at left wing because Nita was out with the flu.

At about two minutes into the game, Maya hooked a thirty-yard shot right into the net. The goaltender never even moved. At five minutes into the game, she did it again. But this time the ball hit the right post and came bouncing back at chest level, right across the mouth of the goal. I dove at it and connected with my forehead, right above the glasses. I hit the ground, and the ball sailed into the back of the net. A beautiful highlight-reel goal.

Victor pulled me to my feet, shouting, "Yeah! Yeah! Come on, let's get another!"

We lined up again quickly, as we always do. The Manatee coach called time-out and came running onto the field to talk to the referee. We had to stand there and wait while the referee signaled Betty Bright to join them. It wasn't until then that I noticed the storm overhead. It had blown in quickly, darkening the field and lowering the temperature. A bolt of lightning shot down; the thunder followed almost immediately.

The coaches' conference broke up, and the Manatee guy waved his players off the field. They seemed eager to get away from us and back into their bus. Betty Bright called us into a circle. "The coach says they can't play in any lightning. It's their school policy."

Victor said, "So they quit? That's the game?"

"No. Right now it's a rain delay. Let's all get inside and try to keep loose."

We ran into the building and congregated around the double doors in the back. The referee, a tall woman with short blond hair, came in behind us just as the rain hit. Victor went up to her. "Yo, ref, what's up with this? Are we gonna have to play some kind of rain-out game?"

The referee wrote something into a little notebook. She replied, "Nope. This is it. You play today, or it goes down as 'No game' in our book."

"What's that mean?"

"It's like it didn't happen."

Victor grabbed me by the shoulder and shook me dramatically. "What about Fisher Man's goal?"

The referee sounded sympathetic. "It didn't happen. Not if we don't play at least half a game."

"Man!" Victor pounded angrily on my back. "We were gonna murder these chumps! It was gonna be, like, fifty to nothing. I was gonna up my numbers!"

Betty Bright kept looking out the window. She said, "It doesn't matter. We might play. If we don't, we're still undefeated"—she paused to point at Victor—"and untied."

"And untied" was a reference to Lake Windsor Middle School and what had happened to them yesterday. Up until yesterday, they'd had the same record as us. Then they took that bus ride to Palmetto Middle School, Home of the Whippoorwills, and got stuck in a 0–0 tie. Maybe they couldn't handle the dirty play, or the acorn throwers.

We hung around near the back door, shuffling in our cleats, for twenty more minutes of pounding rain. Finally Betty Bright called out, "There they go!" We crowded by the doors, and I could see the red taillights of the Manatee bus receding in the rain.

Victor turned to the referee. "They quit, right? It's a forfeit!"

The referee shook her head. "No. Not under these circumstances. You could never have played in this weather."

"We play in any weather, lady. We're the War Eagles."

The referee handed a piece of paper to Betty Bright. "I guess that's up to you. But this is a 'No game' today. All right, Coach?"

Betty Bright nodded. She signaled for us to gather

around. "Nothing more we can do here today. Maya, Paul Fisher, good going with those goals—but they don't count, so we have to forget about them. Everybody get up to your classrooms and get changed, with no horsing around. We have practice tomorrow, our last practice. We have a game on Friday, our last game."

Victor interjected, "Lake Windsor, home of that Gino chump."

The coach replied, "Lake Windsor, home of the only other undefeated team. But they couldn't put the ball in the goal yesterday."

"Yeah. They shut out that Gino fool."

"You forget about him, Victor, or you'll end up the fool. You concentrate on *us* putting the ball in the goal. If we get over there and lose our heads, lose our focus, we lose everything that we worked for."

"But we could win it all, too. Right?"

"That's right. Remember, all of you, we have the better record. The title is ours to win. Like they say in the big leagues, we're in control of our own destiny."

Wednesday, November 8

I must have made an impression on Mr. Donnelly. We're all over the front page of today's *Tangerine Times* sports section. There is a long article about middle school soccer and a "Looking Back" feature about Betty Bright at the Pan American Games.

First the soccer article. It named the top three scorers in the county. Maya Pandhi, of course, is number one, with 22 goals. But check this out—Gino Deluca and Victor Guzman are tied for number two, with 18 goals apiece. The article goes on to point out that Maya herself has scored more goals than most of the teams in the county. The scoring total for

Tangerine Middle School is an awesome 52 goals, which is already ten above the previous record.

The article didn't waste any space describing the records of the lesser teams in the county. There were only two records worth talking about—Tangerine is 9–0–0; Lake Windsor is 9–0–1. The article concluded, "The championship will be decided at tomorrow's big game between the War Eagles and the Seagulls at the Lake Windsor field."

The feature on Betty Bright was more of a picture essay. It had a color snapshot of her in a Tangerine High School uniform. It had a wide-angle photo of her posing with other members of the U.S. Olympic team. And it had a grainy black-and-white photo, taken off a videotape, showing her in midstride clearing a hurdle. Another hurdler's fist extends from the left edge of the photo, right into her eye. Her face is twisted, punched, to the other side. The caption below it says, "A controversial non-call in Buenos Aires."

After I finished reading the essay, I began to worry. Did Betty Bright mind the publicity? I thought about her meeting at the practice field with Mr. Donnelly and the photographer, and Shandra Thomas's frightened run from their camera. Did Betty Bright feel the same way? Did she mind this painful memory being plastered across the front page of the newspaper? Did she mind having to relive that punch in the eye?

Friday, November 10

Today's game, like all away games, began out on the circular driveway at Tangerine Middle. As usual, we gathered around the bus with our cleats slung over our shoulders, waiting for the bus doors to open. What was unusual was the crowd. The people who turned out for our home games—parents, little brothers and sisters, and other locals —had turned out for this game, too.

When Betty Bright opened up the bus door and called out, "Count 'em up, Victor," a caravan of at least twenty-five cars and trucks, including the green Ford pickup, fell into place behind us.

Everyone was quiet, subdued, as we rolled out of the parking lot. Nita was back, sitting with Maya, although she didn't look too good. Neither did Shandra, who was sitting right behind them. She had her forehead pressed against the window and her eyes closed. Was she not feeling well? Was she lost in thought? It was hard to tell.

As we drove past the packing plant and into downtown Tangerine, Henry D. started to tell me about last year's game with Lake Windsor. "It came down to the last game last year, too. That's why they're our archenemy now. They came here last year with the same record as us, 9–1. They beat us in the last game, on our own field."

Victor was listening. He called over, "You tell him about that, Henry D." He raised his voice. "Anybody else who doesn't remember needs to hear about this, too. They stole our championship last year, on our own field, in our own backyard. They must die for that."

I said, "What was the score?"

Henry replied, "Four to one," but then Victor picked up the story.

"Ignazio was last year's captain. Dolly's brother, Ignazio. So Ignazio scored a goal in the first half and we were in control, all the way. We must've had twenty shots on goal to their two." Here he stopped and looked around accusingly. "But in the second half, we let down. We got overconfident. That Gino dude started doing things on his own. He'd get the ball at midfield and take it all the way into the goal. Nobody stopped him! He scored three goals in the second half. And that Chinese dude got one."

I figured he was talking about Tommy Acoso. I said, "He's Philippine."

"Yeah, whatever. Whatever he is, he took the penalty kick after Ignazio finally flattened that Gino kid's butt." Victor's eyes narrowed as he recalled the moment. "It was like a joke to him. I heard him tell that Chinese dude to take the kick, 'cause he was tired of scoring."

Victor grew silent, reliving last year's game, getting angrier and angrier. We drove on, an old bus and twenty-five cars and trucks, toward the developments west of town; toward the developments where I live.

It was strange. Very strange. I was driving past the sights that made up my ride to and from school, every day. But today I looked at them through the hostile eyes of a War Eagle.

Victor had chilled out some, and he started to comment on the scenery. He talked as if he had never been out this way before in his life. "Check it out. It's like *Lifestyles of the Rich and Famous* out there."

Others started to get into it as we caravaned past the Villas at Versailles.

"Check out that gate, man! What is that?"

"That's gold. Look, they got gold on that stuff!"

"That's beautiful, man. That looks like a movie."

They were all sincerely amazed at this stretch of road, this stretch that I took for granted. It *was* like a movie—like a movie set, anyway—painted on plywood and propped up by two-by-fours. As phony as an Erik Fisher football hero smile.

I watched it with them, amazed, too. Amazed that it could be out here, where once only citrus trees had been. I watched it all roll by until we pulled onto the landscaped campus of Lake Windsor Middle School.

I could see crowds of people as soon as we turned around the main building. People were ringing the soccer field. The crowd was two to three people deep on the home side and spilling over onto the visitors' side.

Betty Bright drove the bus onto the grass as the rest of our caravan veered off into the parking spaces. We bumped over the grass until we reached the corner-kick area on the visitors' side. That's where we parked. That's where we always park. The coach has made this same off-road trek at every away game, just in case we need to find shelter or make a quick getaway.

I looked out over the crowd, searching for familiar faces. There were a lot of them. Mom was standing with some other adults along the home sideline. Did she realize that I was a visitor? Joey was near her; so were Cara and Kerri and a bunch of kids from my old classes, from my old life. Mr. Donnelly and the long-haired photographer were set up at midfield. Coach Walski, bald as ever, was out with his players on the field, leading them in calisthenics. They looked bigger than I remembered. Gino, Tommy, and all of those eighth-grade guys seemed to have grown taller and stockier. They looked like a football team.

I pulled on my cleats and tied them tightly. "Listen up," the coach called. "Let me break it down for you. There are three things that we can do today—win, lose, or tie. If we win, the county title is ours; if we tie, the county title is ours; if we lose, the county title is theirs." Betty Bright stood up, all the way up, to the ceiling of the bus. "Let me tell you something else. You have outscored every team in the history of this county, and you are going to outscore this team today. OK, Victor. Lead them out."

She threw open the bus door. Victor strode to the front of the bus and jumped out, followed by his boys, and then the rest of us. We ran down the inside perimeter of the field. The crowd stared, but no one yelled or spit at us. Mom waved. Joey was busy looking the other way. Kerri was looking right at me. So was Mr. Donnelly, who gave me a big thumbs-up sign.

We turned and ran toward the visitors' sideline and heard the loud cheers of our caravan riders. At midfield Victor turned sharply and sprinted toward the center of the field, as he had done so many times before. Betty Bright was already there. We packed around them and chanted our war cry.

"Who are we?"

"War Eagles!"

"Who are we?"

"War Eagles!"

The coach's voice rose up angrily, letting us know that our response was not yet good enough. "I said, 'Who are we?'"

We screamed back, "War Eagles," and fell into the frenzied chant that began each game: "War! War! War! War!"

We broke the circle, and the starting players took their positions. I looked around the field. All the people—the Lake Windsor players, the students, the adults—were staring at us with their mouths hanging open. In amazement? In disapproval? In fear?

The game began at that moment, in silence. I stood in a line with Betty Bright and the smaller substitutes, the kids who only go into the blowout games. I had never minded being a substitute on this team, until that moment. Just about everyone I knew could see me standing there, not quite good enough to be out on the field. I hoped Betty Bright understood that this was the school I used to go to; this was the team I used to play on.

I checked out the Lake Windsor goaltender. He was the same eighth grader who had named me Mars long ago, those many weeks ago. If things had been different, would I have been standing there in his place? Probably. Would I have made any difference? Probably not. They had won nine games without me, and they had played to one scoreless tie. This was a team that did not depend on its goaltender.

The action on the field started slowly. Both teams were sloppy, kicking the ball away. Victor seemed more intent on intimidating Gino than he was on getting the ball. Victor and Gino slid for the same ball near our sideline and got tangled up. The referee blew the whistle and called for a drop-kick, but Victor still had one more thing to say. He got right up in Gino's face and started jawing. Suddenly one of those big fullbacks they have—I don't even know his name—ran up and grabbed Victor by the hair. He spun him around and punched him, full in the face. Victor went down in a heap, hitting the back of his head on the ground. The referee lunged at the Lake Windsor player and grabbed him. He yelled to Coach Walski, "Out of the game! He's out of the game!"

Betty Bright took off toward Victor, and I was right behind her. She reached out and grabbed Tino, who was closing in on the Lake Windsor fullback with murder in his eyes. She pulled him with her to the spot where Victor was lying. His eyes were open, but he had a dazed look.

She said, "Victor, can you understand me?"

He said to her, "I'm OK. I'm ready to go." He was strangely calm, like he didn't know, or remember, what had just happened. He sat up quickly. "Really, Coach. I'm OK. I'm ready."

Betty Bright said, "No, I gotta check you out on the sideline for a while." She called to the referee, "Substitution." Then she turned to me. "Paul Fisher, you're in." Victor struggled to his feet. She held on to him while she called the rest of us around her and said, "This is where it happens. This is where losers act like losers and winners act like winners. This is where they send some fool out here to punch you in the face. If you retaliate, you're playing their game.

If you get focused on soccer, you're playing your game."

She walked Victor off the field and the action resumed. We had a free kick coming from the spot where the foul took place. The referee put the ball down and blew his whistle. The Lake Windsor players, who had huddled together after the goal, were slow getting back into position. I saw this and screamed, "Go!" I kicked the ball as hard as I ever have, over the heads of the surprised defenders. Our front line took off and flew past them. Tino ran the ball down in the left corner, pivoted, and crossed it with his right foot. Maya slapped it to a dead stop on the ground as a Lake Windsor fullback skidded past her; then she powered it into the back of the net. *Bang!* It happened that fast. That's how it had gone all season; that was our trademark. We struck swiftly, with just a couple of passes, and *bang*—into the goal. 1–0.

The Lake Windsor team was in confusion. They were yelling, "Offsides!" But it wasn't offsides. They'd been caught flatfooted. Their goaltender didn't have a chance.

After that Gino and Tommy took over. They started picking the ball up at midfield and either dribbling it themselves or passing it to each other. And they started shooting. Gino can drive the ball harder than anyone I have ever seen, on a straight line, from outside the penalty area. He grazed the top of the crossbar with one that Shandra didn't even get close to. He then made her dive to deflect one away for a corner kick. He and Tommy worked a series of short passes all the way in to the penalty line. Tommy reared back to kick it, and Shandra charged out, sliding into him for a block. But Tommy faked the kick, pulled the ball back, and flipped it over her into the open net. 1–1.

Shandra got up slowly, holding her stomach. The Lake Windsor players ran out to celebrate with Tommy. I watched Shandra stagger back to the goal. She looked feverish, weak. She held on to the goalpost, bent over, and vomited a white liquid into the grass.

I turned and saw Betty Bright hurrying toward her. At the same time, Cesar, our smallest substitute, came running onto the field. Victor had named him Cesar Salad. He only got in in absolute blowouts. He ran right up to me and yelled, "Fisher Man, coach says that I'm in for you and you're in for Shandra." He handed me a red goalie's shirt to wear.

I pulled the shirt on and ran down to the goal just as the coach was leading Shandra away. I placed my heels on the goal line and looked out. The Lake Windsor players had lined up in the distance, ready to come at us again. I thought, *Wait. I'm not ready. I'm not ready.*

I was numb; I felt like throwing up, too. But there was no time to think about it. Gino took the ball away from Henry D. like he wasn't even there and came sprinting right up the middle of our defense. Dolly tried to slide into him, but he was too quick. He flicked the ball to the right, hurtled over her, and came at me one-on-one. I was flat back on my heels when he fired the shot, a bad shot, right at me. I moved my arms to grab it, but they never came together. The ball bounced off my face, knocking my goggles up and knocking me back into the goal net. The ball bounced right back to Gino, who tapped it in. It was 2–1.

Gino himself pulled me out of the netting. "You all right, Mars?"

"Yeah."

"You better get ready, Mars. I'm comin' back."

"Yeah. Yeah."

His teammates mobbed him. Mine didn't even look at me.

I took off my goggles and cleaned them. When I pulled them back on they were smeared with blood. I looked down and saw a dark red spray of blood on the goalie shirt. My nose was bleeding. I bent over, pinched the bridge of my nose, and blew out as much blood as I could. I twisted the shirt around and cleaned my goggles again on the back of it.

Dolly called over, "Fisher Man? You all right?"

I sure was. "Yeah," I yelled. "Let's go."

Now I felt it. I was into it now. They came right back at us. Gino ripped a long shot that I dove for and caught in midair. I leaped to my feet and kicked it away. For the rest of the half I was awesome; I was zoned. I stopped everything they sent my way. I punched shots away; I deflected shots over the goalpost; I came out and slid into them before they could get shots off. The half ended like that—with a relentless Lake Windsor assault that produced nothing. It was still 2–1.

We spent the halftime sitting in a semicircle by the far goal, eating our tangerines. Victor would be going back in for the second half. Nita, who was struggling, would not.

Suddenly, out of nowhere, Coach Walski was standing next to me with his clipboard. He looked at Betty Bright and said, "Coach, this goaltender of yours is not eligible to play. He wasn't eligible to play for me, and he's not eligible to play for you."

Betty Bright stood up and faced him. They were the same height. "Oh? Is that right?"

"This is your official warning. I'm going to talk to the referee next."

"You are? So what makes him ineligible?"

"His address, for one thing. Now, we can talk this over at a hearing, if you like. I'm just here to tell you that the County Sports Commission won't recognize him as eligible, so you're going to forfeit this game if you put him back in."

"Is that how it is?"

"Yes. I'm sorry, but that's how it is."

"Uh-huh. Did you see my other goaltender? Her mother

had to drive her home because she's sick. Did you see her? She's Shandra Thomas."

Coach Walski stared at her blankly as Betty Bright continued.

"Do you know where she lives, Coach? She lives in Tangerine, with her mother and her brother. Do you know who her brother is? He's Antoine Thomas! Your football star at the high school here? Antoine Thomas lives in Tangerine, too. Now, are you sure you want to play that county-eligibility game with me?"

Coach Walski took a step back. His face seemed to flatten out, like she had hit him with a shovel. He said, "I'm sure Antoine Thomas has a different address."

"I'm sure he does. But he doesn't live there. I can take you and show you, or any officials of any commission, exactly where he lives."

Coach Walski continued backing away. This time he didn't stop. "All right. All right. Let's just play ball."

Betty Bright snorted in disgust. "Yeah. Let's all play ball." She jerked her thumb toward the field, and we all hopped up. She pointed an angry finger at me. "Get in that goal, Fisher Man."

The return of Victor in the second half made a huge difference. Lake Windsor could no longer double- and triple-team Maya. Victor took control of the middle of the field, which meant that we started to play the game up at their end instead of down at ours. Gino and Tommy still broke out with the ball and worked their plays, but I was always there. I saw each play as it developed. I thought one step ahead of them each time.

Maya couldn't shake the crowd of defenders around her inside the penalty box, so she started coming out to the wings. She made a neat move with the ball to get loose in the corner, then she crossed it, hard and low, right across the front of the goal. Tino and a Lake Windsor defender both lunged for it and smacked into each other. The ball squirted through everybody and landed right at the foot of the one guy nobody was worrying about, Cesar Salad. He was wide open. He stopped the ball calmly and kicked it into the net. 2–2.

We lined back up quickly. The battle for the middle heated up. The Lake Windsor players started to get desperate, started to kick the ball away. We were playing with confidence, and with the clock on our side.

Tommy and Gino were now going all the way back into their own end of the field to pick up the ball. They had to. They weren't getting any help from anybody on their team. They *were* their team.

The referee was already glancing at his watch when they made a final charge. Tommy picked up a loose ball at midfield and looked for Gino. He drove a long, high, looping pass into the penalty box that Gino and Victor both went up for. They collided and twisted in midair. Victor crashed down on top of Gino, right at the penalty line.

The referee blew his whistle. *No*, I thought. *No! You can't call that a penalty!*

Both coaches came running out onto the field. Victor jumped up, screaming, "I played the ball, man! I was going for the ball!"

But it was too late. The referee grabbed the ball and placed it on the penalty line, twelve yards in front of me.

Coach Walski asked, "How much time is left?"

The referee answered, "This is it." He turned to Betty Bright. "The penalty occurred right before the end of regulation."

"Yeah, sure it did," she snarled. She walked up to me. "You ready for this?"

"Yeah."

"What are you gonna do?"

"He always hits his penalty shots high and to the left. That's where I'll be."

She nodded. Then she smiled, lowered her voice, and said, "Now I wish I'd given you more playing time."

The players from both teams lined up outside the penalty box. Everyone except Gino and me. He looked at me, touched the ball with his foot, and stepped back three paces. The referee blew his whistle. Gino's head snapped up and he sprang forward—one, two, three steps. I catapulted myself into the air, high and to his left.

But Gino didn't kick it there. He had fooled me completely. He went the other way with it. I was a fool, flying through the air. I was a fool, landing on the ground. I closed my eyes and buried my head in my arms, trying to block out the whooping cheers.

Then I snapped my head up. It was Victor's voice that was whooping. I turned and looked back at the goal. The ball was not in the net. It was off to the right, and still rolling away, down into the sinkhole. Gino had missed. He had missed to the right.

The rest of the War Eagles mobbed me and hoisted me up. We all started to jump up and down and whoop together. I stopped and stepped out of the pack when Gino came over. He patted Victor on the back and said, "Congratulations." Then he put his arm around my shoulder and said, "Mars, you were in my head on that shot. You made me miss. You made me choke."

I shook my head vehemently. "You didn't choke, Gino. You missed. That's all."

He wasn't the least bit upset. "It's cool. I don't mind. It's only a game, Mars."

As he walked away, I was still shaking my head. I said out loud, but too low for him to hear, "Maybe to you it is."

Spectators were out on the field now. Someone tapped

my shoulder and said, "Good game, Paul." I knew that it was Kerri, but by the time I turned around she was already walking away with Cara. Joey wasn't with them.

Luis Cruz pounded me on the back and said, "I didn't know you were a goalie! Great game. Great game."

I said, "Thanks, I'm glad you think so."

Then Mom was standing in front of me. She said, "Are you OK?"

"Yeah."

"Now, what does this mean, Paul? Are both teams co-champions?"

"No. We're the champions. We have the better record. We're 9–0–1; they're 9–0–2."

"Oh. Now, do you want a ride home?"

"No. I want to go back on the bus."

"That doesn't make sense, Paul. I'd have to follow the bus all the way over there and then drive you right back here."

"That's right, Mom. That's what you're going to have to do."

She thought about it, then put her hands up in mock surrender. "OK. I give up."

I worked my way back toward the bus, shaking hands with a couple more Lake Windsor players. Mr. Donnelly called out, "Come over here, Paul!" He and his photographer had set up a shot with Cesar and Maya. It was comical. Maya towered two feet over Cesar. "Come on, we need you to balance out this shot."

I shook my head. "No, sir. It shouldn't be me. It should be Victor."

"Then let's get Victor, too. Where is he?" Mr. Donnelly located Victor and posed the four of us for the front page of tomorrow's sports section.

When we all got back to the bus, the coach called out, "How many, Victor?"

"Fifteen, Coach."

Betty Bright closed the door and turned to us. She pointed at us and said, "You're number one. You're second to none."

Victor grabbed Cesar from behind and shook him. He declared, "His name is Julius Cesar now, the emperor of Rome!"

We pulled out of the Lake Windsor campus, whooping and yelling, with our caravan of fans behind us. When we got to the downtown stretch of Tangerine, everybody in the row started honking horns and flashing lights. People came out of the shops along the main street; cars pulled over and stopped to see what all the commotion was about.

I'll never forget that ride home. When we got to Tangerine Middle, the bus doors opened, and the War Eagles got out to find their separate rides, to go their separate ways. I was the last to get off. I was crying when I finally climbed down the stairs with my shoes over my shoulder.

I crossed over to the white Volvo. Mom looked at me funny. Maybe she was wondering why I was crying. But all she had to say was, "Well, that was quite a ride."

I swallowed hard and managed to say, "It sure was, Mom. It was quite a ride."

part 3

Monday, November 20

Today was the day when the science group came over to my house. I guess it was a big deal for me. I had never had anybody over to the house except Joey, and who knows if that'll happen again?

Henry D. and I set it all up with his brother, Wayne. Wayne was due to spray for mosquitoes, so he came by to pick up Theresa, Tino, Henry, and me after school. When he pulled up at Tangerine Middle, I saw that he had already attached the trailer with the sprayer on it. We all climbed into the bed of the pickup and rode over to Lake Windsor Downs in the open air (a fact I neglected to mention to Mom).

Everything was cool when we got to the house. I took the group in through the back and introduced them to Mom. Then I led them into the great room. Theresa looked around and said, "This is a real nice place." Tino didn't say anything. He didn't look around, either. Mom followed us in with a tray of Yoo-Hoos and started to hover around. But then Dad came home early from the office, so she went into the kitchen with him.

We dragged some stools into the alcove. I put Dad's IBM through its paces, showing everybody the different fonts, colors, and graphics that we could use. I printed out examples of the ones that seemed best for our report. Theresa studied the hard copies like she was picking wallpaper. She said things like, "I like this for the title page, but let's have it in orange."

It didn't take long to design the final copy of our report. We still had a half hour before Wayne would be finished with his spraying. He had planned to do our street last, so

I suggested we go outside, while we still could, and kick the soccer ball around.

That loosened everybody up. Theresa played, too. We passed the ball in a big circle. Tino showed off his foot-juggling moves. I set up a goal in front of the gray wall and they took turns shooting at me.

Then, like in a rerun of a bad dream, I heard the sound of Arthur's Land Cruiser racing up the perimeter road. The whole scene with Joey flashed back into my mind; I started to feel sick.

I looked over at the patio doors. No one was inside. I could feel the blood draining out of my head.

I looked at Theresa, and she said, "Are you OK?"

I just stared back at her, paralyzed with fear, while the scene rolled on. Erik and Arthur came in through the gate. They were both carrying gym bags. Erik was in front, followed by Arthur. They stood still and looked at us. Tino, Theresa, and Henry looked back at them, but I couldn't. I just stared straight ahead.

Erik pointed to us and spoke with mock admiration. "Look at this. I think it's great that these farm-labor kids get to spend a day away from the fields."

Arthur nodded, slack jawed. "Yeah. It's touching."

I looked at Tino. He was glaring his mad-dog glare at Erik. I took a step toward Tino and said to him, "Forget it, Tino. They're not worth it."

Tino gave me the strangest look. Was it anger? Pity? He said, "Forget you." He stalked over to Erik with his fists clenched. He stopped two feet in front of him, totally unafraid, and said, "You're a real funny guy."

Arthur took a menacing step forward, but Erik extended his right hand toward him, slowly, casually. I watched that hand, mesmerized. I watched it move like a snake—a slow, casual snake hand—with a gold varsity ring on one finger. Arthur obeyed the hand, but he plunged his own hand into his gym bag and pulled something out—something short, black, and heavy—like a sock filled with lead. A blackjack?

Erik held him in place with the hand and said, as casually as he could, "I don't think we'll be needing that today, Arthur." Then Erik turned his full attention back to Tino, standing insolently before him. The casual snake smile started to slip from his face.

Tino stared up at him and spoke as he had before. "A funny guy, yeah. I see you on the TV, and I laugh all the time."

Erik's face started to contort. The snake smile was gone now, replaced by something else.

But Tino kept it up: "Yeah. I really like that thing you do, Funny Guy, when you pretend to kick a football and then you go flyin' up in the air and then you land right on your ass."

Immediately, faster than I thought he could, faster than Tino thought he could, Erik lashed out, smashing the back of his hand across Tino's face, smashing him so hard that Tino spun halfway around in the air and landed on the grass.

Was it hard enough to knock him out? Was it hard enough to kill him? I didn't know. Tino just lay there flat on the grass. Erik stood over him, his face a mask of rage. Then, like a genie sucking back into a bottle, he regained control. He took a deep breath and motioned with his hand toward the gate. Arthur quickly gathered up their stuff and started back out.

But Erik didn't follow immediately. He stopped in the gateway and stared at me, unmoving, until I dared to return his gaze. When I finally did, when I finally looked right into his eyes, I was surprised by what I saw. It was not hatred, or even anger. It was more like sorrow. Or fear. He gave me that look, then he spun around and left.

Henry and I reached Tino as he was struggling to his

knees, his hands cupped over his head. I saw a trickle of blood coming down from where Erik's ring had struck him beneath the ear. I was panicked. I wondered if I should call Dad. Or an ambulance. Or the police. I looked up at the patio door, and I saw something move. Something white. Out of the corner of my eye, I saw a white shirt move. Dad? Dad's white shirt walking out of the kitchen? Could he have seen it? Could he have seen what Erik did?

I turned back to Tino and tried to help him up. He pushed me roughly away. He looked around for Theresa. She was still standing by the wall; she had never moved. I heard the sound of Arthur's Land Cruiser revving up in the driveway and pulling away. They were gone.

I tried to get Tino to come inside, but he wouldn't. He wouldn't talk to me, or even look at me. Theresa came over to where we were standing. She walked Tino out through the gate without saying a word. Henry D. and I exchanged one pained look, and then he followed.

I walked as far as the gate and watched them. They stood motionless out at the curb. Then I heard the rumbling sound of the mosquito sprayer approaching. I saw Wayne stop in front of the house, the cloud of poison still five yards behind him. He pulled off his ant mask, hopped out, and turned off the spray of white fog. Henry got into the cab, but Theresa and Tino climbed back onto the truck bed. They all pulled away quickly, just ahead of the cloud of insecticide.

I wandered back into the yard, sick to my soul. I stood in front of the wall and replayed the scene in my head. I tried to slow the scene down, to relive it frame by frame. What could I have done? What should I have done?

I stared at that gray wall, waiting. Waiting for some long-dead, long-forgotten scene to come back to life. But none did. Nothing came—no answers, no remembrances, no insights—only the choking white waves of the fog.

We woke up this morning to unusually cold weather. I ate breakfast across from Dad at the round table. He was reading the sports section of the *Times*. I was on the verge of asking him, "Dad? Did you see Erik hit Tino in the face so hard that he nearly knocked him out?" But I didn't. I couldn't. I had the words all picked out, but I couldn't say them.

I sat there agonizing about it. Why couldn't I tell? I'd ratted out Tino at the carnival. Why couldn't I tell my own parents about Erik? What was wrong with me? What was wrong with all of us?

Anyway, I didn't say a word to Dad. I didn't say anything to Mom on the ride in, either. Tino and Theresa were both absent from school, so I didn't have to face them. Henry D. was there, but he and I managed to avoid each other all day.

While I was waiting for Mom to pick me up, I thought briefly about asking her to help me. But try as I might, I couldn't think of any good that could come from it. Even if she believed me completely, what could she do? Get Erik to issue a phony apology to Tino? That stuff doesn't play in Tangerine. Anyway, who's to say she would do anything about Erik? She's never done anything about him before.

So Mom and I rode out of Tangerine the same way we rode in, in silence. Mom has a lot on her mind these days, worrying about not only our home but every other home in Lake Windsor Downs. Now that soccer season is over, I'm back to accompanying her on her endless errands. This afternoon's first stop was out at our climate-controlled storage bin on Route 22.

When we reached the storage place, Mom finally said, "Hey, why doesn't Joey Costello come over anymore? Did you two have a fight?"

"Yeah. I guess so."

"What was it about? A girl?"

"No."

"Then what was it?"

I thought about that one for a long time. I thought about Joey's attitude on that first day. I remembered what he said about Theresa. I finally said, "You're right. It was about a girl."

Mom unlocked the garage-type door and waited for me to hoist it up for her. She went over to some boxes marked WINTER, put her key down, and scanned the labels on them until she found one marked SWEATERS, ETC. She said, "Here. Give me a hand."

I went over to the stack and lifted the top two boxes so she could remove the third one. As Mom handed it over to me, she said, "Do you smell that? There's insecticide in here, too."

"Yeah. That's life in Florida."

Mom quickly headed back out, into the fresh air. "Tell me about it. I hate that smell."

I lifted the SWEATERS, ETC. box onto my shoulder, stepped outside, and pulled the bin door down. It clicked and locked.

Mom patted the pockets of her jeans. "Oh no!"

"What?"

"My key. My key is inside!"

"They must have some way to let people in. Do they have a master key in the office?"

Mom looked shocked. "I hope not. This is supposed to be our private space. They're never supposed to come in here."

"Then how would they get in to spray for bugs?"

Mom thought about that. "They wouldn't." She snapped her fingers. "Erik! Erik has a key. He can stop in here and get mine."

We climbed back into the car. I said, "Why does Erik have a key?"

"I don't know, honey. Because he asked for one. You can have one, too, if you want."

I said, "I don't need one. Where are we going now?"

"I have to be at the high school at four o'clock. I have a meeting. I figured you could watch the football team practice. OK?"

"What's the meeting about?"

"It's about Erik. I'm meeting with his guidance counselor."

"Yeah? Why? What did he do?"

"Do? Nothing, Paul. I mean, there's no *incident* that they called me about. Is that what you mean?"

"Yes."

"Why? Why would you say that?"

I thought, *Because Erik is a psycho, Mom. Do you really not know that?* But I didn't say it. Mom and Dad don't like it when I say things like that.

Mom asked again, "Has Erik done something that I need to know about?"

I thought to myself, *That you need to know about?* And I answered honestly, "No."

Mom nodded, then she explained, "This is more of an academic conference. Erik's grades have slipped." Mom looked at me and added, "It's not unusual for an athlete, during the season, to slack off a little."

"I didn't."

"What, dear?"

"I'm an athlete. A champion athlete, in fact. And I didn't slack off during the season."

We turned at Seagull Way and drove to the south

entrance of the high school. Mom parked in the shadow of the steel gray bleachers and turned off the car. She finally said, "I know you had a good season, Paul. A great season. Remember me? I'm the one who drives you back and forth to that place every day."

I looked at her, but I didn't say anything. She got angry. "Give some credit where credit is due. Who do you think makes all of this possible? Who do you think holds this whole thing together? Your father?"

I had the answer to that one. "No."

She got out and walked inside. I sat in the car for a minute, then moved cautiously toward the sounds of football practice. I was determined to avoid Erik and Arthur, so I ducked under the bleachers. I picked my way over the steel bars, getting closer and closer to the front, until a row of seats was resting on top of my head. To the right I could see Antoine Thomas and another black guy with huge muscles practicing center snaps. To my left I could see Erik and Arthur. They were at the center of a group of admirers that included Tina, Paige, and a couple of skinny football guys. Just about everyone else was trudging toward the western exit of the field. Practice was over.

I watched as the first group of players passed through the opening at the far end of the bleachers, heading toward their cars. Suddenly a familiar color caught my eye.

A green Ford pickup rolled into view and parked in a space near the gate. The old Ford looked odd, out of place among the expensive imports, sports cars, and 4 × 4s. What was it doing here?

Luis Cruz got out and stared intently at the people who were leaving. He stopped one player and spoke to him. The player listened and then pointed down toward Erik's group. Luis started walking, in his limping style, through the gate and down the sideline. He continued on past Antoine and the muscle man, who were now sitting on the bleachers, watching him. What was he doing here? He stopped right in front of my hiding place, and he waited.

Erik and his group had gathered up their gear and were preparing to leave. Luis stood in their path, like the brave sheriff of a town full of cowards. When Erik's group got close enough, Luis called out, "Which one is Erik Fisher?" He looked right at Erik. "Is that you?"

Erik opened his eyes wide in mock terror. He turned to Arthur and said, "We may have a situation here, Bauer." The others in the group seemed amused.

Arthur started to walk slowly west. His hand fumbled inside his gym bag.

Luis continued in a loud voice, "I think you are. But I think you are not man enough to say so."

An "Ooohhh" sound rose up from the group. Erik just smiled and met Luis's stare.

Luis held his long arms out and extended his palms. "You would smack a little kid in the face, right? Why don't you come over here and try to smack me?"

The "Ooohhh" grew louder.

Arthur Bauer was still walking forward, with his head down, but Luis was paying no attention to him. He called out again, "Come on! Why don't you try to smack me!"

Arthur reached Luis, turned, and whipped the blackjack around with a loud *whack* against the side of Luis's head. Luis's arms shot up to cover his head as he staggered to the right and fell on one knee. Arthur stuck the blackjack back into his gym bag and continued walking, as if nothing had happened.

Erik walked quickly past Luis. He explained, for the benefit of his group, "Arthur takes care of all my light work." Erik and the rest of them caught up with Arthur at the gate. I could see that they were laughing.

Antoine and the muscle man were not. They stood up. They walked out to Luis and examined his injury. From where I was, I couldn't see any blood. They helped Luis to his feet and talked to him for a few minutes. Then they walked with him to his truck. Luis seemed pretty steady. I remained frozen in my spot as he got back in the Ford and drove off.

I don't know how much later it was when Mom came out from her conference and found me there. She called out, "Paul? Are you playing under there? What are you doing, hiding?"

I pulled myself together and picked my way back over the steel bars. We drove all the way home in silence, except for one remark. Mom said, "The conference went very well. The guidance counselor thinks this football stardom business has gone to Erik's head. She thinks he'll be better off once football season is over. And it *is* nearly over."

Nearly over? In our family, it's never over. The Dream lives twenty-four hours a day, seven days a week, twelve months a year. The Dream has four years at a big-time college ahead of it. And then who knows? Maybe the NFL.

Thursday, November 23, Thanksgiving

Yesterday morning I dug out my old Houston Oilers hooded sweatshirt, a thick pair of corduroy pants, and a wool shirt that has always been too large for me to wear. The weather has turned very cold and very windy. The guy on my clock radio called it a Thanksgiving freeze. Down in the kitchen the TV weather girl called it a fall freeze.

I answered the phone on the kitchen wall and heard my grandmother's voice. "Paul? You're on CNN again. You're having record cold temperatures down there."

"I know, Grandmom." She made some more small talk with me about the cold in Florida versus the cold in Ohio. Grandpop got on the extension, and the two of them asked me about myself—about my school, about my friends. That's one thing about Grandmom and Grandpop—they couldn't care less about the Erik Fisher Football Dream. They never, ever mention it. And when Dad brings it up, they do their best to change the subject.

Mom got up and took the phone away. She talked a little but mostly listened, while Dad, Erik, and I sat and ignored each other. Then she said, "Great. We'll look forward to seeing you then."

Mom hung up and announced to us, "Grandmom and Grandpop are stopping by on their way to Orlando."

Dad asked glumly, "When?"

"A week from Sunday."

"For how long?"

"An hour or two."

Dad perked up. "Is that all?"

"They've booked a week at Epcot. They just want to stop in to see our new house."

Dad thought about this. "So, they can drive to Florida to see Mickey Mouse, but not to see their own grandson play football?"

Mom was ready for him. "Well, maybe we can talk them into changing their plans."

Dad managed a weak smile. Mom turned the conversation back to the unseasonably cold weather. She said, "I'm going out to the storage bin today to get winter clothing for all of us. If there's anything particular you want, let me know."

Dad said, "Whatever you packed up in Houston—I'm sure that's OK."

Mom said, "Erik, you'll need to give me your key. We locked mine in the bin yesterday."

Erik looked up. "Oh yeah. I got it in my locker at school."

"What's it doing there? I need it now."

"That's where I keep a lot of my stuff."

"OK. How can I get it?"

"I'll bring it home today."

I could see that Mom didn't like that answer, but she was stuck with it. On the way to Tangerine, she started thinking out loud. "I'm sure they have some way of letting their customers get into those bins. I'm sure I'm not the first person in history to have locked a key inside."

We pulled up to the school. There were no karate kickers. No gangstas. There were no human beings of any kind hanging around outside. Kids from the cars ahead of us sprinted into the building with their heads down, clutching their books to their bodies.

I didn't. I stood outside the car door, unflinching, like a northern kid.

Mom asked, "What winter clothes should I bring for you?"

"I don't know. What do I have?"

She looked me up and down. "I swear, Paul, you've grown half a foot this year. You probably don't have anything that fits. Including what you have on now."

"Thanks, Mom."

"Are you at least warm?"

"Yeah. I'm at least that."

"OK. You had better get inside. I'll see you later."

I walked into the building. In those few yards my ears were turned red and raw by the wind. A lot of kids were absent from first period. Wimps, I figured. By second period, though, I realized that something bigger was going on. At least ten kids were absent from science—so many kids that we had to waste our time with worksheets. I walked over to Henry D.'s desk and asked him, "Where is everybody? Are they all sick?"

"No. I reckon they're out fighting the freeze."

"What? What does that mean?"

"It's a tradition in Tangerine. Kids from families that are in the citrus business, or the vegetable business, can stay out of school whenever there's a freeze. Their families need them to help."

"It's like a snow day."

"I don't know about that. The kids aren't playing, they're out working. I remember my daddy and my granddaddy talking about getting out of school to fight the freezes."

"What do you fight with?"

"Anything you got. Most people around here are small growers. They use whatever. They haul old tires out and start a bonfire in the grove. They burn up old brush. They do anything they can to create heat and smoke."

"So all of these kids are out building bonfires?"

"Some of them are. They might be out filling up the smudge pots, or hauling out pipes for the water pumps. Whatever a family has to fight with, that's what the kids are working on."

"Do you think that's what Luis and Tino are doing?"

"Most definitely. And Victor and those guys. They're trying to save those Golden Dawn tangerines, and the rest of the trees out there."

Immediately, without a doubt, I knew what I had to do. I said, "Can your brother drive us out there today?"

Henry looked at me uncertainly. "I expect he can."

"What do you say we go help them fight the freeze?"

Henry thought it over and nodded. "Yes. I suppose we should." He added, "We're all War Eagles."

We shook on it, and I went back to my seat. The rest of the day dragged by. Henry told me some more about the freezes in Tangerine. He explained that the first night is dangerous, but the second night is the real killer. The trees are injured already; they're weak and vulnerable. Luis and his crew had probably worked all night in the groves. They would sleep during the day, and then the battle would resume at sunset. And we would be there.

I called Mom at lunchtime, but she was out. I left this message: "Mom? We're having a combination science meeting and sleepover party at Tino's house. I have a ride there with Henry Dilkes. I hope it's OK to go because I already said I would. The good news is that you don't have to pick me up after school. I'll call you when I get there. Bye."

After last period was over, I looked out of the second-floor window. I was a little worried that Mom had not gotten the message, or that she *had* gotten it but was not buying it. Anyway, when I stepped outside Mom's car wasn't there. The car riders were once again running, panic-stricken, through the punishing gusts of wind.

I followed Henry across the street to where Wayne was parked. Henry pulled his hood on against the stinging wind, so I did the same. We climbed into the cab, and Henry said, "We're not going home, Wayne. We're going back out to the Tomas Cruz Groves. Can you take us?"

It was all the same to Wayne. He smiled. "Yeah. I'll take you. I gotta go right back to work, though. There's emergencies all over the county on account of the freeze. I don't know when I can pick y'all up."

"That's all right, Wayne. We don't need to be picked up. We're gonna help them out in the groves tonight."

Wayne looked at me with genuine surprise. "Is that right? You're gonna get out in that nasty cold?"

Wayne wouldn't say it, he was too polite, but I knew what he was thinking: *How come you're not back at Lake Windsor Downs with the rest of them, complaining about the mosquitoes, and the termites, and the muck fire?*

We pulled off Route 22 at the Tomas Cruz sign and bumped down the dirt road. The cattail pond now had steel gray and rust brown pipes running up from it toward the groves, like someone had connected straws together in four crooked lines. Wayne pointed at them. "Looks like they're icing down their new grove."

"What's that?"

"They'll pump water over the trees all night long, probably a quarter of the grove at a time."

This was all new to me. I shook my head. "Why is that a good thing to do? Won't that kill the trees sooner?"

Wayne answered patiently, "If you cover 'em with ice, their temperature will never drop below thirty-two degrees. Thirty-two degrees won't kill a tree; thirty-one degrees will, if it stays that cold long enough."

"So why don't they just ice all the trees and be done with it?"

"Probably 'cause they don't have the water, or the pumps, or the sprinklers to do it all. It's expensive enough to do one part. Even then it might not work. The ice has to be kept just like slush. If ice gets thick and hard on a tree, that thing'll crack in half like a Thanksgiving wishbone."

"So what if they start this slush thing and they run out of water?"

"That won't happen. That there's a spring-fed lake. It'll just keep fillin' up. Now they might run outta diesel fuel. Water won't do you any good if you can't pump it where you want to. Look over there." Wayne pointed at something that I hadn't noticed before. On the rising ground behind the house, barely visible from the road, was a vertical orange tank twenty feet high. It looked like a giant can of frozen orange juice stuck there on its side. "That tank's full of diesel fuel. That diesel's your life's blood tonight."

We drove around the house and stopped outside the Quonset hut. Luis and his father were standing by the back door. They were both dressed in layers of old clothes, and they both had blue knit ski caps pulled down over their ears. Wayne waved to them and pulled away. Luis said, "What can I do for you guys?"

I thought of Luis facing down Erik and his gang at the high school. I answered earnestly, "We want to help you fight this freeze tonight. We'll do anything we can."

Luis looked at Henry, then back at me. His doubts seemed to be directed at me. So were his words. "Why do you want to do that?"

I didn't know what to say. Was he looking at me as Erik Fisher's brother? Was I now the enemy? Tino came out of the house, and I thought of Henry D.'s line. I said, "Because we're all War Eagles."

Luis turned to his father and said a few words in Spanish. Tomas Cruz walked up to me immediately and stretched out his hand. He said, "Thank you for your help." He shook hands with both of us and continued on into the Quonset hut.

Luis said, "Our daddy thinks that's great. But he doesn't worry about the insurance and stuff. Do you guys have your parents' permission to do this?" We both nodded. Finally Luis shrugged. "OK. You're on Tino's crew. He'll show you what's up." He looked directly at me, like I was the one who was a potential lawsuit. "But you're responsible for your own health and safety. Right? If you get too cold, you come into the hut here and you warm up. If you get too tired, you come in and lie down."

Luis went inside, leaving us with Tino. He was dressed like I was, but his sweatshirt said MIAMI DOLPHINS. He had a walkie-talkie in one hand and a white bag from Kmart in the other. He was all business. He said, "There ain't no lyin' down on my crew. You got that?"

"Yeah."

"Anybody has to do any bathroom stuff or anything like that, you do it now."

I half raised my hand, like I was in school. "I have to make a phone call."

Tino opened the door and led us into the Quonset hut. It had been transformed. Most everything that had been in there last week was gone, replaced by hundreds of baby trees, each about a foot high. We marched through them to the far end. The desk was still there, but now it had a big aluminum coffee urn sitting on it, with Styrofoam cups, creamer, and sugar spread out around it.

I picked up the phone and called Mom. I said, "I tried to call before. Were you out at the storage bin?"

She didn't sound too happy. She said, "Yes. I was."

"Did you need Erik's key?"

"No. I filled out a form and the manager let me in."

"Uh-huh." Mom didn't say anything else. Was she angry at me? Was she going to come and drag me home? I changed the subject. "So what's happening there?"

She paused a moment, as if thinking the whole thing over. Then she changed gears and answered conversationally, "Your father bought a case of those fake logs. He's going to get the fireplace going. And we're going to break out the Christmas music."

"Uh-huh."

"We'll probably make hot chocolate, too. Too bad you're going to miss it."

"Yeah."

"Now, what is this thing, Paul? A sleepover party? Why didn't we have any notice about it?"

"I wasn't invited until today." I half covered the mouthpiece and whispered, "I don't know. Maybe I was an afterthought."

"You don't have a change of clothes. You don't have a toothbrush."

"I'll use my finger."

There was a long pause, and then a long sigh. "Paul,

I trust people. I trust them until I have a reason not to. Do you understand me?"

"I understand."

There was another long pause and some mumbling. "Your father says you have to be back here by nine tomorrow morning. It's Erik's last game."

"OK. You can pick me up at eight if you like."

"I hope I can find that place."

"Look for the sign that says TOMAS CRUZ GROVES."

The door at the far end of the hut burst open. Victor, dressed in black sneakers, pants, and hood, like a cat burglar, walked in, followed by his boys. I said, "I have to go now, Mom. Enjoy your fireplace and all." She didn't say anything else, so I cradled the phone.

Victor, Hernando, and Mano went right to a stack of shovels that were piled up next to the baby trees. Tino said to Henry, "You should have been here last night. We must have hauled a ton of dirt from the old grove to the Golden Dawns." He pointed to the stack and said, "Grab a shovel." Then he held up his Kmart bag. "Check it out." Tino dumped out a pile of thick black work gloves onto the desk. Everybody grabbed a pair and pulled them on. Tino was smiling. "I bought twenty pairs of these gloves, for you boys with delicate hands."

Victor said, "Yeah? I'll mess up your face with some delicate hands."

Tino said, "My daddy and my Uncle Charlie are out in the Cleopatra grove startin' the fire. They're gonna call us out to haul tires and brush. Luis is gonna stay in the new grove and run the pumps. He's gonna call us to chop ice off the trees." He smiled at Victor. "In our spare time, we're gonna do what we did last night. We're gonna keep the Golden Dawns packed with dirt."

Then Tino extended one gloved hand toward us and held it there, just like Victor did before each soccer game. We crowded in and put our hands on top of his. He said, "You know what's up. Time and temperature. Luis says it's gonna be ten hours of hard freeze tonight. Trees are gonna die no matter what we do. We gotta save what we can."

Victor said calmly, "Let's do it," and the circle broke up. We filed outside with our shovels into the cold sting of the wind. The sun was dropping in the sky. The temperature was dropping, too.

We headed into the old grove of trees, now bare of fruit, the grove of the Cleopatra tangerines. Their leaves seemed to be withering, shriveling. We walked through the sights and smells of last night's battle, to a high point of land. Tino gestured in a slow circle. "Check this out."

The trees in this spot were tall, weathered, and cracked —haunted-house trees. "Luis says to use these to keep the brushfire going. Daddy and Tio Carlos will do the chopping, and we'll do the hauling." Tino looked at Henry D. "These trees are all dead. We call them the lightning trees. They're at the highest point in the grove, so they get zapped by lightning. They've been dead for years. We don't chop them down, though, 'cause they act like lightning rods. I hope we'll get away with just chopping down one or two for the fire tonight."

Tino started downhill and we followed. Henry pointed out a line of metal contraptions that were about four feet high. Each had a wide, round base and a narrow stovepipe sticking up from it. "Those are the smudge pots. Wait'll you see them when they're burning. Fire comes shooting out of the tops of them." He called out, "Tino, are we gonna be haulin' the diesel for these smudge pots?"

"Ain't nobody else gonna do it." Tino turned at the end of the row and stopped. He pointed out a skinny three-sided wooden box, about five feet tall. Henry and I looked inside. It was a glass thermometer, attached to a white metal plate that had PEPSI written across it. The temperature read

215

thirty-five degrees. "You'll see these at different spots, high spots and low spots inside the groves. I call Luis with the temperatures, and he calculates what we have to do and how much time we have to do it in. Time and temperature."

As we approached the lowest point in the grove, the trees began to look scorched; they smelled like smoke and rubber. We reached a clearing that had obviously been the site of a fire the night before. Tomas Cruz and his brother were placing dead branches in a crisscross pattern, laying the foundation for tonight's fire. A revolting smell of burnt rubber seeped up from the debris.

Tino poked at his uncle as we passed by. *"¿Qué pasa, Tío?"*

"Tu saves," he replied.

We emerged from the old grove into the wide, square field of the Golden Dawn tangerines. How different this field looked now! Tino and his crew had dumped a thousand small mounds of dirt in here. Like a thousand giant anthills, they covered up all of those black irrigation hoses. Each little tree was now packed with dirt about a foot high, with a few green leaves sticking out at the top.

Tino spoke again to Henry. "We have to make sure that these trees are packed above the bud union, right here." He pointed to a spot halfway up one of the dirt mounds. "If we don't, the Golden Dawns are dead, and we got ourselves a thousand rough lemon trees." He paused for emphasis. "That can't happen."

We continued along the back of the square field until we entered the new grove. There were twice as many tall, skinny sprinklers as last time. In the distance I could see that one part of the grove was already being watered by them, from high above.

We walked toward the sound of a diesel pump until we came to a rickety corrugated-iron shed, kind of a lean-to that was open on one side. Luis was inside it, looking at the dials on a pump and making notes. We formed a group around him, and he said, "Tonight's the night, homeboys. All over this town, all over this part of the state, people are gonna get hurt by this freeze. It's a killer. It's gonna kill right down to the wood, right down to the ground."

He looked up at us. Actually, he looked up at me. He said, "You understand the plan, right? We're icing the new grove, we're packing the Golden Dawns, and we're burning the old grove. What's alive in the morning is what's alive in the morning." He pointed at Victor. "Did you guys get some rest?"

"Yeah, we crashed all day."

"You ready for another night of this?"

"Sure. You know we're always ready to rumble."

"Yeah. I know that. Just be careful. All of you."

Luis looked to the west, so we all turned to look with him. The sun was sinking low. The Cleopatra trees stood black in the orange light, like Halloween cutouts. The temperature was dropping by the minute, and the wind was whipping up.

I thought about my phone call to Mom. In Lake Windsor Downs, the people were inside, welcoming the freeze with hot cocoa and fake logs and Christmas CDs. In Tangerine, the people were heading out to fight it with shovels and axes and burning tires.

That turned out to be our last moment of peace. For the next twelve hours, we waged a fierce and increasingly desperate battle to save the Cruz family's trees.

We began with the smudge pots in the old grove. A hundred smudge pots had to be filled with fuel, fired up, and kept burning all night. We set out in pairs to do it. Henry and I were given two gas cans and a lighter, and we soon figured out what to do with them. The smudge pots were hellish machines, belching foul-smelling smoke and shooting a dangerous wild flame out the top, like upside-down rockets.

We made hundreds of trips to the big orange diesel tank. Diesel generators pumped the water that Luis spread over the new grove. Diesel generators lit the new grove and the Golden Dawn field. Whenever we weren't responding to a crisis, we were hauling diesel.

But there was one crisis right after another. A crisis might begin with a call from Tomas that the brushfire was going out. We'd take off on the run through the Cleopatra grove, choking on the smoke, tripping in the dark. Tomas would be there hacking apart a lightning tree, and we'd drag the dead limbs to the bonfire. Then we'd run back to the diesel tank. Soon Luis would call, and we'd take off for the new grove. We'd use our shovels to scrape at trees that were getting too heavily coated with ice, trees that were about to crack.

On and on it went like that, repacking dirt, hauling tires—we battled against the ever-dropping temperature: thirty degrees, twenty-eight degrees, twenty-six degrees.

But we were losing. The fire in the old grove was blazing high and wild, scorching the leaves off anything near it. By midnight we had chopped down four lightning trees. The ice was forming too rapidly in the new grove; the coatings on the trees were too thick. The loud cracking sound of trees splitting off branches like amputated limbs, or splitting in two like they'd been pole-axed, hung horribly in the frozen night air. We were losing.

For all of our frantic efforts, the temperature continued to drop. It must have been about two o'clock when I saw Tino and Victor standing in front of one of those Pepsi thermometers. Victor was screaming at it, "Twenty-four degrees! Twenty-four degrees!" It was like his frozen breath was spelling out the awful words.

Tino got off the walkie-talkie with Luis and announced, "Luis says this: If it stays twenty-four degrees for ten more minutes, then it's all over. He's calling it off. We're all going home."

I stopped in my place, in a row of Golden Dawns, and I set down my can of diesel. One by one, I pried my black-gloved fingers back, trying to straighten out my warped hand. For the first time that night, I felt the cold. And I felt exhaustion.

I dropped to my knees on that frozen piece of earth, weary to the core of my body. I looked over to my left. The new grove was glistening like an angel on a Christmas tree, lit from within by the light of a diesel generator. Every tree dripped frozen icicles, from the top down to the ground. And the glow of all of them together was more beautiful than anything I had ever seen.

To my right, the smudge pots and that bloated bonfire were spewing out over every living thing. I saw Tomas and his brother emerge from the black and billowing smoke, marching toward Tino. I turned back and saw that Luis was coming down, too. They all met at the thermometer and talked for five minutes. Finally Tomas and his brother broke away and marched back into the scorched grove. Luis said one more thing to Tino and then went back to his duties.

I got back up on my feet as Tino called us to him. He announced, "Our daddy and Tio Carlos are going to keep trying. Luis says that the rest of us have to go inside. Right now. He'll call me when we can come back out."

We all trudged obediently over to the Quonset hut. I walked inside, felt the blessed heat, and collapsed on the floor. Victor picked me up into a sitting position. Then Theresa appeared in front of me with a cup of coffee. She said, "Do you like cream and sugar?"

I shook my head dumbly and said, "I don't know."

She smiled. "Let's find out." I tried to take the cup from

219

her, but my fingers wouldn't close around the handle. Theresa stooped down, held the cup up to my mouth, and I took a sip. It made me shiver. I took another one. And then another. Finally I was able to hold the cup in my hands.

Tino said, "Fisher Man, last time you were here you collapsed because it was too hot. Now you're collapsing because it's too cold? What's up with you?"

I couldn't even think of a reply, much less make one. I sat there in a kind of coma for a long, long time. Finally Tino's walkie-talkie crackled to life. I heard him say, "All right! That's what we're waiting to hear." He turned to Victor. "Luis says the new grove is holding steady at twenty-nine degrees, and the high spots in the old grove are showing twenty-eight. He says that the worst is over; the temperatures are goin' back up."

Victor and Tino clasped hands, but Victor was solemn. "So how much dead wood you got out there?"

"I don't know, man. Anything in those low spots has had it." He turned to include me. "It got too cold down there for too long. But, hey, we're still in business." Tino, Victor, and the boys got up to go back out, so I struggled to get to my feet. Tino turned to Theresa. "No way he's going back outside. Orders from Luis."

Theresa pointed a stern finger at me. "You heard that. Now don't move from here. I'm going to go get you some blankets."

I could barely move. I could barely speak. But suddenly Luis entered, and I knew I had to.

He said, "Paul, are you all right?"

I looked up at him and tried to focus my eyes. I stared hard at his left temple. There it was! I could see it in this light. It was a dark red bruise, deep set, like a birthmark. It curved over his eyebrow like a dark red crescent moon. I whispered, "Yeah."

"Tino said you were in bad shape."

"I was a little frozen. I'm OK now."

"Do you want to go to the hospital?"

"No. No way. I'm feeling better already."

He studied me doubtfully. I blurted out, "Listen, Luis. We only have a couple of minutes, and I have to tell you something. I saw you at Lake Windsor High School. I saw what you did."

Luis straightened up.

"I saw you face down Erik and those other guys, and I saw Arthur Bauer hit you with a blackjack."

His hand moved automatically up to his temple. "Is that what it was?"

"Yes. And you have to believe me, Luis. They're dangerous. They're very dangerous."

Luis, to my amazement, smiled. He was about to reply when the door at the far end opened and Theresa returned. He just said, "I'll talk to you about this later."

Theresa came up and handed me two thick green blankets and a white pillow. Luis went back out, and I crashed.

The next thing I knew it was six-thirty, and the crew was coming back in. Henry D. said to me, "The sun's coming up. We made it through the night."

I pulled off the blankets and stood up, humiliated. But Tino came right up to me and said, "Hey, Fisher Man, thanks for helping us tonight."

He held out his hand, and I shook it. I said, "Tino, I'm really sorry about what happened."

"What? Hey, man, you're not used to this kind of work."

"No. Not that. I mean at my house."

Tino shook his head. "Oh, that. Well, we never should have gone over there."

"Yes! You should! You should go over there. You're my friends. Or . . . I want you for my friends. You're welcome at my house."

Tino nodded and then said, "You can be our friend over

here. All right?" I shrugged and nodded. He added, "Our daddy's driving to the takeout for some Egg McMuffins. You down with that?"

"Yeah."

"OK. Oh, and Luis says he wants to see you outside."

"All right."

I went out back and found Luis kneeling by a Golden Dawn tree with his face buried in the green leaves.

I said, "Can you smell anything now?

He laughed. "Yes. I can." He sat back and looked at me. "I can smell what it will be like."

"So the Golden Dawns survived?"

"Oh yeah. They all survived. They were the safest ones. When you're little like this, we can just cover you up with dirt, and you'll be OK." He checked behind me and said, "I want to finish our conversation, because I want you to know what's going to happen."

"OK."

"You know those two black dudes who were there? One of them is Shandra's brother?"

"Yeah. Antoine Thomas."

"Right. Well, Antoine and the other dude, the muscle man, don't care too much for Erik Fisher or his friend."

I said, "Arthur Bauer."

"Right. They told me to come back on Monday and we'd take care of business. They said that all the players have to be there on Monday to turn their equipment in. Is that right?"

"I don't know. That sounds about right."

"I'm just telling you this so you'll know. You seem kinda scared of Erik and Arthur Bauer."

"Yeah. I am. Who wouldn't be?"

Luis answered simply, "I wouldn't be. They're punks." He pointed one ropelike finger at me. "And you shouldn't be, either. You watch what happens on Monday. If Antoine keeps his word, two punks are gonna have new attitudes, right around three o'clock."

Luis's uncle walked up and started talking to him, so I drifted back inside, thinking about my fear of Erik. How could I be so totally afraid, and Luis be not the slightest bit afraid, of the exact same thing? Which one of us saw it wrong?

Theresa brought out a nine-inch portable TV, and we all gathered around it to eat our Egg McMuffins. The news people said that the cold front was now moving out of our area, but it had left a lot of damage behind, and it had "put some area growers out of business." They showed pictures of a grove that had been iced over; it was now dripping in the sun. Everyone in the hut watched in silence.

After the news, Victor and his boys headed for home. I stood outside and waited for Mom. She pulled up right at eight o'clock. Her first words were, "Did you stay up all night?"

"No. I slept."

"Paul? You look awful."

"I slept, Mom. But I think I'm coming down with a cold."

Mom reached over and put the back of her hand against my forehead. "Yeah. You and half the population of Lake Windsor Downs." She sighed. "Well, I'm not going to have you sitting in a freezing-cold football stadium. You need bed rest."

"You're right. I'd be better off at home."

Mom thought for a minute and added, "Your father isn't going to like this."

"I know. Just tell him I need my sleep."

Mom sighed again. "I will. But you had better sleep."

"I will."

And I will. Just like the rest of the crew. But first, I had to write this all down.

Friday, November 24

I slept for eighteen hours yesterday. No one woke me up to go to the game. That was good. No one woke me up for Thanksgiving dinner, either. That was weird.

It was four-thirty on my alarm clock when I finally opened my eyes. I lay there in the dark for another hour, then got dressed and went down to the kitchen. I was starving. As I was finishing a turkey sandwich, I heard the sound of the newspaper plopping onto the driveway.

I walked outside. The air was cold, but nowhere near freezing. The wind was blowing from west to east, blowing the smoke of the muck fire through the starry sky.

I walked back inside with the *Times* and sat on the floor of the great room. The headline of the sports section was "Lake Windsor Defeats Tangerine." Underneath that it said, "Antoine Thomas throws for 3 TDs, runs for 2, in 30–0 rout."

I started to read about it, but then Dad wandered through in his pajamas on the way to the kitchen. He stopped and scowled at me. He said, "I thought you had a cold. I don't hear any coughing or sneezing."

I answered, "Sorry, Dad, but I'm feeling better today."

We locked eyes for a few seconds, then he continued into the kitchen. When he came back out he had a cup of coffee, and he had lost the scowl. He sat down on the floor next to me and began to talk about his favorite subject. "You didn't miss much of a game. You know that big center, Brian Baylor?"

"Is he the one who hangs out with Antoine?"

"Right. He's been snapping the ball to Antoine perfectly all year. Yesterday, I guess he forgot how. The kicking game stunk to high heaven, and it was all because of him. I think Coach Warner should have benched him." Dad pointed to the sports section. "Do they even mention Erik in there?"

"No. They just say that the score should have been higher, but Lake Windsor missed all five extra points."

Dad's eyes shot fire. "Missed extra points? Is that what it says? Erik didn't miss anything! He never even kicked the ball. The ball never got anywhere near him. Brian Baylor made five bad snaps in a row!"

I couldn't resist. I said, "Well, at least we won. That's the important thing."

Dad didn't even hear me. He was shaking his head back and forth. "It would have been nice to finish the season on a high note. With a big game. But this Baylor kid ruined it." He took a sip of coffee. "I don't know. Maybe he just wasn't used to snapping the ball to Arthur."

"Arthur? You mean the coach actually put Arthur Bauer in the game?"

"Oh yeah. He put all the seniors in. It was their last game. And it was a blowout. Of course he was going to play them all." He pointed at the paper. "Is Antoine the big story?"

"Yeah. He's pretty much the whole story."

Dad brooded about that. He finally said, "It's like Brian Baylor did it deliberately. Like he wanted to make Erik and Arthur look like fools. All five snaps were wild. They were high, or wide, or they bounced before they got there. He made Arthur jump for them, or dive for them, or chase them down. The last one went so high that Erik had to run it down himself and fall on it. If those Tangerine linemen had been faster, Erik could have gotten hurt."

I thought, *Just wait until Monday, Dad. Erik is going to get hurt. Arthur Bauer, too.*

We heard Mom in the kitchen rattling some pans, so Dad got up and joined her.

I turned to page two and saw a large composite photo with this caption above it: "All-County Middle School

Soccer Team." I studied the names and faces. I knew them all—four were from teams that I'd played against, and the other seven were from teams that I'd played on. The faces of the players, actually their school photos, were arranged in three rows, the way that a team would pose. Under each photo were the player's name, school, and position. One face, however, was missing.

Across the top row the strikers included Maya Pandhi, Gino Deluca, and Tommy Acoso. The middle row, of halfbacks, included Victor Guzman and Tino Cruz. Across the bottom row one of the fullbacks was Dolly Elias, and the goaltender was Shandra Thomas. It was Shandra's face that was missing. There was an empty frame where her photo should have been.

I stared at them for a long, long time. Did I want my own face to be up there? Yes, I did. Did I want to change what had happened to me this season? No. Not a minute of it. Not ever. Shandra had earned her place on this team. I wondered if she felt proud to see her name, if not her photo, in the *Times*.

I walked out to the kitchen, found the scissors, and started to cut it out. Mom and Dad looked up.

Dad said, "What's that?"

"The All-County Middle School Soccer Team."

"Yeah? Are you on it?"

That question really hit me the wrong way. I couldn't believe he had asked me that. And yet it was so typical. I answered, "Sure I am, Dad. They picked me as the All-County Benchwarmer."

He looked annoyed. He sounded annoyed, too. "Come on, Paul. Did you make the team or not?"

We locked eyes again. "How many games did I play in, Dad?"

He pulled back. "I don't know."

"What position did I play when I did get into a game?"

"How am I supposed to know that?"

"OK. Here's one: How many field goals did Erik kick this year?"

He stared at me, and then he blinked rapidly. "All right. Your point is taken."

"What's that supposed to mean?"

"It means I understand what you're saying. You're saying that I know everything about Erik's season and nothing about yours. You're right, and I'm sorry."

Mom looked up at him with interest.

"All I can say, in my own defense, is that this was the critical season for Erik. College recruiters are watching him. A lot is riding on this season. His entire future in football is riding on it."

Mom asked quietly, "What if Erik has no future in football?"

Dad stared at her blankly, so she repeated, "What if Erik has no future as the placekicker for some big-time college football team?"

Dad let out a short, uncomfortable laugh. "What are you talking about?" He looked at Mom, then me, as if we had lost our minds. Or worse, as if we had forgotten the Erik Fisher Football Dream. He said, as if to two morons, "Erik can kick a fifty-yard field goal."

Mom continued, "I know he can. What if that's not enough?"

Dad answered calmly. "Well, that's *not* enough. You have to have good grades. You have to show good character."

Mom looked down at her coffee. Was she thinking what I was thinking? Did she know that Erik had no good character? Or was she still as clueless as Dad? Did she still believe blindly in the Dream?

No one else spoke, so I went back to cutting up the newspaper. In the column next to the photo there was a notice, bordered in black, that caught my eye.

The annual Senior Awards Night at Lake Windsor High School will be held on Friday evening at 7:30 P.M. in the school's gymnasium. This year's ceremony will include the dedication of a laurel oak tree in the memory of Michael J. Costello, the Lake Windsor football captain, who was killed by lightning on September 5.

I said, "Do you two know about this Senior Awards Night next Friday?"

Dad was still trying, unsuccessfully, to make eye contact with Mom. He answered, "Sure. We'll all be going. They're honoring Mike Costello. And all of the other senior players, of course. Bill Donnelly is going to be the master of ceremonies."

I folded the sports section back up and handed it to Dad. The phone rang, and Mom picked it up. She looked concerned. She said, "No, we just got up. We haven't been outside at all." Then she said, "Oh my God." She got off the phone quickly and pointed at me. "Paul, you're dressed. Check all around the house. All around the outside."

"What's wrong?"

"That was Sarah from next door. She said somebody has smashed up all the mailboxes and spray-painted all over the wall."

I went out through the front door. Mom hurried to watch me through the side window in the great room. I saw our neighbor's mailbox first. It was smashed, all right, like an aluminum can, and it was hanging by a thread from its pole. Then I looked over to where ours should have been. All I saw was the pole, bent at an acute angle. There was no trace of the mailbox. I looked up and down the street. About every other mailbox had been smashed, probably by a baseball bat.

Then I went into the backyard. There was no paint on

228

the inside of the wall, so I climbed up on top of it and vaulted over. I hit the ground, turned around, and saw it— swirling lines of white paint, like fake snow, against the gray of the wall.

I was too close to make out what it said, so I started to back across the frozen mud ruts of the perimeter road. The wind was whipping up. The smoke was in my eyes, and my nose. I had to back all the way across before I could read the message. It said, SEAGULLS SUCK.

I'm not sure what happened next. I stood there staring at this sight, breathing in the stench of the muck fire, and I started to get the feeling. I started to remember something. Some place. Where was it?

The wind raised up brown clouds of dirt from the perimeter road and mixed them with the black clouds of the muck fire. The sun started to darken, like the moon was passing in front of it. And I started falling backward, as straight and as stiff as a tree.

That's how Dad found me, stiff and unconscious. He had to pick me up and carry me across the road. He started yelling over the wall to Mom to bring the Range Rover around. I remember telling him, "I'm OK. I'm OK." And I *was* pretty much back to normal by the time they got me onto the couch in the great room.

Mom said, "I'm going to call the doctor."

I said, "No. No, really, I'm all right."

Dad was totally stressed out. He started yelling at me, like it was my fault, "What happened to you? What did you do? Did you walk into a car?"

I said, "No. No, nothing like that."

Mom put her hand on my forehead.

I said, "I don't know. I can't remember. I really can't remember."

Mom looked into the backs of my eyes. She said, "This is all my fault. You had a cold to begin with, and then I sent you out into that disgusting air." She started into the kitchen. "I'm going to make you some tea."

Dad stared at me for a few more seconds. Then he joined Mom in the kitchen and talked to her about the mailboxes and the spray paint. He said, "I bet kids from Tangerine High did it after yesterday's game. They were mad about getting blown out like that." He's probably right.

Mom brought me a cup of hot tea with lemon. All day long she and Dad kept looking at me and asking me how I felt. I kept saying, "OK."

That was true, and yet it wasn't. The whole truth is—I feel very weird. But I can't say why. I can't *remember* why.

Not yet.

Monday, November 27

Today was supposed to be the day.

Mom insisted that I stay at home, although I told her that I felt fine.

I thought all day about Erik. About Erik and Arthur. At 10:00 A.M., I thought to myself, *Erik and Arthur have no idea, at this moment, that they're going to face Luis again this afternoon. And that this time he won't be alone.* At noon I thought the same thing. And I thought it again at two. I wondered if Erik would walk through the kitchen door with his eyes swollen and black. Or with his nose broken. I wondered what kinds of questions Mom would ask him. And would he answer them? I figured that Erik and Arthur would take the time to make up a mutual lie—like they had gotten jumped by ten guys from Tangerine High School, maybe the same guys who had vandalized our neighborhood. That would sound a lot better than the truth—that their own teammates despised them so much that they helped a stranger beat them up.

Anyway, Erik did walk through the kitchen door, but something, obviously, had gone wrong. He went straight to the refrigerator and grabbed a can of soda. I looked right at his face. There wasn't a mark on him. It hadn't happened. Something had gone wrong.

I was disappointed, but still confident. Something had gone wrong. That was all. I sat down at the kitchen table and tried to think. *Could it still happen to Erik and Arthur? When? How?* Then it came to me: *Yes, it could still happen. It could happen on Friday, outside of the Senior Awards Night. If Luis asks me about another time and place, that's what I'll tell him.*

Mom walked in with the phone. I hadn't even heard it ring. She said, "Not too long, please. I have calls to make before the homeowners' meeting tonight."

I pressed the button. "Hello."

"Hi, Paul? It's Kerri."

I held the phone out at arm's length. Then I shook my head, like a wet dog, trying to clear my thoughts. I finally said, "Hi."

"Yeah, hi. I, uh, I figured you were never going to call me, so I decided to call you."

"Uh-huh. Look, I'm sorry. I've been meaning to call you." I held my hands out in a gesture that she would never see. "I just didn't."

"Well, that's OK. Do you want to talk to me now?"

"Sure."

"I guess the last time I saw you was at the soccer game. You guys have a really great team."

"Thanks."

"I think it's great that you have girls and boys."

"Yeah. It was great. Did you see the paper yesterday?"

"I sure did."

"Three girls from our team made All-County."

"I saw that. Yeah. Did you see that thing about planting a tree for Mike Costello?"

"Uh-huh."

"Are you going to go? It's Friday night."

"Oh yeah. I'm going."

"Because I'm going, too."

"Oh yeah?"

"Yeah."

There was a pause, then she said, "Joey's having some kids over to his house afterward. Would you like to come with me? As my date?"

I didn't hesitate at all. I said, "Sure."

"Great."

I added, "Thanks for asking me."

"Sure thing."

"Does Joey know that you're asking me?"

"Oh yeah. He knows. He says we can ride over there with him and Cara."

I had a sudden, crazy picture in my head. Could Joey be listening to this? Could he be on the extension? Mom came in and pointed at the clock. I said, "I'm sorry, I have to go. I'll see you at the gym on Friday."

"OK, great. Bye."

"Bye."

Mom said, "Who was that?"

"Kerri Gardner, from Lake Windsor Middle. We're going over to Joey's house on Friday night, after the ceremony."

Mom took in this information. She waited—I guess, for more. But I didn't say anything else, so she started making her calls to the homeowners. It didn't sound like too many were interested in her meeting.

Mr. Costello arrived first, at about eight o'clock. I answered the door and let him in. He gave me a friendly greeting, as usual. I claimed my seat in the alcove at Dad's IBM. I pulled up the "Erik—Scholarship Offers" file as Mom and Mr. Costello settled into the living room.

Dad has been working on the file again. He has added the names and phone numbers of scouts and alumni boosters from the three Florida schools—people like Mr. Donnelly and Larry and Frank. He has also noted that a "press packet" from the *Times* has been sent to those schools. He hasn't added anything more to the other page 1 schools, and get this—the page 2 schools are gone. Deleted. Trashcanned. The Houston schools, and any other noncontenders for the national title, are gone. They have no place in the Erik Fisher Football Dream.

I clicked out of the file and started listening to the meeting. Mom was taking notes as Mr. Costello rattled off a series of items: a Rolex watch, a diamond stickpin, a twenty-four-carat gold bracelet.

I logged off and walked into the great room. Mom didn't suggest that I leave, so I joined them. I asked, "What are you writing down, Mom?"

Mom looked at me with a pained expression. Was I being a pain? "These are items that were stolen from the tented houses."

Dad came in and sat in one of the folding chairs. He didn't say anything to us; he didn't even look at us. It was like we weren't there. He just stared straight ahead at the fireplace, like he was waiting for it to flame on.

The doorbell rang, so I went to answer it. I let in a group of four homeowners. Mom suggested that they begin the meeting right away since no other people were expected.

It was smaller and friendlier than most homeowners' meetings. The eight of us listened as Mr. Costello read the financial reports. Then he turned to the old business. "We have good news on a couple of fronts. All I can say is, thank God for that freeze. It killed off all the mosquitoes, so we were able to cancel that guy with the gas masks and the sprayer."

Mom said, " 'Thank God' is right."

"The freeze also signals the end of the thunderstorm season. This is a fact that Mrs. Fisher and I have both brought to Bill Donnelly's attention. We have suggested a compromise to him—that he remove his string of lightning rods for now and put them back up next summer. He has agreed to think about it."

The man from the yellow Tudor asked, "What about the termites?"

"The freeze might have helped us there, too; I just don't know. Three houses have tents now, which makes a total of twenty-five so far in the development."

"And the robberies?"

Mr. Costello nodded solemnly. "There were two more robberies of tented houses since our last meeting. In both cases, robbers smashed a window, ran in, and ran out with cash and jewelry. The deputies say they have some leads, but that's all they're willing to tell us at this point."

The same man said, "I saw a guy sitting outside a tented house with a shotgun." Everyone reacted to that, and he continued, "He's one of your neighbors, Jack. He's sitting outside in a lawn chair, all night long, with a shotgun across his lap."

Mr. Costello said, "Thanks for telling me. I'll talk to him. If that doesn't do any good, I'll have the Sheriff's Department talk to him. We can't have that." Everyone agreed. "He's gonna wind up shooting some late-night jogger."

The woman from the white York asked, "What about the front, Jack? That's looking kinda run-down."

"The front is looking bad because of the freeze. Those plants are supposed to be cold-hardy, but nothing is going to come through a freeze like that completely undamaged."

The same woman asked, "Did the freeze kill off the rest of your fish?"

"No. We can't blame the freeze for that. Those koi are cold-hardy. That pond could freeze a foot thick and they'd be OK under the ice. We believe that some local person stole them and sold them."

I said, "I don't believe that."

They all turned and stared at me, as if they had just noticed that I was sitting there. Then they all turned back. They were about to ignore me and go on when I added, "That doesn't make any sense." They turned toward me again. "Think about it. How could some local person, some koi thief from Tangerine, stop at the front of our development, in that wide-open space, without anyone seeing him? How could he fish for, catch, and drive away with a string of big orange shiny fish with no one seeing him?"

Mr. Costello answered, "I don't know, Paul. Maybe because he does it in the middle of the night, when people are asleep. Anyway, it's the only theory we have. Unless you have a better one."

"The ospreys," I said. They all stared at me blankly. "The ospreys, the birds of prey, from those giant nests out on Route 89. They swoop down, snatch up the koi, and fly back to their nests. No one sees them; no one thinks about them; no one suspects them."

Mr. Costello seemed annoyed. They all did. He said, "You've seen this happen?"

"I've seen them flying west with the fish in their talons."

"How do you know they were our fish?"

"They were big and orange and shiny."

They all looked at each other. No one spoke. Finally, Mom said to me, "Paul, if you knew about this, why didn't you ever tell anyone?"

"No one ever asked me."

She looked at me with the pained expression again. "Is there anything else that we should ask you about?"

"What do you mean?"

"Do you know anything about the robberies?"

"No."

"Are you sure?"

"Yes."

Mom nodded. She believed me. The rest of them now seemed to be waiting for me to leave, so I got up. She winked at me and said, "Thanks. Good night."

As I started out, I heard one of the homeowners ask, "Did anybody see that *Eyewitness News* team report on the sinkhole? The one where they found out the county never surveyed the construction site? Why can't we get that *Eyewitness News* team out here? They can shoot pictures of the muck fire. We show them to the county and demand action." The guy looked around for support. Nobody moved. He added, "And if that doesn't work, we can sue the county."

Mr. Costello half smiled and pointed at Dad. "We'd be suing our host here."

Dad jumped to his feet and gestured for the crowd's attention. He looked absolutely frazzled. "I want you all to know something. I am determined to change things. That sort of nonsense, an unsurveyed construction site, will never happen again in this county. I can't change the past, but I'm putting some big changes in place—for now and for the future."

The homeowners listened, then turned to other matters. I continued on upstairs. I have to wonder about Dad, though. He was a wreck just now. He was coming unglued. What is going on in his head?

Tuesday, November 28

Luis Cruz is dead.

When I walked into first period this morning, there was a group of kids standing around and whispering. Henry D. came up to me and said, "Did you hear what happened?"

"No."

"Tino and Theresa were waiting outside yesterday for Luis to pick them up, but he never came. Theresa called home and told their father. He went out into the grove and found Luis lying there dead."

"Found him what?"

"Dead. Right out in the new grove."

I stared at Henry like he was crazy. "Dead? Are you saying that Luis is dead?"

"That's right. Their father called 911. Wayne was one of the guys on call. He said Luis was dead when they got there; that he had been dead for hours."

"Dead? Dead of what?"

"Wayne said it might have been an aneurysm, like a blood clot. He thinks Luis got hit on the head, it formed into a blood clot, and that killed him."

My mind was racing in circles. I finally said, "What? Someone hit Luis on the head and killed him?"

"No. Wayne said the sheriff's deputies don't think it was a murder or anything like that. They think Luis might have gotten hit on the head last Wednesday night, when all those frozen tree branches were breaking off. They think maybe one of the branches hit him on the head and started that aneurysm thing going. But they don't know anything for sure."

I put my hand over my mouth, afraid that I would throw up. I whispered, "He got hit on the head on Wednesday night?"

"They don't know that, they're just saying maybe."

"One shot to the head? Five . . . six days ago? How is that gonna kill anybody?" Henry could see how upset I was getting. He didn't reply. "I mean, you see these guys in these kung-fu movies getting hit on the head a thousand times, and they keep on fighting. Right?"

"Right."

I raised my hand and got Ms. Pollard's attention. I said,

"I gotta go. I'm sick again." I hurried into the hall, pushing past a stream of kids all the way to the office. I asked to use the phone and left a quick message for Mom. "Come back. Right away. I'm sick again." An aide led me into a sterile black-and-white room that turned out to be the nurse's office. I slumped down into a black chair and waited there—dry eyed, speechless, numb.

Mom returned at nine o'clock to sign me out. She told Dr. Johnson, "I guess we sent him back to school too early."

I rode home in a painful trance. Finally, when we pulled into our development, Mom said, "This cold of yours is really bad. It's really persistent."

I nodded slowly. "Yeah." I thought, *How could she believe that? How could she believe that I'm in the sixth day of a severe cold, when I have not coughed or sneezed even one time? Has it even occurred to her that that isn't the truth? That I might be making it all up? Probably not.* I decided to share part of the truth with her. I said, "Luis Cruz is dead."

She thought for a minute. "Who, honey?"

"Luis Cruz. He's Tino and Theresa's brother. He was at the grove the day you drove me out there. I guess you didn't see him. He came to nearly all of our soccer games. But I guess you didn't see him there, either. He used to pick tangerines on Merritt Island. He injured his knee doing that. He played goalie for Tangerine Middle School. He invented a new variety of citrus. Then a tree branch broke off and hit him on the head."

I looked over at Mom. She was nodding sympathetically. Did she want to hear more? Maybe the whole truth? Did she want to hear anything bad? Should I come right out and say, *Actually, Mom, he wasn't killed by a tree branch. He was killed by Arthur Bauer, on orders from Erik.* What would she do if she heard that? Would she swerve into a utility pole? Or would she do what she always did back in Houston—take my temperature and threaten to call the doctor?

I didn't say anything else. When I got into the house, I went straight to Dad's IBM and logged on. I put in a CD-ROM called *HealthText* and searched for "aneurysm." I found out that it's not a blood clot at all. It's a "weakening of a blood vessel," like a little bubble that swells out from a vein or an artery. That's all there was about it, so I got online, searching for a medical home page. The Tangerine County Medical Center listed one called "Ask-a-Nurse." I got into it and typed, "Can you get an aneurysm from an injury to the head?"

I received a reply right away: "No. You are either born with an aneurysm, or you are born with the tendency to get one."

I typed in, "Can an aneurysm kill you?"

"Yes. An aneurysm can burst, causing a massive stroke and death."

"What could cause it to burst?"

"The aneurysm gradually deteriorates due to the constant pressure of the blood passing through it."

"Could an injury to the head cause it to burst?"

"Yes. An injury to the head could further weaken the aneurysm and cause it to burst."

"Would this happen right away, or could it happen a week later?"

"It could happen right away, or a week after the injury, or a month after, depending on the condition of the aneurysm."

I typed in "Thank you," and logged off. I had my answer. Luis had been killed by Arthur Bauer on Tuesday, but it had taken six days for him to die. That shot from the blackjack had been just as deadly to Luis as a shot from a gun.

I went upstairs and lay on my bed until three-thirty. Then I called Henry D. "Henry, what else did you hear about Luis?"

"I haven't heard anything new from Wayne. I did hear from Dolly that Luis's funeral is going to be on Thursday at noon."

"Oh. All right. I'll be there. Do you think the whole team will go?"

"I expect so. They all knew Luis. A lot of us owed Luis for things. A lot of us got rides from him in that truck of his."

"Yeah. Look, if you hear anything else, anything at all, especially from Wayne, will you please give me a call?"

"I sure will."

At dinnertime, Mom knocked lightly on my door and brought in some vegetable soup and a basket of rolls. I pretended to be asleep. She put them down quietly and started to leave, but she turned and saw that my eyes were open. She said, "How are you feeling, Paul? How is that cold of yours?"

I didn't answer, so she just smiled weakly and continued out.

Wednesday, November 29

I stayed out of school again today. I got dressed at about ten and went out back to sit for a while. Mom came out with the telephone and handed it to me. "Another girl," she said. "A different one."

I waited until she went back in to press the button. "Hello."

"Paul Fisher?"

"Yes."

"This is Theresa Cruz."

"Theresa? I'm really sorry to hear about what happened—"

She interrupted me; her tone was all business. "Yeah,

I know that. Look, I have to tell you something: Don't you be coming to Luis's funeral."

I stammered, "Uh, OK."

"Henry says you're talking about coming. But Tino and Victor and those guys are saying some bad stuff. So you had better not show your face at Luis's funeral. I'm calling to tell you that."

"All right."

"I don't want any more bad stuff to happen, especially not at the funeral."

"No. Of course not."

"So I'm just telling you." Then she hung up.

I sat there with my mouth wide open. They knew! They knew everything! Theresa, Tino, Tomas and his brother, Victor and the others—they all knew the truth! They knew that Luis came looking for Erik last Tuesday. And they knew what happened to him at the school. They knew that he didn't get hit by any frozen tree branch. How did they know?

I jumped up and hurried through the gate to the front of the house. I turned left and headed down the sidewalk. I had to get away. I had to think.

My mind was racing with questions: *Did Luis tell someone about it? Of course he did. If he told me about it, he told other people, too. Did I really think I could keep this a secret from them all? Does everybody in Tangerine blame me now? Am I just as guilty as Erik?*

I was all the way down at the entrance pond before I stopped. I stood there and stared at the dark water until I finally understood. And it was so very simple. *There's no big mystery here. The truth about Luis is obvious to all of the people around him.* Their *lives are not made up of bits and pieces of versions of the truth. They don't live that way. They know what really happened. Period. Why would that seem so mysterious to me?*

I sat on the bank and stared at the lifeless water. After a few minutes I heard a noise behind me and turned. A little boy on a little bike had pulled up about ten feet away. He looked to be about five years old—not old enough to be out on the road by himself. He sat there staring at me, astride his red twenty-inch bike. Then he pointed at the pond and said, "They say there's a gator in there."

I looked back at the pond. I wanted him to leave, but he went on, "They say a gator came outta there last year and ate a kid."

I turned back toward him. "Oh yeah? Who says that?"

"My mom and dad."

I shook my head. "Well, forget it. That didn't happen."

He shook his head right back. "My mom and dad say it did."

I thought about that. I thought about my own mom and dad, and I looked him right in the eye. "Then they're lying to you. They're telling you a story just so they can keep you scared. They want you to be scared. Do you understand?"

He stiffened. "My mom and dad don't tell me stories."

I rose up onto my knees so that we were eye-to-eye. "Oh no? Did they ever tell you a story about a kid who went swimming right after he ate, and he got cramps, and he drowned?"

"Yeah."

"Well, did you ever meet that kid?"

"No."

"OK. Did they ever tell you about a kid who climbed a utility pole to get his kite back, and he got electrocuted?"

"Yeah."

"And did you ever meet that kid?"

"How could I meet him if he's dead?"

"How about a kid who got bitten by a stray dog, and he got rabies, and he started foaming at the mouth? Did they ever tell you about him? And did you ever meet him?"

The boy straightened out the front wheel of his bike and started to back away.

"My mom and dad don't lie to me."

I got onto my feet. My voice was rising. "No? How about this one: Did they ever tell you about the kid who went out to play football in a thunderstorm, and he got struck by lightning, and he got killed?"

He shook his head.

"Or this one: Did they ever tell you about the kid who climbed a tree with a sharp pair of clippers in his hand, and he fell out of the tree, and he stabbed himself? Did they ever tell you about either one of those kids? Did you ever meet either of them?"

"No."

"Well, I did. I met both of them."

He continued to back away. I shouted after him, "What about this one: Did you ever hear about this kid, this stupid kid who wouldn't listen to anybody, and he stared at a solar eclipse, and he went blind? Did you ever hear about him? Did you ever meet him?"

The poor kid pedaled away as fast as he could. I didn't watch him go. I bent over and looked down at my own murky reflection in the water. Like the final words of a ghost story, I muttered, "Well, you have now."

Thursday, November 30

Mom left the house at ten o'clock this morning. She was gone for most of the day. I was here alone.

At exactly twelve noon, I pulled out my blue suit from the closet, the suit that I had worn to Mike Costello's funeral. I put it on, without a shirt, shoes, or socks, and walked out through the patio doors, into the backyard. I must have looked like an idiot.

I walked straight out until I was facing the gray wall. I had no clear idea what I was going to do. I just knew that I had to do something. For a while I stood there staring at the ground, like an idiot. Then I bent forward and wedged both hands into the space between the wall and the sod. I pulled the sod up and toward me, so that the whole piece of it rolled back onto my feet with its roots sticking up. Beneath it was a rectangle of white sugar sand two feet long and three feet wide.

I got down on my knees, like an idiot, on that upside-down piece of sod, and started to scrape away the sugar sand. I scooped up big handfuls of it, piling them on either side of the rectangle, until I reached the dirt below. I stared at that dirt in fascination, thinking how odd it was that I had never seen it before. This was the dirt that we lived on. The dirt of the tangerine grove that we burned, and buried, and plowed under, and coated with sand, and landscaped over. Here it was.

The sweat started to drip off my forehead, fogging up my glasses. I yanked them off and threw them over to the side. I didn't even know where they landed. Then I bent over that hole in the dirt until my face was an inch above it. I thought about Luis Cruz, a man I barely knew. I thought about Luis Cruz being lowered into this ground, never to come back up. I felt the tears start to well up deep inside of me. Once they started to come, there was no stopping them. I wept, and sobbed, and poured tears into that hole in the ground. Like an idiot? No, I don't think so.

When I was finished I stood up, brushed the dirt from my knees and my elbows, and located my glasses. I pushed the sand back into place and rolled the sod back into position. Then I came back in here and threw my suit into the garbage.

It's remarkable. Strange and remarkable. I feel like Luis is a part of me now.

I feel like a different person.

Friday, December 1

It's nearly midnight on Friday. It's been a night to remember.

I just got off the phone with Joey. He called to find out if I'm all right. I think I am. In fact, I think I'm more than all right.

Joey said that everybody at his party was asking about me. I guess that would include Kerri, the date I never had. I told Joey everything that I knew about tonight, and he told me what he knew. Between us, I think we managed to piece together what happened at the Lake Windsor High School gym.

Let me start at the beginning. I took another bogus sick day today. Mom didn't care. She seems to be having problems of her own. She spent a couple of hours on the phone this morning, holding a yellow legal pad in her lap. I went walking through and I heard her talking to someone at the Sheriff's Department.

Anyway, both Mom and I managed to do what Dad asked—to be ready at six o'clock to go to the Senior Awards Night. I wore black pants that were too short for me and a white shirt that was too tight. Mom commented, "That's it, Paul. We have to get you some new clothes this weekend. Definitely."

The seniors had to be at the gym at six-thirty so they could learn where they were supposed to stand and what they were supposed to do. To Dad this meant that we had to arrive at six-thirty, too, even though Erik was riding with Arthur Bauer.

So there we were, standing outside the south entrance to the gym an hour beforehand. Some members of the football team were still carrying risers in and setting them up on the hardwood floor. The principal, Mr. Bridges, was pacing nervously and gesturing to Coach Warner. He finally settled down when a pickup truck arrived towing a boat trailer. It wasn't hauling a boat, though; it was hauling a tree—the laurel oak that would be planted in Mike Costello's name. The tree was a lot bigger than I had expected. It was about fifteen feet tall, and it was growing in an enormous plastic tub full of black dirt that was almost as wide as the trailer.

The driver of the truck swung around and backed up toward the gym door, following Mr. Bridges's hand signals. Mr. Bridges called out to the coach, "All right, now what do we do? How do we get it from here to the basketball court?"

Coach Warner disappeared inside and came back with four of his biggest seniors, including Brian Baylor. They spread out around the trailer and started talking about how to move it. Mr. Bridges opened the double doors for them. As soon as he did I could see Joey and his parents standing inside.

On the count of three, Brian Baylor and the other guys hefted the trailer up and off of the truck hitch. They started walking the trailer into the gym like a huge wheelbarrow. Everything went fine until they got to the spot where they were supposed to set it down. When Brian Baylor let his end all the way down, the big tub tipped toward him, the tree branches crashed down onto his head, and a huge pile of black dirt came pouring onto the gym floor.

Coach Warner ducked into his office beneath the bleachers and came out with a board and a pair of cinder blocks. Brian hefted up the trailer again and the coach slid the board and the blocks underneath it, straightening out the tub.

Mr. Bridges clapped his hands together and called out, "All right. Now let's get this dirt cleaned up."

Brian Baylor and the other football guys drifted away. They had no intention of touching that dirt. I walked over and started to scoop some back into the tub. Joey joined me right away. In a few minutes we had it all cleaned up.

Joey said, "Fisher, are you being a hero again?" I looked at him, but I couldn't tell if he was being serious or sarcastic. Then he took one of his black-smudged hands and made like he was going to press it onto my white shirt. I backed off, and we both laughed. Mr. Costello led us into Coach Warner's office, where we used the bathroom sink to wash up. The only other thing that Joey said was, "Do you need a ride to my house tonight? You and Kerri?"

I said, "Yeah."

When we came out from under the bleachers, there was a lot more activity in the gym. Mom and Dad had staked out seats just above us, about six rows up and on the aisle. Mom leaned over and said to me, "Paul, get a program from that girl."

I looked over and saw a Student Council girl in a blazer standing on the basketball court, right next to the tree. She was holding a pile of programs. Joey and I went up to her. She turned to him and said, "You're Mike's brother, aren't you?"

He said, "Yeah."

She smiled and told him, "Mike was a really good guy."

Joey just nodded. Then he pointed at me and said, "And this is Erik's brother."

The girl showed some mild interest. "Erik Fisher?" I shuffled uncomfortably. She handed me a program and added, "Mr. Generosity?" I must have looked really confused. She laughed, said, "He sure is a great kicker," and turned to greet some new arrivals.

Mr. and Mrs. Costello started gesturing to Joey to come. They had joined Mr. Donnelly on a low riser near center court. I said to him, "I'll catch you later," and climbed up the steps to sit with Mom and Dad.

I could see that the low riser was going to be the focal point of the ceremonies. There were six chairs on it, a table covered with trophies, and a microphone stand. Behind it were three rows of risers; each one was six inches taller than the one before it. All of the bleacher sections on our side of the gym had been pulled out, and they were filling up quickly. On the far side of the gym, only the center sections on both sides of the exit had been pulled out. The marching band, the Seagirls, and the rest of the football team, the guys who weren't seniors, were sitting there.

I caught sight of Kerri and Cara. They were in the top row, about five sections to the right of us, near the east entrance. They were looking right at me. They smiled and waved, and I waved back. I saw a few other kids from Lake Windsor Middle School come in, Joey's friends. They all climbed up to that same section. That Adam kid was with them, but he didn't sit next to Kerri.

A high-pitched wail of feedback snapped my attention back to the front riser. Mr. Bridges was standing at the microphone, getting ready to begin. He said, "If everyone will take their places, we can get started."

Everything was arranged in descending steps. Across from us, against the far wall, the blue uniforms of the band members filled two sections from top to bottom. Then the white-and-blue robes of the chorus singers filled three risers, from high to low. On the front riser were Coach Warner, Mr. Bridges, Mr. Donnelly, and the Costellos. To their right, or my left, was the laurel oak tree. And in the space in between, at floor level, were the other honored guests of the evening—the senior football players.

The leader of the chorus raised her hand, and we all got quiet. The chorus and band performed a song called "Try to Remember."

After the song, Mr. Donnelly took over the microphone. He talked about sportsmanship, and about how Mike Costello was a role model. He read some lines from a poem called "To an Athlete Dying Young."

Mr. Donnelly then called on the president of the Student Council, a tall guy in a blazer, to come up and read a statement about the laurel oak tree. The statement was a lot longer than it needed to be. He read a long list of names of "people who helped make this possible." I found my attention drifting back to the right, about five rows up. But when I looked over there, my eyes never got past the east entrance. I bent forward and heard myself whisper, "Oh my God."

There they stood—Tino and Victor. It was like a mirage. It was impossible. They couldn't be there. And yet they were. They were standing together on the sideline staring straight ahead, hard-eyed, totally focused, like the wrath of God.

They continued to stare at the front, and I continued to stare at them, as the Student Council guy finished and Mr. Donnelly returned to the microphone. He began to introduce the senior football players, reading from the program listing: "Brett Andrews, Arthur Bauer, Brian Baylor..."

I looked back at Mr. Donnelly. He was relaxed, smiling, totally unaware of any problem. As he read each player's name, the player walked out and stood facing us, in front of the people on the riser. "... Terry Donnelly, John Drew, Erik Fisher..."

I looked back at Tino and Victor, and my blood turned cold. I became terrified. What had they come here to do?

I didn't have to wait to find out. Tino took off at a brisk walk down the sideline, Victor right behind him. They silently closed in on the front riser as Mr. Donnelly continued to read the names.

But then, suddenly, Mr. Donnelly became aware of their presence. He stopped reading, looked up at the two of them marching forward, and smiled. You could almost see the wheels turning in his head. Something like: Had he forgotten to introduce these youngsters so they could come up and read the poem they had written?

He soon had his answer. Mr. Donnelly, and the rest of us, watched in absolute silence as Tino crossed the hardwood floor and walked directly up to Erik.

Erik never saw it coming. Tino brought his right leg up and around in a vicious karate kick that doubled Erik over and filled the gym with a sickening *Hoooh!* sound from his emptying lungs. Then Tino stepped back, measured the distance, and brought his knee up into Erik's face. A sharp sound, like the snapping of a twig, echoed in the gym. Then Tino, his voice trembling with rage and choked with tears, shouted, "That's for Luis Cruz! I take care of his light work."

I could sense Dad standing up next to me. But that's all he did. He stood up and stared at Tino. Everyone on the floor, on the risers, and in the stands seemed frozen in place.

The first person to move was Arthur Bauer. He moved toward Erik, I suppose to protect him from further damage—but he never got there.

Victor took off at a full sprint. Arthur turned just as Victor's head drove into his midsection. Arthur went flying backward into Brian Baylor, who pushed him away.

Suddenly all of the people in the stands were released, and they went crazy—jumping up and screaming and yelling.

Victor jumped on Arthur and started pummeling him furiously, landing roundhouse blows to his head so fast that his arms were a blur, like the nylon strings on a Weed Whacker.

Coach Warner bellowed above the rest of the voices, "Grab them! Grab them!"

Some of the players obeyed. They jumped Victor from behind and pulled him off of Arthur Bauer. Coach Warner himself grabbed Tino, who was still standing over Erik's prostrate body.

But Victor could not be held. One of his captors slipped and fell on the blood that had spilled out of Erik's nose. Victor broke free and ran. The seniors chased him and trapped him, like a snarling wolf, up against the emergency exit door. They charged at him, hit him, and drove him into the red bar that says ALARM WILL SOUND. And that's exactly what happened. The alarm went off. The door flew open. Victor slipped their grasp and was off, running into the night.

Mr. Bridges took the microphone and started pleading for order, but Coach Warner was screaming over him, screaming at the players who'd let Victor get away. He twisted Tino's arm into a hammerlock and started walking him quickly toward the sideline, toward his office, toward me.

All I remember next is Mom shouting "Paul!" as I took off, flying through the air. I landed hard on Coach Warner's back and held on tight, riding his neck and shoulders. He lurched to one side, losing his grip on Tino. I felt one huge hand come around and grab my hair, yanking me forward, right over his head. I bounced off the floor just as Tino hit the exit door. He, too, was gone into the night.

I got pulled to my feet by a couple of football players who dragged me under the bleachers and into the coach's office. I thought they were going to beat me up, but then Dad burst into the room, along with Coach Warner. I was relieved for about two seconds. And then Dad himself was in my face, grabbing me by my shirt and screaming, "I oughta kill you for that! Are you crazy?"

Coach Warner seemed a little more in control. He pointed a big finger at me and demanded to know, "Who are they?"

I stared him down, which made Dad even madder. He screamed, "You heard the man! Who are they?"

I stared Dad down, too. He turned to Coach Warner and reported, "My wife thinks they're from his soccer team. The Tangerine Middle School soccer team."

The coach shook his head slowly and asked Dad the big question, the question that everybody in that gym had to be asking. "Why?"

Dad worked his jaw muscles, at a complete loss for words. At the same time, he loosened his grip on my shirt. Out of the corner of my eye I saw that the coach had an emergency exit door of his own. I didn't hesitate. I hit that red bar at full speed and never looked back. I sprinted across the parking lot, around the football stadium, and out onto Route 89.

I ran for my life, at full speed, like I was sprinting down the sideline of an endless soccer field. I kept that pace up all the way to Lake Windsor Downs. I veered off onto the perimeter road and stumbled along over the packed dirt until I found myself at the wall behind our house. Then I stopped still, clutching my side, gasping for air, doubled over in pain.

When I was able to, I looked up at the wall. The paint had been cleaned off, but the words were still faintly visible in the moonlight: SEAGULLS SUCK. I stood studying that wall for many minutes. Then I felt headlights on me, too high up to be a car's headlights. I turned and watched the Land Cruiser pulling up slowly and unevenly in the rutted dirt.

Erik and Arthur stayed inside for a minute, invisible behind the tinted glass. Then a bolt of light shot into my eyes, snapping my head back. It was the Land Cruiser's center spotlight—huge, bright, and powerful, like a setting sun.

Erik and Arthur opened their doors and got out, leaving the motor running and the headlights on. They stepped around in front, so that the lights were on me while they remained in shadow. Still, I could see that their faces were swollen and bloody. And I could see that Erik was holding a metal baseball bat in one hand. I understood that I was supposed to be terrified by this spectacle—these two demonic creatures on this dark, lonely road. But for once in my life, I wasn't.

I stepped forward and faced them, just as I had seen Luis do. I held my hands out, as he had done, and said, "I'm not afraid of you, Erik. Come on."

Erik stood in his pose, not moving. But Arthur did move. He produced the blackjack and began to tap it into his hand. I thought to myself, *Can you really be that stupid? Can you really still be carrying around the murder weapon?*

When they finally spoke, it wasn't terrifying, it was lame. They started in on the same routine as always. Erik made his remarks, and Arthur repeated them, as if nothing in their pathetic lives had changed. As if they had not just been beaten up by a pair of seventh graders in front of the entire football team and five hundred other people. Erik posed and talked, and then Arthur repeated:

"You're going to pay for what happened tonight."

"Oh yeah. You're gonna pay."

"You're gonna wish tonight had never happened."

"Oh yeah."

I couldn't stand it. I took another step forward and challenged him, "Come on, Erik, let's see if you can do any better with me than you did with Tino."

Erik stopped, his rhythm broken. I could see that his nose was pushed over to one side. He tried to ignore my interruption. He poked the bat at me. "We'll decide what's going to happen to you."

"We'll decide."

"Maybe you'll be in the right place, but maybe it'll be the wrong time."

"Oh yeah. It'll be the wrong time."

"And then it'll happen."

I took another step forward. Now I could see swelling

around Arthur's eyes. I said, "I've already been in the right place at the wrong time, you lowlife creeps. You pathetic losers. I was under the bleachers on Tuesday afternoon." I raised my finger like it was loaded, and I pointed it at Arthur. "I saw you kill Luis Cruz."

Arthur's swollen eyes widened, and he took a step backward. Erik shot a quick look at him. Then he turned back to me. "Who's going to believe you, you blind little geek? You're blind! You can't see ten feet in front of you. Nobody's going to listen to you!"

Erik stared at me with growing fury, with growing hatred, moving the bat in a tight circle. I could see that his eyes, too, were starting to swell closed.

I ignored him. I continued to speak to Arthur. "And I'm not the only one who saw it."

Erik snapped, "He's lying!"

But Arthur had heard enough. He said, "Come on. Let's get outta here."

Erik shouted, "He's lying! He's lying! He's lying!" Until he completely lost control. He started smashing the bat into the mud ruts in front of him, grunting with rage at every blow. Then he turned and unleashed a furious shot at the right headlight of the Land Cruiser. The glass exploded, sparks flew, and the light sputtered out.

Arthur's voice was trembling, pleading, "Come on! Come on! Let's get outta here!"

Erik was still in his rage. He was talking to Arthur Bauer, but he was staring at me when he roared, "Shut up, Castor!"

Then, deep breath by deep breath, the rage started to recede. Erik backed up, step-by-step. He turned and threw the bat into the Land Cruiser. He got in, and Arthur got in, and they drove quickly away. They drove away leaving that name, Castor, hanging in the air like some horrible apparition, like the key to a lock, like the solution to an unsolved crime. I turned my head slowly back toward the wall, and I remembered something from long ago:

A silver-gray wall.

It surrounded a development called Silver Meadows, where we lived when I was four and five years old. I remembered Castor. Vincent Castor. He was Erik's goon back then. He followed Erik around and did whatever he was told.

I remembered spray paint on that wall. Erik and Vincent Castor had found a can of white spray paint, and they had painted something on that gray wall. I don't even know what it was. I never did. I just knew that Erik and Vincent Castor had done it. All the kids in the development knew that. But I never told anybody about it.

I remembered coming out to play in the morning and not being able to find any of my friends. Where were they? Did they know something? Did they know what was about to happen to me?

I remembered walking into our garage and hearing Erik's voice, cold and menacing. He said, "You're going to have to pay for what you did."

I said, "What? I didn't do anything."

"You're going to have to pay for telling on Castor. You told who sprayed paint on the wall, and Castor got into trouble. Castor doesn't like getting into trouble."

I turned around and saw Vincent Castor. He was holding a can of spray paint. Then I felt Erik grab me from behind, easily pinning both of my arms with just one of his. I could hear my voice crying, "I didn't tell! I didn't tell!"

And I remembered Erik's fingers prying my eyelids open while Vincent Castor sprayed white paint into them. They left me screaming and rolling around on the floor of the garage. Mom came out and tried to drag me over to the hose to rinse out my eyes, but I fought like a wildcat. She managed to push me into the backseat of the car and drive me to the hospital.

Somewhere around that time, so they say, there was an eclipse of the sun. I didn't remember that. But I remembered all the rest.

I stood for a little while longer, until I was sure there was nothing else to remember. I climbed over the wall, hopped down, and crossed the yard to the back door. Mom and Dad were sitting on stools at the breakfast nook, looking at a yellow legal pad, when I walked in.

They were ready to jump on me, no doubt about it. But I jumped first. I said to Mom, "Do you remember Vincent Castor? From Silver Meadows?" Mom and Dad looked at each other. There was no question about it. They remembered. "Do you remember him, Mom? Dad? He was the Arthur Bauer of his day."

Mom turned deathly pale. She said, "What's this all about, Paul?"

Dad tried to regain control. "Listen, there are questions that need to be answered about tonight."

I exploded. "No! No, sir!" I yanked off my Coke-bottle glasses and shook them at him in a rage. "There are questions that need to be answered about these! Am I such a stupid idiot fool that I stared at a solar eclipse for an hour and blinded myself? Is that who I am? Am I that idiot?"

They didn't answer. They didn't look at me. They didn't even seem to be breathing.

Dad was looking down at the yellow legal pad when he said, "You were five years old, Paul. There was only so much you could understand. All you could understand was that something bad had happened."

Mom spoke with her eyes closed, as if she weren't really there, as if she were coming in over the radio. "I was so terrified that you would be blind. But the news wasn't all bad. They told me that you would *not* be blind. They told me that your eyes would heal, slowly." Her eyes opened, but her voice started to fade away. "They told me that you might lose your peripheral vision. Or you might not. But you would not be blind. That was the good news." Then Mom started to cry. With her face still frozen, like a statue, she started to cry.

I lowered my voice and said to her, "Let me ask you one thing, Mom. When you got home from the hospital that day, did you see the white paint on Erik's hands?"

She didn't hesitate. "Yes."

"Did you know what happened?"

"Yes."

No one spoke for a couple of minutes.

Dad continued to examine the legal pad in front of him. Then he said, "The doctors told us that you might never remember. And we figured that that was the best way to handle the situation." He shook his head sadly. "We wanted to find a way to keep you from always hating your brother."

I answered, "So you figured it would be better if I just hated myself?"

That did it. Dad was finished. He broke down. It was frightening to see. He didn't cry like a statue, he cried like a baby. After a minute I left them sitting there, snuffling and feeling sorry for themselves, and I came upstairs.

That brings me up to Joey's phone call asking me if I'm all right. I *am* all right. I'm more than all right. Finally.

Saturday, December 2

Joey was back on the phone with me at nine o'clock. He said, "Fisher? They haven't arrested you yet?"

"No. Not yet."

"Hey, doesn't Betty Bright have a yellow Mustang?"

"Yeah."

"Well, it's parked in front of Mr. Donnelly's house."

"Yeah?"

"Maybe she's in there rattin' you guys out for last night."

"No, she wouldn't do that. Anyway, she doesn't have to. They know who I am. And they know where to find Tino and Victor."

"Yeah. I guess so. Well, I thought you might want to know."

"Sure, thanks. I'll check it out." I hopped on my bike and hurried to Mr. Donnelly's. The air was hot and still and smoke-filled. I saw the yellow Mustang up ahead. Someone was sitting in front, on the passenger side. I pulled up next to the window and saw a familiar face.

"Shandra?"

Shandra turned her dark eyes toward me. She seemed to be miles away, lost in thought. She finally said, "Fisher Man, you live around here?"

"Yeah."

She nodded and pointed at Mr. Donnelly's house. "Do you know this guy?"

"Uh-huh. Mr. Donnelly. The sportswriter."

She explained, "Coach Bright and my brother, Antoine, are in there talking to him." She seemed to drift away again, but then she said enthusiastically, "Hey, I heard what you did last night!"

"Oh yeah? Did Antoine tell you?"

"No. Antoine wasn't there."

"No?"

"No. He stayed at home." She slipped back into her far-away voice. "You know, he's the star of the Lake Windsor High School football team, but he doesn't live in Lake Windsor. He lives in Tangerine."

"I understand. I kinda do the same thing. I live in Lake Windsor, but I play in Tangerine."

"But you don't have to lie about what you do, do you? You don't have to live a lie every day of your natural-born life, do you?"

I shook my head no, and she continued. "That kind of lie eats away at people, day by day, till it makes them sick at heart. And that's why Antoine didn't show up to collect any awards last night. He was feeling sick at heart."

I sat back on my seat and asked her, as casually as I could, "Is he just feeling guilty about lying, or what?"

"I don't know. I guess it's not just one thing. He felt real bad after that last game, beatin' up on Tangerine High like that. They were all his homeboys, you know, the kids he hung out with just a couple of years ago. He didn't want to beat them that bad, embarrass them like that." Shandra looked down and lowered her voice some. "And I know he felt bad about me, about me not being able to put my own picture in the paper, even though I earned the right to. About me not being able to show pride in myself, because I'm afraid of giving him away. Because I'm afraid of somebody looking at me and saying, 'That's Antoine's sister. How come she plays for Tangerine and he plays for Lake Windsor?'"

I thought about her running from the camera and from Mr. Donnelly. Now here she was, sitting in his driveway. What was going on? I said, "Shandra, is there something else? Is there some other reason why Antoine is feeling so sick at heart?"

Shandra's eyes burned into me. She answered intensely. "Yes, there's something else. They won't tell me what it is, but there's something else. Antoine was on his knees crying last night. And that wasn't about his homeboys, and that wasn't about me. He couldn't stop himself. I got scared, so I called Coach Bright. Coach and Antoine stood outside and talked for a long time, then they came in and called up Mr. Donnelly. Now here we are."

259

I heard the front door slam. I turned to see Betty Bright coming down the walkway toward us. Antoine Thomas and Mr. Donnelly were still standing in the doorway, shaking hands.

Betty Bright looked tired, sad eyed, but she managed a smile when she saw me. "Paul Fisher. Hey, I heard what you did last night."

"Hi, Coach."

She looked down at me. "Are you coming back next year?"

"I sure hope so."

"My girl Shandra here is moving up to the high school. I was thinking of maybe trying out a boy in the goal."

I laughed, but then I said, "I'll do what you say, Coach. But I don't want Shandra's job. I want Maya's."

"Is that right? OK. Whatever. I want you back."

I heard the front door close again. Antoine Thomas came toward us, walking slowly. He's Betty Bright's height, but wider and all muscle. She said to him, "You OK?"

He answered, "Yeah," in a low, calm voice.

"Then it's all taken care of?"

"Yeah. He'll be running the story tomorrow." He looked down at Shandra. "We're telling the truth now. Understand? Don't tell anybody anything but the truth from now on."

Antoine looked over at me casually. Then his eyes narrowed.

Betty Bright said, "This is Paul Fisher. He's one of my players."

Antoine studied my face. He said, "You're Erik Fisher's little brother?"

I tightened up at the sound of Erik's name. I mumbled, "Yes."

Antoine said quietly, "It's time to start telling the truth, little brother. Do you understand what I'm saying?"

I nodded like I understood. But I didn't. Not really. Not until he added, "Don't spend your life hiding under the bleachers, little brother. The truth shall set you free."

I nodded with real conviction now. I said, "Yes! Yes!"

Betty Bright and Shandra were clearly puzzled, but they didn't ask any questions. Antoine said to them, "Come on, we've got one more stop to make." He looked back at me. "We've gotta tell somebody else the truth."

The three of them backed out and drove away quickly, without another word, leaving me alone in Mr. Donnelly's driveway.

I repeated to myself, "Under the bleachers!" And I knew what the next stop was going to be. Antoine was going to the Sheriff's Department to tell them what he had witnessed, to tell them that he had witnessed the murder of Luis Cruz.

Suddenly I was startled by the sound of the garage door opening and the sight of Mr. Donnelly backing toward me at high speed. I had to push off quickly to get my bike out of his way. He slammed on his brakes and rolled down the window. He was all flustered.

"Are you OK, Paul?"

"Yes, sir."

"I'm sorry. I should have been looking. There are too many kids around here. I should have been looking."

"That's OK. I'm all right." He didn't say anything else, so I did. "I just talked to Betty Bright. She said that she brought Antoine Thomas to see you."

"That's right. Did she tell you what we talked about?"

"No, sir."

Mr. Donnelly thought for a few seconds. "Then I'd better not tell you, either. Let's let everybody find out the right way, in tomorrow's paper. OK, Paul?"

"OK."

Mr. Donnelly pulled away, leaving me wondering what

Antoine could have told him. I pulled out onto the road and started pedaling, thinking, *I guess we'll all have to wait until tomorrow*.

I managed to avoid Mom and Dad for most of the day. I know they were in the alcove for hours with that yellow legal pad. At five o'clock the three of us sat down in a circle around a pizza, but no one was hungry.

Mom said to me, "We're going to have an important meeting here tomorrow at noon, Paul. We'd like you to attend."

I said, "OK."

Dad added, "We've invited some people. You should be one of them."

"OK."

We all picked at the pizza in silence, and then we all reacted to the same disturbing sound. It was the sound of a chair scraping on the floor overhead. Erik, apparently, was holed up in his room—hiding his face.

Sunday, December 3

I was up before dawn today, waiting for the news. The bad news. I was standing on the sidewalk when a white van with squeaky brakes drove up. A thin arm reached out of the passenger-side window and tossed the Sunday edition of the *Tangerine Times* onto the driveway. It was oversized, and heavy, and double-wrapped in a plastic bag.

The same thing was happening all over Lake Windsor Downs; the same thing was happening at all the other developments. The white vans were pulling up, and these fat plastic bags were flying out the windows, bursting like water balloons in the homes of the football fans of Lake Windsor High School. It sure was a mess.

Our phone started ringing at 7:00 A.M. Dad answered it upstairs and heard the bad news from another football father. I don't even know which one.

I was already down in the great room, reading all about it. The story filled the bottom right-hand corner of the front page. It took up two columns there and was continued on page 10. The headline said, "Lake Windsor Athlete Confesses in Football Scandal." There was a photo of Antoine Thomas leaving the Tangerine County Municipal Building with the caption "Star quarterback Antoine Thomas leaves emergency meeting of the Tangerine County Sports Commission."

The front page was just the tip of the iceberg. The article continued inside, with photos, charts, and quotations spread across all of pages 10 and 11. There were photos of Antoine, Coach Warner, and the three members of the Tangerine County Sports Commission. There was a chart showing the territorial boundaries of Lake Windsor High School and Tangerine High School, and another chart showing the Lake Windsor football records before and after the arrival of Antoine Thomas. The quotes were from Coach Warner and Mr. Bridges. They were both "shocked" by the news. Neither admitted to knowing anything about anything.

The article itself began, "The Tangerine County Sports Commission, meeting in emergency session last night, voted to nullify all victories by the Lake Windsor High School football team over the last three seasons. This drastic action was taken in response to a confession made by Lake Windsor quarterback Antoine Thomas to the Commission members. In a signed statement, Thomas confessed to lying about his eligibility to attend Lake Windsor High School."

The article quoted a Commission member as saying that Antoine "had contacted them, had met with them, and had presented them with a notarized statement." The same member said they "had no choice but to uphold the regulations of the Commission and to nullify all the victories in which Mr. Thomas was involved."

I couldn't believe what I was reading. I had thought that *maybe* Lake Windsor would get fined. Or they would have to forfeit their last victory against Tangerine High. But not this. I never even suspected that the Commission had such power. It was like they were rewriting history.

Lake Windsor had had a 7–3 record in Antoine's first season; they were 9–1 the next season and 10–0 this season. That's a total of 26 wins and 4 losses. Now they're 0–30. 0 wins and 30 losses over the last three seasons.

And if that's not bizarre enough, every record that they set with Antoine on the team has been nullified, too. There was a boxed list of those. Most of the records belonged to Antoine Thomas, but Erik Fisher was in there for the longest field goal, the highest field-goal percentage in a season, and the most extra points in a season.

Not anymore. They're all nullified.

There was another article that focused on a guy who lives in Tangerine, on the same street as Antoine Thomas. He's a black guy about twenty-five years old, who had played football at Tangerine High and then at Florida A & M. This is part of what he said: "Everybody knows how it is. If you want that big-time football dream, that Heisman Trophy thing, you get out of Tangerine. No big-time scouts ever come here. Ever. So you get yourself an address in Lake Windsor. You have your mail sent there, but you continue to live here. You live a lie. Everybody knows what's happening. Nobody asks any questions . . . But now Antoine is the one standing up saying that it's all a lie, so people have to listen."

I had finished reading all of the articles in the front section by the time Dad walked into the great room. He still had the phone in his hand, and he had forgotten to turn it off. I could tell by his face that he had already been told the basic facts. I handed over the front section without comment, and looked to see what there was in the sports section.

Dad sat down in a heap on the floor. He finally turned off the phone, and he started to read. But the phone rang again immediately. He listened impatiently, then said, "I have no idea. I haven't even had a chance to read the paper yet." He hung up again and held the paper in front of him with both hands, like he was grabbing some guy by the lapels.

I left him alone and examined the front page of the sports section. The left side had a column written by Mr. Donnelly, with the strange title "Thoughts on an Imaginary Porcelain Plate." I almost didn't read it, thinking he had written the column before all of this Antoine Thomas stuff had happened. But I was wrong. Here is the entire column:

Not too many people know this.

For twenty years I held the Tangerine County record for the most passing yards in a single game. How I got that record had as much to do with the weather conditions as it did with my talent as a quarterback, but I didn't care. The record was mine, and I was proud of it.

On the night when I set my record, Tangerine High was playing Suwannee High during a violent thunderstorm. By all rights the game should have been called off, but no one in authority had enough sense to do that. As the lightning flashed and the thunder cracked, I, the unsung quarterback of an unsung team, rose up out of that mud not once, but twice, to achieve football immortality.

Twice we were pinned on our own five-yard line, and twice I dropped back, slipping and sliding, and heaved the ball. Twice a receiver ran under that heave and kept on running, 95 yards into the end zone. In two plays, I had passed for 190 yards. In the rest of the game, I would pass for only 37 more, but the damage had been done. The old record had been shattered. The new record was mine. It went into the record book this way: "Most passing yards in a single game, 227, William F. Donnelly, Tangerine High."

I have actually seen this record book at meetings of the Tangerine County Sports Commission. It's an old red book. And yes, I have looked up my name. That name, written by hand in a fat old book, is *it*. It's all you get. There is no trophy, no plaque, no certificate, no plate. You get that one handwritten line plus the knowledge, inside of you, that you hold the record.

Well, that wasn't enough for me. I needed something more splendid, something that I could picture in my mind. So whenever I thought about the record, which was often, I imagined a fine porcelain plate. It was a large white plate, encircled with fourteen-karat gold edging. A plate that you would display proudly on the back wall of a trophy case. A plate that gleamed at visitors and invited comment. But it was also a fragile plate, one that would last only until fate smiled on some other quarterback rising up out of some other mud puddle.

Miraculously, my plate hung intact for twenty years. When it was broken, when my record finally fell, it had nothing to do with a lucky heave or a slippery surface.

Antoine Thomas of Lake Windsor High School broke my record midway through his sophomore season. He broke it on a sunny Saturday up at Lake Windsor High, playing against my old school. In that game, he threw for 250 yards and 5 touchdowns.

But that was just the beginning. Antoine Thomas would break my record six more times. (Actually, after the first time, he was breaking his own records.) He would go on to rewrite that old red record book in dozens of single-game, single-season, and career categories, becoming the most dominant player of his, or any other, generation.

Now all that has changed.

The Tangerine County Sports Commission has ruled that Antoine Thomas was not legally eligible to play for Lake Windsor High School. Therefore the records that he broke were not legally broken.

Do you realize what this means?

The Tangerine County Sports Commission has gathered up the shards of my porcelain plate, Krazy-Glued them together, and handed it back to me.

I'm looking at it right now. I guess they meant well, but they did a lousy job. I can see the cracks, like the lines of age on a face. I can see the globs of glue, like tears that will not fall. I can see chips and missing flakes in the gold edging where the circle has been broken.

Thanks, Tangerine County Sports Commission, but no thanks. I'm not putting this thing back in my trophy case. I wouldn't even put this thing out in a garage sale. This is nothing to be proud of.

Antoine Thomas holds the record for the most passing yards in a single game. Antoine Thomas is the greatest quarterback in the history of Tangerine County.

Everybody knows that.

I was glad that Mr. Donnelly had put in one good word for Antoine, because it was clear that no one else was going to. The phone kept ringing.

A strategy was emerging from the calls that Dad received and made. They were going to blame Antoine, and Antoine alone. The families, the coaches, the teachers, the fans were all denying that they even dimly suspected that anyone was breaking any rule at any time.

Give me a break. After I heard Dad telling an assistant coach that he, too, was "shocked by the news," I couldn't take it anymore. I said, "Dad, have you ever seen any of the Lake Windsor High football guys out running?"

He looked as if he was surprised that I was there. "What?"

"Have you ever seen any of the Lake Windsor High football guys out running? Like, along the roads?"

"Yeah, sure. Why?"

"Have you ever seen them riding tenspeeds, or shooting hoops, or playing tennis?"

"Yeah."

"Have you ever seen them driving their cars?"

"Yes."

"OK. Now, have you ever seen Antoine Thomas doing any of those things? Have you ever seen Antoine out running or biking or driving anywhere around here?"

Dad looked at me curiously, but he still didn't get it. He answered, "No. I can't say I have."

"Have you seen him at the supermarket? Or at a pump at the gas station? Or getting some fries at McD's?"

Dad was nodding his head now, but he wasn't agreeing with me. He was getting annoyed. "What is this about?"

"I guess it's about your eyesight, Dad. Your eyesight, and Coach Warner's, and Mr. Bridges's, and everybody else's who's 'shocked' today. Because I've seen lots of those Lake Windsor guys in lots of places. Everywhere we go, in fact. But I've never seen Antoine Thomas. I've never seen him anywhere except at the football stadium. That's because he doesn't live around here, Dad. He lives in Tangerine. Everybody knows that."

Dad looked down. He knew that I was right. He knew the truth. The phone rang again, but he didn't answer it.

Sunday, December 3, *later*

With everything else fighting for room in my head, I must confess that Mom and Dad's "important meeting" didn't seem very important to me. That's why it took me by surprise.

As I came downstairs I heard Mom's voice, tense and upset. "I want this thing to be over with, completely finished, everyone gone, by the time my parents get here."

Dad was just as tense. "What? And you think I don't? I don't want them butting in on this."

They were setting up the great room, setting it up as if for a homeowners' meeting. They arranged ten chairs facing the fireplace for the "guests" and another ten chairs off to the side, by the kitchen. These chairs, as it turned out, were for the "families"—two families—the Fishers and the Bauers.

As the guests arrived, they were handed sheets of paper by Dad. I took one for myself and read it. It was a list of items, items that had been stolen from houses in Lake Windsor Downs, as compiled by the Tangerine County Sheriff's Department. There were notations like "Rolex watch, $900, recovered" and "Pearls, antique, $500, not recovered."

By one o'clock all of the guests had been seated. I knew who most of them were. They were from Joey's street, the street where all of the houses had been tented. That's what they all had in common. The white Tudor, the gray

269

Lancaster, the yellow Stuart—today they were all the same. Today they were all the Blue Tents.

The chairs off to the side were occupied by Mom, Dad, Arthur Bauer, Sr., Mrs. Bauer (who I had never seen before), and Paige Bauer. Arthur Bauer, Sr., looked angry; the rest of them looked sick at heart. Arthur Bauer, Jr., had joined Erik out on the patio, where the two of them were slouching silently. Mom and Dad had set out a pair of chairs for them next to their families, but they weren't sitting in them. I wasn't sitting in my family chair, either. I chose a place on the couch, next to the coffee table.

Mom stood up to open the meeting. But before she spoke, she turned and looked outside at Erik. Then she walked into the kitchen, opened the patio door, and said, in a trembling voice, "Erik, would you come in here, please?"

Neither Erik nor Arthur moved.

Mom waited them out, in front of everyone. Silence filled the great room like an embarrassing smell. Finally, Mom repeated, "Erik, would you come in here, please?"

Arthur Bauer, Sr., leaned around the corner and barked, "Arthur! Get in here!"

First Arthur, then Erik, staggered to their feet and moved slowly inside to the empty chairs next to their families. When they sat down there was a low gasp as the guests looked upon their horrible faces. Erik's nose was blood red and swollen. His eyes were mere slits and rimmed with black, like a raccoon's. Believe it or not, Arthur looked worse. Arthur's face was covered with purple bumps and red cuts. His lips were cracked and swollen, too. He looked out of place among humans, like an ogre in a storybook.

Mom picked up her notebook, opened it, and started to speak in an even, formal voice. "On behalf of the Bauer family and the Fisher family, I want to thank you for coming. It is my duty to inform all of you of the following." She looked down at her notes and read: "On November twenty-second, I made a shocking discovery. While out at our storage bin, searching for boxes of winter clothing, I found a gym bag that did not belong there. When I opened this gym bag, I found a U.S. Army gas mask, a pair of rubber gloves, and a plastic supermarket bag filled with diamond earrings, watches, gold rings, and many other types of precious jewelry."

This time there was a loud gasp from the audience, including me.

"That afternoon I spoke with Sergeant Edwards of the Tangerine County Sheriff's Department. You probably know his name. Sergeant Edwards confirmed that the items in the gym bag matched the descriptions of the items that were stolen from your homes while they were tented."

Mom closed the notebook and made eye contact with the guests. "It didn't take a genius to figure out the rest. These items were stolen by Erik Fisher and Arthur Bauer. They have admitted as much. They have had no choice but to admit it. Arthur used the gas mask to enter the tented homes. Then he stole items from those homes while Erik kept watch outside."

She pulled out a copy of the sheet that each guest had been given. "We have recovered some of the items already. My husband will tell you more about that. Erik and Arthur gave some of your things away, and we are working on getting them back." Mom nodded at Paige. "Paige Bauer has already returned the items that were given to her. Her friend Tina Turreton, who agreed to come here today but who obviously has not shown up, has already returned what was given to her. They have also provided us with names of other Lake Windsor High School students who received stolen items from Erik and Arthur. We have contacted the parents of all of those students and are confident that we will be able to get back those stolen items." Mom stared blankly at the guests for a minute, then said, "My husband has more to say to you."

Dad stood up as Mom sat down. He picked up where she left off. "That's right. Sergeant Edwards is the Tangerine County officer in charge of all of your cases. He has allowed us, and by 'us' I mean the Fishers and the Bauers, to approach all of you with a plan to make restitution. That is, Erik and Arthur will make full restitution to all of you for all of your stolen property. If any item cannot be recovered and returned, Mr. Bauer and I will guarantee its full value to you in cash." Dad held up his copy of the list of stolen items. "You can see what we have already recovered. Those items could be released to you as early as tomorrow. If we can get all of you to agree to this restitution plan, and it has to be *unanimous* agreement, then the Sheriff's Department will not pursue further charges against Erik and Arthur."

I felt sorry for Dad at that moment. He just couldn't give up. He had too much invested in the Erik Fisher Football Dream, and he just couldn't give up. I wanted to say, *Look at Erik's face, Dad. That's what he really looks like.* But I kept quiet.

The phone rang, so I leaned over the coffee table and grabbed the portable. It was Joey, and he was practically screaming into the receiver. "The sheriff's deputies are at Arthur Bauer's house! They're sitting in a car out front."

"Oh yeah?"

"Yeah. They stopped me on my bike. They asked me if I knew where he was."

"I know where he is."

"Yeah? Where?"

"He's right here."

"Whoa! Can I tell them?"

"Yeah. Why not?"

Joey slammed down the phone.

Arthur Bauer, Sr. was speaking now. He was angry. "I've talked to my son about this. He has admitted his wrongdoing, he has said he is sorry, and he has made full disclosure of the facts. The question today is, Do you want to prosecute these two dumb kids and possibly ruin their lives? Or do you want them to make full restitution to you, like men, and get on with their lives? Do you want to give them a second chance or not?"

I searched the faces of the people from the blue tents. Their jaws were set. Their eyes were focused on the ugly faces of Erik and Arthur. The Blue Tents clearly felt no pity for those two thieves sitting in their chairs, staring at the floor—voiceless, useless, lifeless—like a pair of mannequins in a Dumpster.

One man spoke up against Mr. Bauer. He said, "Don't go blaming me for ruining your kid's life. I didn't ask your kid to break into my house."

Mr. Bauer answered coldly, "No, of course you didn't."

The man turned to the others and continued. "Why should they escape all punishment for their crimes? That's not justice. What if the cops had nabbed two kids from Tangerine for robbing our houses? They'd be in jail now."

Mr. Bauer waved the list at him. "Yeah. And you'd never see your property again. If this gets into the court system, you might never get your things back."

The man shouted, "What is this? Blackmail? If I don't agree, I don't get my stuff back?" He looked at the others. "We're getting robbed all over again."

Mr. Bauer was furious, but controlled. "Yeah, well, maybe you're the one person in the world who never did anything wrong in his life. Maybe you were born perfect. Maybe you were never a dumb kid once."

The man didn't back down. "I'll tell you what I never did. I never broke into an old lady's bedroom, and ransacked through her underwear drawer, and stole her pearl necklace that was handed down to her by her own grandmother, and then gave it to my girlfriend like I was a big man or something. I never did that. And I don't know anybody else who did, either. Your kid, and that other kid, are in a class all by themselves."

Mr. Bauer didn't reply. He was so angry that he walked back to his seat and sat down, leaving no speaker at all in front of the meeting.

Dad got up again, looked at them all, and asked simply, "Do you accept our plan for making restitution or not?"

What choice did they have? In the end the Blue Tent people accepted the plan, reluctantly. They agreed, reluctantly, to give Erik and Arthur that second chance. The second chance you get when your parents can guarantee full restitution. The second chance you get when you can kick a fifty-yard field goal.

The meeting broke up quickly. Mr. Bauer led his family directly to the door. The other guests started to file out, solemnly, silently. But then they stopped in their tracks. Something was blocking their passage. I hurried over to the side window and looked out.

The first thing that I saw was Joey. He was straddling his bike out on the sidewalk. He was squinting in the sun. I looked to his left, and there they were! Two sheriff's deputies—one thin with blond hair; the other big and muscular, with a black mustache. Joey pointed out Arthur Bauer, and the two deputies started toward him. Arthur and his father stopped still, right in front of my window, while the rest of the guests and the families squeezed out onto the driveway. The big deputy asked, "Are you Arthur Bauer?"

Arthur nodded meekly. The deputy said, "Extend both hands, please, Mr. Bauer." Arthur did, and the deputy calmly clicked a pair of handcuffs onto his wrists. His partner circled Arthur and started to pat him down, looking for a weapon.

I hurried to the door and pushed my way through. The big deputy was reading Arthur his rights: "Arthur Bauer, you are under arrest in connection with the murder of Luis Cruz. You have the right to remain silent..."

Arthur's father was paralyzed, in a state of shock. But when he heard the charge, he yelled out, "Wait a minute! Arthur, is that the guy you told me about? The guy at football practice?"

Arthur, terrified, nodded his head rapidly. His father continued, "Listen, officer. This is not right. This is a mistake. Arthur told me all about this guy, back when this first happened." The deputy, whose name tag said SGT. ROJAS, started walking with his prisoner, not listening.

"Arthur told me about a guy who showed up at football practice looking for a fight. He didn't belong up there. He was just looking for trouble. Am I right, Arthur?" Arthur continued to nod. "He came up to Arthur and took a swing at him, so Arthur hit him back. One time. Am I right?" Arthur nodded. "And that was the end of it. The guy came up there looking for a fight, and he found one. The guy didn't even belong up there."

I couldn't listen to any more of this. I shouted, "He belonged up there!" Arthur's father turned to see who had said this. I went on, "He belonged up there as much as you and your stupid kid do." I looked at the blond deputy. "The weapon that he used to kill Luis Cruz was a blackjack."

This made Sergeant Rojas stop in front of the open door of the police cruiser. He turned and stared at me. So I added, "It's probably still in his Land Cruiser, back at his house. It was there on Friday night, anyway."

Sergeant Rojas called over, "How do you know he used a blackjack?"

"I saw him do it. I saw Arthur Bauer sneak up on Luis Cruz, like a coward, and hit him on the side of the head. Luis never even saw it coming."

Sergeant Rojas told the blond guy, "Get on over there and guard that vehicle until I get back." The blond deputy took off running.

Sergeant Rojas turned back to me. "What else did you see?"

I stood up straight and faced them all, like I had seen Luis do. "I saw—I heard Erik Fisher tell him to do it."

The heads in the crowd all turned together toward Erik. Sergeant Rojas pointed one finger at him and ordered, "You—get over here."

Erik shuffled forward, like he was already wearing leg irons. The sergeant demanded, "Is that true?"

Erik looked at Dad. Dad repeated the words, "Is that true?"

Erik hesitated for just a moment, then started to nod. At Dad, at the sergeant, at everyone in the crowd. Steadily, up and down, he nodded to us all.

Sergeant Rojas instructed Dad, "You keep this young man in the house—not in the neighborhood, not in the yard—in the house. I may call or come back at any time, and I expect him to be here."

Dad whispered that he understood. The sergeant turned his attention back to me. "Do we have your statement, son?"

"No, sir." Then I felt compelled to add, "I wasn't brave enough to give my statement."

He eyeballed me. "Are you willing to give a statement now if called upon?"

"Yes, sir."

He put one hand on Arthur's head and pushed him down into the seat in the back of the cruiser. The rest of the Bauers hurried into their car to follow. I stood there with Joey and watched them pull away.

The people from the meeting drifted off toward their homes, shaking their heads and talking. Joey held out his fist, and I banged my fist down on it. He said, "I'm gonna hustle over to Bauer's and see what that deputy does."

"OK."

"I'll talk to you later."

Once Joey rode away we found ourselves alone—Mom, Dad, Erik, and me. We walked together back up the driveway and into the garage. Erik stopped by the door, turned, and looked at me through his swollen eyes. I looked back through my thick lenses. He seemed to be struggling with something. Maybe a memory. Maybe he was reliving a scene from long ago.

The four of us remained posed there, like we were frozen in time. Four frozen figures from the Wonders of the World exhibit. Mom finally broke the spell when she whispered to herself, "Oh no. Not now."

We all turned to see Grandmom and Grandpop walking up the driveway. Mom whispered again, "What are we going to tell them?"

I knew the answer to that. "We're going to tell them something bad, Mom."

Grandmom and Grandpop stopped at the top of the incline, framed in the rectangular opening. Grandmom said, "Caroline? Have we come at a bad time?"

Mom shook her head. "No. You're right on time. You're here right when you said you'd be."

Grandpop looked hard at Erik. He asked him, "What the hell happened to your eyes?"

Erik answered him in a surprisingly strong voice. "I got kicked in the face, Grandpop. Some kid kicked me in the face."

Grandpop glanced over at me, and then back at Erik. He gave him a short nod, like he understood.

Erik said, "Excuse me." Then he opened the door and disappeared inside.

Dad gestured to Grandmom and Grandpop to come in, too. They exchanged a worried look and then started forward. Mom and Dad led us into the kitchen and sat at the round table.

Grandmom and Grandpop looked me up and down. Then Grandmom asked her usual question, "How are you, Paul?"

"All right. I'm all right."

Grandpop clapped me on the shoulder. "That's good."

I dragged over a stool from the counter so the five of us could sit around the table. Erik wasn't anywhere to be seen. I figured he'd gone upstairs to his room.

Mom and Dad took turns talking, just as they had at the meeting. Grandmom and Grandpop didn't seem surprised by any of what they heard. They took it all in without even blinking.

When it was over, when we had told them every bad thing there was to tell, we paused and waited. Grandmom put her hand on her heart, sighed deeply, and said, "You know what I'm going to tell you, Caroline."

Mom closed her eyes.

"You're paying now for what you didn't do back then."

Mom agreed with her completely. "I know. I know."

But Dad wasn't so quick to surrender. He said curtly, "That's easy to say now. It's easy enough, seven years after the fact, to say I-told-you-so."

Grandmom replied flatly, "We're not saying that."

Grandpop leveled a stare at him. "We *did* tell you so. Erik did need help. He needed a doctor's help."

Dad countered with, "No. Erik did not need a doctor's help. He did not need drugs. He did not need to be one of those medicated kids who float around all the time like they're underwater."

"What drugs? We're not talking about drugs. The kid

278

needed to know which end was up, that's all. First off, he needed to get his backside whipped for hurting Paul."

Dad looked away. He clearly wanted out of this conversation. I guess we all did, because we all sat for a long minute in silence.

Grandpop finally said, "OK, let me be the one to apologize. I don't have all the answers. I'm not saying I do." He said to Mom, "We're family. That's all I know. We'll help you any way we can." He said to Grandmom, "I think the best thing we can do right now is get down to Orlando and leave them alone."

Mom tried halfheartedly to talk them out of it. Dad didn't say a word. He drifted off toward the great room.

Mom said, "At least take a tour of the house. That's what you came here for."

Grandmom and Grandpop exchanged another look. Grandmom said, "A quick tour."

I tagged along behind them on a fast lap around the ground floor. We passed by Dad sitting in his alcove in front of the IBM. I watched him as Mom pointed out things in the great room. He was sitting in a trancelike state in front of the screen, with the green light of the "Erik—Scholarship Offers" file washing over his face.

Mom described the top floor briefly, but she didn't take them up there. The tour ended in the foyer at the front door. Grandmom said, "It's a lovely house," and stepped outside.

Grandpop, however, was not quite finished. He signaled "just a minute," climbed the stairs, and turned left. He knocked, waited a moment, and then spoke quietly to Erik through the door. Then he came back down to Mom. He told her, "It's a beautiful house, all right. Nothing like those places I made you live in. Huh?"

Mom looked like she might cry.

Grandpop put an arm around her shoulder. "Good luck

279

to you in it, honey. Good luck to you from here on." Then he hurried out to catch up with Grandmom.

Mom watched them drive away down the street until the ringing phone pulled her back inside. She picked it up, listened briefly, and answered, "We'll be there." Her eyes drifted over to mine. She spoke in a weary voice—a voice beyond anger, beyond upset. "That was your principal, Dr. Johnson. She wants to see both of us in her office tomorrow morning, at seven-thirty sharp."

Monday, December 4

Mom and I had to leave a half hour earlier today in order to be at Tangerine Middle School by seven-thirty. I packed my books and my lunch like I was going for a normal day. What did I know?

Mom drove tensely, silently, angrily. I can't say that I blame her. In just one week both of her sons had gone from success to failure, from public praise to public shame. I tried to picture Mom in our climate-controlled storage place: Finding that gym bag. Not recognizing it. Wondering whose it was. Deciding to open it to find out. Staring at the items inside. Pulling them out one by one. The awful truth appearing to her gradually, like a slowly developing Polaroid.

We pulled up in front of Tangerine Middle at seven twenty-five. Absolutely nothing was happening. None of the karate kickers were on the sidewalk. None of the gangstas were hanging out. None of the buses were pulling into the loop. I had never been there so early before.

We walked through the front doors and climbed the stairs to the main office. Dr. Johnson was just inside the glass doors talking to two other adults—Tomas Cruz and a woman who I recognized from the soccer games. She looked a little like Victor, so I guessed she must be Mrs. Guzman.

Dr. Johnson shook hands with my mother, very seriously. She looked at me and said, "Paul, why don't you wait out in the hallway for a few minutes? We'll call you."

Dr. Johnson led the adults to her inner office. I drifted back through the glass doors, into the hall. I heard light footsteps on the stairs, so I started watching the second-floor landing. A familiar brown ponytail appeared. Then a familiar face. I said, "Theresa! Hi."

She didn't really look at me. She came to the top of the stairs and said, "So there you are."

I said, "Did they call you in, too?"

"No, not me. Just Tino and Victor. They're inside."

"They are? I didn't see them."

"Yeah. They're in there. Dr. Johnson probably put them in the nurse's room. That's where they usually wait."

"Oh? Why are you here?"

"Me? I'm always here early. For my job."

"Office aide?"

"Yeah, right. That's me."

Theresa and I stood together, with our backs to the glass wall of the office. We stood for a whole minute like that, in silence, like two strangers waiting for a bus. Then I remembered, and I reached into my backpack. I pulled out the science report, laser-printed in four colors, with a clear plastic binder. I handed it to Theresa. "Here. I was hoping I would run into you. I finished putting together the report. I hope you like it."

Theresa took it and studied the title, printed in tall orange letters with black shading. She read it out loud, "The Golden Dawn Tangerine."

She leafed through the report, looking at the pie chart for "The Varieties of Citrus Grown in Tangerine County" and the bar graph for "The Decline of Citrus Acreage in Tangerine County." She whispered, "This is beautiful. This is an A-plus for sure."

Theresa looked me in the eye and smiled, but not for long. Suddenly, like they had sprung a leak, her eyes filled up with big tears that rolled down her cheeks. She shook her head from side to side and demanded to know, "Why did you do this?"

"What? Do what?"

"All of it!" She held up the report. "All of this! All of it! Why did you come to my school? And come to my house to work? And jump on some coach? Are you crazy? You messed up your whole life. Do you know that?"

I had never seen Theresa angry or upset. Now she was both. I tried to calm her down, but she went on, "Listen! You're not one of these guys. Do you understand that? You're not one of these guys who're sitting in the office all the time waiting to get punished. You don't even belong here. You don't live in Tangerine. You live in Lake Windsor Downs. And you're going to have to keep on living there. You're going to have to go to that high school. You're going to have to face that coach and everybody else who was in that gym. Tino and Victor don't have to do any of that. Tino and Victor are going to walk away from all of this." She looked away, shaking her head at my absolute stupidity. She took several deep breaths, then she looked back at me and repeated, calmly, "So why did you do it? Why did you jump on that coach?"

I raised up my shoulders and let them fall. "I've thought about that a lot over the last three days. I spend a lot of time thinking about stuff. Probably too much. But that night, in the gym, I didn't think at all. I just did it."

Theresa wiped her cheek on her sleeve. "Yeah? Well, you really messed up. Tino and Victor got caught anyway. They always do."

We fell silent again and settled back into our positions against the wall. I tried to lighten the mood. I said, "Maybe this is all your fault. You're the first one I met here. You're the one who took me around."

She didn't know if I was kidding or not. She said, "So how's that make it my fault?"

"You introduced me to Tino and Victor."

"Yeah. Well, you said you wanted to play soccer."

"But you didn't have to do that. You could have let me sink or swim on my own."

Now she smiled, slightly. "Yeah. I could have let you sink." She pointed to the office. "Dr. Johnson told us that some kids were coming here from Lake Windsor because their school fell down a sinkhole. I don't know. I guess I figured you'd all be looking down your noses at us. And some of those kids were. But not you. You acted like you were happy to be here. You liked it here. Then you said you wanted to play on the soccer team ... I don't know. I guess I felt sorry for you. Especially when I thought about what Victor and those guys might do to you."

The door to Dr. Johnson's office opened. Theresa and I both looked in that direction. She said, "Whenever Luis talked about you, he called you Paul. I'm gonna start calling you that, too." She took me by the arm. "Come on, Paul."

She led me into the office. Dr. Johnson walked out and said, "Theresa, would you go ask Ms. Pollard to come up here and to bring Paul Fisher's file with her?"

Theresa gave me a silent squeeze on the arm and took off to do the errand. I peered into the inner office. I could see Mom's profile. She was crying. Dr. Johnson said, "OK, Paul, come with me. You can wait in the nurse's room. We'll be calling you boys in one at a time."

She led me down the short hall and opened the door to the nurse's room. Tino and Victor were in there, sitting in black chairs against the white wall. They seemed smaller, younger, than I remembered. Like little kids. They certainly weren't nervous. I guess they had been in here too many times.

Tino continued to stare straight ahead, but Victor popped up in his seat and started in on Dr. Johnson. "Oh no, Dr. Johnson! You're bringin' the wrong boy in here now. Fisher Man was just sittin' up there with his mama and papa. He just fell outta those bleachers like he fainted or something. He's lucky he landed on that dude. That broke his fall." He turned to Tino for support. "Fisher Man fainted out there in the grove last week. Am I right?" Tino ignored him. "Dr. Johnson, he might have a brain tumor making him faint like that. That boy needs an X-ray."

Dr. Johnson shook her head and said quietly, "Things are bad enough, Victor. Don't make them worse. Now come along with me."

Victor opened his eyes wide and looked at me. Then he got up and followed Dr. Johnson out of the room. I sat down in his chair, next to Tino.

He surprised me by speaking right away. "When you get in there, don't be runnin' your mouth like that fool Victor. All you say to Dr. Johnson is 'Yes, ma'am,' 'No, ma'am,' and 'Thank you, ma'am.' Understand? You take your three weeks' suspension, and you go home."

I said, "Three weeks? You figure that's what it'll be?"

"Yeah." Tino shifted around in his chair, but he still wasn't looking at me. He went on, "And you can tell Tuna for me that we weren't disrespecting his brother or anything like that. We just had to take care of business."

"I think he knows that."

"Yeah, well, you tell him I said so."

"OK."

Suddenly Dr. Johnson opened the door and signaled that it was Tino's turn to follow her. I was left in the nurse's room by myself, staring at the eye chart. It seemed like it was about two minutes later when she came back for me.

I followed her into the inner office. Mom was sitting in the same spot. Her eyes were red, but she was no longer crying. Dr. Johnson stood behind her desk, held up a thin white booklet called *The Student Code*, and said, "I've already explained this to your mother, Paul. The school board has set down its policies in this booklet, and we are all obliged to follow them. It is my duty to explain to you what violation you committed and what penalty you will receive." She held the booklet out in case I wanted to read it. She explained, "Your violation is called a 'Level Four Infraction,' in this case, 'assaulting a teacher or other School Board employee.' This is the most serious level of infraction. The penalty for this and for any other Level Four Infraction is expulsion."

Dr. Johnson paused to make sure I understood. I don't think I did. I was thinking to myself, *Three weeks, I'm supposed to get three weeks*. She continued, "As of today, you are expelled from all Tangerine County public schools for the remainder of this academic year."

She paused again and looked at me. I heard myself say, "Yes, ma'am."

Dr. Johnson set down the *Student Code* booklet and asked, "Do you have any questions about this?"

I thought of *No, ma'am* and *Thank you, ma'am*, but I couldn't say them. I was too confused. And I did have questions. I said, "What about Victor and Tino? Are they expelled, too?"

Dr. Johnson frowned. I could tell that she didn't want to talk about them. She pointed back at *The Student Code* and said, "No, Paul. Their violation falls under the Level Three Infractions, 'fighting with another student.' The penalty for that is three weeks' suspension."

I nodded. What else could I say but, "Thank you, ma'am."

Dr. Johnson moved toward the door, so Mom got to her

feet. Dr. Johnson said, "Your mother has decided to waive your right to appeal. Basically, Paul, you did it, you got caught, and you got punished. On the positive side, you have already completed enough days to get credit for this semester. There are options available to you. Your mother has selected the option of enrolling you in a private school to complete the second half of seventh grade."

We were all moving out the door by now, into the main office. Other kids were coming in and out. Dr. Johnson held out her hand, and I shook it. She said, "I wish you well in that option, Paul. Good-bye, Mrs. Fisher."

And she was gone. Just like that. I guess I had expected more. I guess I had expected a pep talk, or a stern speech. But she got rid of me as quickly as she had gotten rid of Victor and Tino. The office was starting to fill up with kids, and Dr. Johnson was needed elsewhere. The day had begun. The students at Tangerine Middle School were doing what they always did, but I was not among them. I was no longer one of them. That realization hit me suddenly, like a smack in the face.

I followed Mom down the two flights of stairs, keeping my head lowered so that I wouldn't have to look at anybody. When we got to the front door, I could hear the sounds of the mob of kids outside.

The karate kickers had arrived. So had the gangstas. They were all doing what they did every morning. Being wild. Being loud. Until they saw me. Then, in a heartbeat, it all stopped. They all stopped what they were doing to stare at me.

Mom and I stood at the top step and stared back at them. She said, "Paul? What do they want?"

I could hear mumbling from different areas in the crowd. They were saying stuff like, "That's him," and "That's Fisher."

One of the biggest and baddest eighth-grade gangstas

moved toward us with his boys right behind him. Mom let out a frightened noise and whispered, "What are they doing?"

I turned toward her and said, out of the corner of my mouth, "No fear, Mom. Show them no fear."

I walked slowly down the steps. Mom stayed where she was. The mob parted slightly, just enough to swallow me up. That big eighth grader held his fist out, and I put mine down on top of it. He said, "All right, Fisher!"

Suddenly they were all on top of me, all these guys I didn't really know. Guys who didn't really know me. They started pounding me on the back, rubbing my hair, shaking both of my hands at once. They were all saying stuff like, "Way to be, Fisher." "Hang tough." "Keep your head up, man." It was a strange moment for me, among these big, bad strangers. Their words surrounded me, and picked me up, and moved me along toward the car.

I could hear Mom yelling over the top of them, "Paul! Are you all right in there?"

Mom had worked her way around to the driver's-side door and was fumbling with the keys. I opened my door and turned back to the mob. I couldn't think of a thing to say, so I just stuck my thumb up in the air, awkwardly, and slipped into my seat. They all turned and headed back to their usual places.

Mom quickly locked the doors, and we peeled out. By now she was more puzzled than scared. She waited until we were safely away to ask, "What was that? What was that all about?"

I curled up my lip. "They know a bad dude when they see one."

"Paul! You are not a bad dude."

"Oh no?" I jerked my thumb back toward the mob. "Do you see any of those wusses getting expelled? From every public school in Tangerine County?"

Mom breathed a loud sigh. "You'd think those would be the worst words a mother could hear." She shook her head back and forth. I didn't know if she was going to laugh or cry. She laughed. "Not in this family!"

We drove through downtown Tangerine. Mom said, "Well, I'll tell you, I for one am glad you're out of that place."

She wasn't glad for very long. I informed her, "I'm going back, Mom. Next year. I already talked to the coach about it. And I'm going to make the All-County Team."

Mom said with certainty, "You can't do that." And then with less certainty, "I don't think you can do that."

I quoted Gino's words. "They make exceptions for lots of guys. They're gonna make one for me."

"We'll have to see about that."

"There's nothing to see about. I've made up my mind."

Mom shook her head some more, but she didn't seem to be upset. She certainly wasn't crying. Maybe she had gone over the edge. Maybe we both had. For whatever reason, a strange feeling of calm had come over us. We reached Route 89 and turned south. I said, "Wrong way, Mom."

"Depends on where you're going."

"Where are we going?"

"The mall. We're going to buy you some clothes that fit."

"OK."

"And some uniforms."

"Some what?"

"Blue pants. White shirts. Blue ties."

"You're kidding."

"Nope. This is your option."

"You're sending me to St. Anthony's?"

"That's right. Dr. Johnson called the principal for me, Sister Mary Margaret. She agreed that you could start there on Wednesday, in the seventh grade, on a trial basis."

"A trial basis? You mean she wants to find out if I'm too bad a dude to keep there?"

"Yes. I guess that's what she means."

"You mean that I'll be walking in there with a bad reputation? That kids will fear me?"

"I wouldn't go that far."

"Well, I would. I know all about fear." I thought about other new schools that I had entered. "Do you realize, Mom, that I've never been anything but a nerd? And now I'm going to enter this nerd school, not as a fellow nerd, but as a feared and notorious outlaw?"

"It's not a nerd school."

"Oh yes it is. I've been there. October twelfth. Some of them may remember me from that day. I rode up there with the War Eagles. We laid them to waste, 10–0. There was fear in their eyes. And there will be again when I walk in on Wednesday."

"Paul, please. You need to take this 'option' very seriously. Not everybody gets a second chance."

I thought, *Yeah, tell me about it, Mom.*

We pulled into the mall. Then we went on an enormous shopping spree, unprecedented in my lifetime. Mom was out of control. She let me buy everything that I even thought about wanting. She never said no; she never even hesitated. Bag after bag. Store after store. Sneakers, jeans, jackets, shirts, socks, underwear.

When we got home, I went upstairs with a pair of lawn-sized garbage bags. I dumped out the old clothes from my dresser. Then I pulled out the old clothes from my closet. I filled both bags and went back for two more. I put everything into those big green bags and then piled them in the garage for the Goodwill pickup.

Then I started to work on my new stuff—pulling out pins, cutting off tags, throwing away paper. Drawer after drawer, hanger after hanger, I filled up my dresser and my closet with new clothes that fit.

Tuesday, December 5

Dad had to take Erik down to the police station this morning to talk to Sergeant Rojas. They were there from seven-thirty until ten-thirty. When they got back, Erik went straight up to his room.

Dad came into the kitchen and told Mom and me, "Arthur Bauer is trying to blame Erik. He's saying that Erik put him up to it. Erik denies it. He says Arthur misunderstood him. It's a big mess." He poured himself a cup of coffee and added, "The police will sort it out. It's their job, not mine."

I said, "What do the witnesses say?"

"I know that Antoine Thomas and Brian Baylor have given statements to the sergeant. They both say that it was Arthur who actually assaulted the guy."

"The guy's name was Luis."

Dad nodded and corrected himself, "I'm sorry. Luis."

I thought about Erik's group of flunkies. I asked, "What about friendly witnesses?"

"Erik and Arthur don't have any friends. Not since we started rounding up all of that stolen jewelry. No. Nobody but Arthur Bauer, Sr., is saying it was a fair fight."

Mom had her elbows flat on the tabletop and both hands up under her chin, like she was holding her own severed head. She asked, "So what's going to happen now?"

Dad answered calmly, almost casually, as if it didn't have anything to do with him. "Now the wheels of justice will turn. Slowly but surely. Each of them will have to answer for whatever it was that he did. I'm not interfering anymore."

I looked back at Mom. She, at least, seemed worried about her firstborn son. Dad, on the other hand, seemed more like those friends who had abandoned Erik, who now regretted ever getting involved with him in the first place. He turned to me. "Paul, Sergeant Rojas wants a statement from you, too. He wants you to type up a paragraph or two describing exactly what you saw and what you heard. You know, what really happened. You can give it to me, and I'll drop it off at the Sheriff's Department."

I said, "OK. I can do that."

The phone rang in the great room. I walked over to the coffee table and picked it up. I heard a familiar voice. "You gotta get yourself a better lawyer, homeboy."

"Tino? Yeah, I guess you're right."

"So . . . what's up? What are you gonna be doing with yourself?"

"I'm starting up at St. Anthony's on Wednesday."

Tino snorted with contempt. "St. Anthony's! Those losers? You gotta be kidding me."

"Hey, I didn't say I was going to play for them. I'm playing for the War Eagles next year."

"Oh yeah? You don't think you're gonna start, do you?"

"I know I'm gonna start."

"Yeah, well, we'll see about that."

"What about you?" I asked him. "What are you gonna be doing?"

"Oh, I got lots to do. You know, it's what they call a blessing in disguise. Luis has been advertising the Golden Dawns in all the trade papers. There's a big response, just like he said there would be. He's got orders from growers all over Florida, from Texas, from California, even from down in Mexico. I gotta help our daddy get all those orders filled. I gotta help him with a lot of the other stuff that Luis did, too." Tino paused, then he said awkwardly, "Hey, uh, Fisher Man, anytime you want to come out and work in the groves, you come on out. You're on the crew. You know what I'm sayin'?"

I knew what he was saying. I answered, "Yeah. Yeah, thanks. I want to. That's something I really want to do. You just tell me when."

"You know when. Time and temperature, right? When the sun's goin' down, and the wind's comin' up, and the temperature is thirty-nine, thirty-eight, thirty-seven. You know what's gonna happen next. And you know where we'll be."

"I'll be there, too."

"All right."

"Maybe I'll even stay awake this time."

Tino snorted again. There was a pause, then he said, "Hey, uh, good luck at that St. Anthony's place. I don't know anything about it, except that we beat their butts every year."

"They gotta wear uniforms."

"Is that right?"

"Yeah. And they got nuns teaching there."

"No way! Nuns?"

"Yeah."

"All right. Well, don't you go gettin' wild like you do. I don't want to hear about you jumpin' out of the bleachers on the Pope or anything like that."

"No. You won't."

"You take care of yourself, brother. I'll see you in the groves."

"Yeah. Bye." I hung up. But I heard that word "brother" echoing long afterward. I looked up at the ceiling, and I heard Erik pacing back and forth, back and forth, in the cage that he had made for himself.

Tuesday, December 5, *later*

I came upstairs after dinner to write out my account of the crime for Sergeant Rojas. I logged on and went back through all my journal entries, from Houston until today. Then I started writing. I didn't finish until after 9:00 P.M.

I started with the basic facts, a paragraph or two, but I couldn't stop there. I had too much to say. I started writing about Luis, and what he meant to the people around him, and how they depended on him, and why they looked up to him. Then I tried to write the same thing about Erik: What did he mean to the people around him? How did they depend on him? Why did they look up to him?

I don't suppose the police are interested in all of that. That's not their job. But it's a part of the truth. A big part. And as Antoine Thomas told me, "The truth shall set you free."

I went downstairs, handed the disk to Mom and Dad, and said, "Here. Here's the whole truth. Here's what really happened."

I went into the kitchen and poured myself a glass of orange juice. When I walked back through the great room, Mom and Dad had both pulled up chairs in the alcove. They were both staring hard at the computer screen.

Wednesday, December 6

The first day of school. Take three.

I got into my blue pants, white shirt, blue tie, black socks, and black shoes and went down to the kitchen. Neither Mom nor Dad mentioned my disk over breakfast. But I was surprised to hear Mom say, "Paul, we've talked about it, and we've decided that your father will drive you to St. Anthony's today."

At seven-thirty, Dad and I walked out into the cold Florida morning. A light wind was blowing to the west, carrying the muck fire away from us, toward the Gulf. To the east, the sun was rising behind a long row of gray clouds. I stopped to look at them, jagged and red peaked, looming there like a distant mountain range.

We pulled out of the development and headed north, past the gates and guardhouses, past the high-tension wires and the osprey nests, toward the Lake Windsor campus. When we stopped at the light at Route 89 and Seagull Way, Dad pointed over to the right. He said, "Do you see that? That's Mike Costello's tree."

I looked where Dad was pointing and saw it, the big laurel oak. It had been planted on the front lawn of the high school, between the road and the bus lanes. It looked healthy enough, strong enough. But it was bound in a crisscross of wires attached to white metal stakes. Dad added, "Those stakes are just temporary. Until it can stand on its own."

We drove on to the next light and turned right. We headed east, toward the glowing colors of the mountain range, and toward the glowing colors of the citrus groves. I thought to myself, *Mike Costello has his tree, and that's good. But Luis has his tree, too, and he will have many, many more.*

Soon the road narrowed to two lanes and we were surrounded by the groves, surrounded by the beauty of it all. I stared through the window at the endless rows of trees— orange, tangerine, lemon—flying past us on either side. I rolled down the window and let it all in. The air was clear and cold. And the car immediately filled up with that scent, the scent of a golden dawn.